CHAPTER 1

Caffe Lattes and Cold Canberra Mornings

Claire Baxter had always known that she wanted to travel the world. When she finished high school and her friends were grappling with what brush to paint the rest of their lives, Claire had already sketched the canvas. When her friends were beginning university and deciding what electives they wanted to study, Claire was working two jobs and goal setting; every cent in pursuit of the one dream she knew was right for herself. When people were complaining about sleepless nights from overdue assignments and study stress on Facebook, Claire was sleeping soundly, dreaming of all the places her feet would take her. The fear, the anxiety she had heard so much about in her early twenties had completely evaded her – for her dream was so all-encompassing it had never entered her mind there would be a time when that idea of herself, that dream for her future, would come to an end.

Claire had had anything but a boring life in her twenty-six rotations around the sun, but her life did feel boring now. Having run out of money and feeling the pangs of homesickness, she had come back to Australia to once again live at home with her parents in their three-bedroom house in Narrabundah, Canberra.

Six weeks ago, Claire had been living in a small brick house in Vietnam along the Mekong Delta, a homestay, with other backpackers constantly coming and going. When she was away, Claire was the envy of her friends and family, with a busy Instagram of exotic people and places. Now, she found herself in her mid to late twenties and thrown straight back into the same life she had left as a teenager, working at the Bookshop Café in Kingston Old. Most of her friends had either moved to Sydney or were working very adult jobs and getting engaged. Claire didn't even own a car in Canberra, but used her old bicycle to get to work in the mornings – a similar system to what she had in Vietnam; only far less romantic when it was your sister's hand-me-down that your father had found in the back shed.

"Claire, Earth to Claire?" A voice echoed in her mind, bringing her back to the present-day reality of a whirling coffee machine.

"Hmm? Yes, what's up?" Claire blinked, focusing on Sarah, the part-time waitress her boss Ainsley would bring in on busy weekends.

"Table five want another flat white."

Her boss, Ainsley, had owned the Bookshop Café for the past fifteen years. A former school teacher, she had bought the small store with the money from what was, as far as Claire could understand, a very messy divorce, at a time when Kingston was far less busy and popular than it was today. As long as Claire had known her, Ainsley had always been single, despite being a very attractive woman in her late forties.

Her thoughts elsewhere, Claire made the flat white for table five and went back to her inner wallowing. It was like she was living in a time capsule, as if her entire life overseas – the incredible sights, feelings, experiences, friends, places, foods – just hadn't happened. It was as if her life in Canberra had just paused one day eight years ago and re-started again six weeks ago when she returned.

At first, there had been some fanfare. There were welcome home dinners with the remainder of her friends who had stayed – like Anna and Daisy. They had all wanted to hear the stories of her adventures, the places she had been to and the crazy things she had gotten up to. It didn't take long, though, for the questions to come less and less often, and for it to become very evident that that part of her life was over now. As if it had never even begun.

Claire was not upset about this change in circumstances. She had her health; she had seen some wonderful things and had made friends all over the world. It was just this feeling, this feeling of uncertainty about the future that she just couldn't shake. A problem she had never had before, as she was always looking forward to the next place, the next adventure.

"You good to close up this afternoon?" Ainsley asked, leaning against the front bench.

"You got it, boss lady." Claire gave her an exaggerated wink.

When the couple at table five finally bundled themselves out into the cold, leaving the café empty, Claire put all the chairs on the table, swept the crumbs off the wooden floors and quickly mopped as well. Ainsley was standing with her arms crossed, lips pursed, as she glared at the bakery across the road.

"Hey, Ains, is there anything else you needed doing today?" Claire asked, pushing the mop bucket into the kitchen, ready to clean out.

Ainsley glanced back at the café behind her as if surprised to see the chairs stacked on the table and the day's business drawing to a close.

"Sorry, what was that dear?" She dragged her gaze back from across the road.

"Just seeing if you needed anything else, before I get hypothermia cycling home?"

Ainsley snorted, "It's not that cold! This is but a fresh autumn breeze…you've become soft, Claire."

"Fresh!" Claire exclaimed. "Do you know how many scarves I had wrapped about my head this morning? I felt like a marshmallow man." She puffed her cheeks out in what was no doubt a very attractive, upset pufferfish kind of way.

"Well, that's what happens when you gallivant from one tropical paradise to the next." Ainsley nodded wisely. "You lose that little bit of Canberra winter cynicism that keeps us all bitter and warm inside."

"Oh, I feel I've acquired a lot of that over the past six weeks. All those years of acclimatisation as a child, gone, lost." Claire threw her hands in the air melodramatically. *No exaggeration there either*, Claire thought with a shiver. *Christ on a bike this place gets cold.*

"Probably flung into the Mediterranean Sea along with some young Spaniard's shorts."

Claire sighed wistfully. "If only Ains, if only."

Ainsley resumed her glaring through the café window. "Look at that store, what a bloody monstrosity!" she grumbled.

"What's so wrong with it?" Claire asked, standing beside her while they peered across the street together. The bakery had only opened a week ago, and Ainsley had been huffing and puffing about it ever since, which was out of character for the normally happy-go-lucky café owner. Over the years, even when other restaurants would pop up that competed directly with theirs, Ainsley had never seemed to mind. This bakery, however, for some reason had rubbed her the wrong way.

"Oh, it's just so..." Ainsley paused, looking for the right word to hang her ill-feeling on, "pretentious, you know?"

"I don't know." Claire laughed. "It looks the same as any other café around here if you ask me."

"Oh no, it's the whole hipster works, Claire! You should see the inside!" Ainsley nodded seriously. "So I went over there on Wednesday, to welcome them to the neighbourhood and all that as I do, being friendly and what have you. The décor is very gauche, very '*Oh look at this exposed brick*', even though that building doesn't have any brick. I know they installed the brick, then went to all that trouble to make it look like they hadn't. Ridiculous."

"Lordy! It's a conspiracy" Claire held back her laughter. Something had definitely rattled her older friend.

"And that's not even the worst part, the owner is this twelve-year-old in flour-covered overalls called *Brian*."

"Well, that's hardly a crime…"

"And when I pointed out our store to this *Brian*, who I am not convinced is legally old enough to vote, he said he didn't even realise we were here, said he thought it was just a bookshop!"

"To be fair, we kind of do sell books…and the name would impl-"

"Fifteen years we've been here, fifteen years! He's been here fifteen minutes. Just a bookshop indeed," Ainsley ranted. "We will see how long this little hipster baker lasts around here – I'm not convinced it will be long."

Ainsley continued to quietly mutter under her breath while Claire finished cleaning up and began the process of reapplying her ten thousand stolen scarves from her mother's closet. Claire made a mental note to go check out this new bakery; she had a sense that Ainsley was feeling exposed by something other than the brick.

"I'll see you later Ainsley, I've gotta get home so my parents can get in their daily dose of disappointment at my life choices."

Ainsley didn't register her comments, her mind clearly on someone or something else, turning to the cash register to begin counting the till. "Cycle safely, see you Sunday," she said. "We will discuss this bakery foolishness further then."

"You're the boss! To Sunday scheming!" *A little intrigue might make the shift pass a bit quicker, in any case.*

Claire left Ainsley to her pondering and began the short ten-minute bike ride from the Kingston café to her parent's small, three-bedroom brick cottage. Years earlier, when her grandfather had been sick and getting treatment, he had lived with her parents and they had added a small studio granny flat at the back of their large backyard. It had a shower, a bed and a small kitchenette and was the place where Claire had dumped her worn backpack and taken over several weeks before.

As much as Claire liked to make fun of her parents, they were amazing people. Everyone said Claire looked a lot like her mother but with more of her father's temperament. Her mother, Dianna Baxter, was a petite woman with curly, short, greying hair. She had worked for the National Gallery of Australia for the past twenty years; she refused to retire because she loved the work so much. Currently, she was the Senior Curator for Australian Prints, Drawings and Illustrated Books; a role that was starting to seep into their Narrabundah house. There were vintage 'Australiana' paintings all over their home, depicting ironbark huts, beautiful Snowy Mountain ranges, billabongs and unwieldy bush scenes. She also collected vintage homewares; every available surface was covered with old Arnott's biscuit tins, rusting irons and even horseshoes.

On the other hand, Claire's father, Harvey Baxter, used to be a journalist and political reporter, but was semi-retired now. Unlike his workaholic wife – who would probably die in the National Gallery, crushed under the weight of some giant painting of a waterlogged gumtree – Harvey spent his time pottering away at home. Whether he was secretly reading Danielle Steele novels, re-mowing the already perfectly acceptable lawn or trawling Facebook Marketplace for power tools he probably wouldn't ever use, Harvey Baxter found a way to make the quiet life work for him.

Dianna and Harvey had three children, of whom Claire was the middle child. Her older sister, Lynette, was married with two young children in western Sydney. Her younger brother, Ben, had just joined the Royal Australian Navy and was in the middle of his boatswain training, having only left home six months ago. Claire's mother was so busy with work she didn't seem to mind the empty house so much. Her father Harvey, however, was not coping so well with the change. Ever since Claire had moved into the empty granny flat at the back of their yard, her father had taken it upon himself to try and spend time with her when she was home.

That was why Claire was not surprised at all to find him in her little studio apartment when she wheeled her bicycle down the side of her parents' house and opened the flyscreen door. As just one large, open room with a double bed in one corner, a couch, TV and the small kitchenette, there wasn't much room for more than two people at any one time. The bathroom was a small shower and toilet, separated by a flimsy wall that didn't quite meet the ceiling. Claire had lived in far less glamorous places during her travels and liked the separation it gave her from the main house. It was not much, but at least made her feel that tiny little bit less like the twenty-six-year-old who had just moved back into her teenage room. Not that she could have, even if she wanted too, her mother having taken over that room years ago to create extra storage for her collectables.

"Ahh, my second born!" Harvey exclaimed when Claire walked in. He was holding a drill, crouched down behind the small television against one side of the wall.

"It is I, the middle child," Claire said, unwrapping her many scarves and throwing them on the small two-seater couch. "What are you up to?"

"Well, being the magnanimous man that I am, who also happens to have a lot of time on his hands, I am installing your TV aerial." Harvey waved said drill about, far too close to his nose. "You just can't tell your mother, because the whole time your grandfather stayed with us last Christmas I put it off, even though she subtly mentioned it at least three times."

"Your secret's safe with me." Claire flopped down onto the couch. "I'm behind on *The Bachelor* anyway, so this is perfect timing."

Harvey continued to connect a bunch of cords around the back of the television, and Claire watched with vague interest while she procrastinated about taking her shoes off. Her dad must have only just put the heater on before she'd arrived, so the room was still a bit chilly and Claire was in no real rush to move from her frozen stance on the couch.

"What have you been up to today, anyway?" she asked, picking the fluff off an exceptionally bright-pink woollen scarf.

"That, my dear, is an excellent question," Harvey replied, turning the television on and frowning when it only responded with pixelated grey static. "I spoke to your sister on the phone – she asked when you were going to come to visit. She feels like you are avoiding her, having been back in Australia for six weeks and not having stayed once. She told me to tell you to call her to organise something."

"Of course I'm not avoiding her," Claire groaned. "Lyn gets so worked up. I haven't been back that long; I'm just finding my feet. I haven't done anything except work, so she can't feel left out."

"You know your sister." Harvey shrugged, tuning the channels. Now and then, a scene would pop up out of the static. "She's probably just a bit lonely; you know Gary is in Brisbane again? I feel like he spends more time there than with the boys...Ahh well."

As he flicked through the blurry channels, the reception suddenly went crystal clear and Harvey let out a triumphant cry.

"Here we go! A bit of telly, now you can stay up to date with those Kardashian girls."

"Dad, pulling out the pop-culture references, I'm impressed."

Claire nodded appreciatively. *Another one of Dad's quirks*, Claire remembered. *Trashy magazines.*

"I need something to distract me from the quiet of the house...and I think that Kourtney is the best of them all, if you were wondering," he added smugly.

"I wasn't, but okay," Claire laughed.

"So what are you up to tonight, anyway?" Harvey asked, walking over to the small kitchen and washing his hands in the sink. "It's Friday night. Your mother and I are going out to dinner – you can come if you want."

"No way, you crazy kids go and hit the town. I'm probably going to make a blanket fort to ward off the cold and then go to bed."

"No plans with Anna or Daisy?" Harvey asked, picking up the drill and putting it back into its hard plastic case.

Anna and Daisy were Claire's closest Canberra friends. Anna and Claire had been best friends since primary school. Anna was beautiful, smart and aloof; even when they were younger, people would not know how to take her dry, solemn nature. Anna had met Daisy at university and had introduced her to Claire. The three of them had quickly become fast friends.

"No, I assume they are busy with their respective, domesticated love interests."

Harvey looked over at her enquiringly.

"And what about you, daughter of mine? I've been waiting for the day when some handsome stranger from a foreign land knocks on our door, having tracked you down after you broke his heart while you were drifting about the globe."

"Don't be ridiculous, Dad." Claire threw a cushion at him from the couch. "You should be expecting way more than one."

"Noted. Your mother and I will increase the dowry," Harvey chuckled, warding off her bad aim easily. "Nether mind any of that, though, you do just as you please. Don't feel pressured by your sister, or your meddling parents. We love having you back and if you want to just lounge around in the flat watching television and drowning in scarves, we will support you." Harvey put the cushion back on the couch and patted her leg gently.

Claire laughed and rolled her eyes exaggeratedly. "I knowww."

"Though there is no pressure for you to go anywhere, you can stay as long as you like. If there's anything else you would like that I can stretch my handyman muscles out on let me know, I want you to be comfortable here."

Claire smiled. She knew that her father missed her brother Ben terribly and also found it hard having Lynette and his grandchildren just a bit too far away. He was probably going to keep going a little bit overboard until the excitement of her arrival back in Australia calmed down.

"You, old man, are a legend among semi-retired men."

"Well, yes, this we know."

With that, Harvey gathered up his things and left her flat. Claire watched him from her open blinds, whistling as he crossed the backyard and went back into the house. It was a little strange for her, being able to spend so much time with her dad now. Growing up, both he and her mother had been so busy with work and focusing on the other two children's soccer games and homework, as well as hormonal teenage tantrums. Since she had been back, it had just been the two of them around the house a lot of the time – and while her coming home felt very similar to when she left, this was one area that had distinctly changed. The relationship had gone from one of parent to more of a friendly housemate, who occasionally installed television aerials and always mowed the lawn.

Claire stretched and finally removed her shoes and jacket, throwing them on the couch next to her. Picking up her laptop, she moved over to the bed and sprawled out along the floral doona bought for her grandfather when he had stayed here years earlier. Claire could call Anna and Daisy, but they already had plans for tomorrow night and Claire wasn't in the mood to do anything except eat an entire block of something chocolate-covered and start researching her next adventure.

Everywhere Claire had lived over the past few years, even when she had stayed there for a while, there had always been something else. Something in the future, something new that she was looking forward to or working towards. Whether that was a location, a country or a job; Claire always had something in mind, no matter where she was in the world. Ever since coming back to Australia this time, though, it had seemed like something was missing. She felt a bit rudderless, lost in new-found territory while living in the very familiar territory of her parents' backyard.

Typing into Google, Claire trawled through some travel blogs to try to find some inspiration for her next adventure. Somewhere with a beach, where she could wear shorts and burn these accursed scarves. *Or maybe somewhere with no beach but a forest?* Claire wondered. *Being warm was definitely one of the criteria though...how about the Amazon?*

I could book some kind of fabulous adventure trek, Claire thought spontaneously, *and fight off leeches and eat fried piranha with beautiful, albeit barbaric, mythical tribeswomen.* She hurriedly tapped away on her laptop, looking through image after image, waiting for that moment of inspiration to seize her and life to set a new course.

After about half an hour of this and no success, she found herself on Instagram, looking back through her own pictures. Maybe she was overthinking things, maybe she just needed to relax and see where the future took her. Living at home wouldn't be forever; what she needed was a hard timeframe. An expiry date, for when she would have to leave her parents' flat and set back out on the road again.

Two months, maybe three? Was that enough time? She had already been home for almost two months and still hadn't even managed to visit her sister. *Four months? Was that enough time to save money until she found a job again overseas?* Potentially, she would have to live frugally, and she had a few things coming up with Daisy's wedding, which would no doubt cost money. *Six months?* Six months was doable – enough time, but not so much time that living in her parents' backyard would begin to feel permanent.

Six months, Claire decided. In six months, she would be on to her next adventure, whatever that looked like. Claire felt a little better than she did at the café this morning. *A timeframe was a direction, wasn't it?* Or at least something similar.

CHAPTER 2

Home or at least a House
My Mother Yells at Me in

Anna Cardwell and Claire Baxter had been best friends since primary school, when Anna and her mother had moved to the house next door. Anna had grown up in Richmond in north-west Sydney until her parents' divorce when she was nine. Her father, a banker, still lived there, with his new wife and horde of stepchildren. Anna and her mother Patricia, however, had moved to Canberra, where her mother got a job as an administrative assistant at the University of Canberra. Anna and Claire had immediately bonded over Anna's dog, Honey.

All through primary school and high school, Anna had been the more reserved of their girl gang. Anna with her long, straight, black hair and beautiful Korean skin. Claire loved her because she was always unapologetically frank and honest and had a talent for being impossibly dry. Where Claire was emotional, impulsive and bubbly, Anna was practical, reasoned and solemn. When Claire had run off to work in pubs in England, Anna had been diligently studying Engineering at the University of Canberra. While she was there, Anna had met David. David was handsome, sweet and an all-round nice person. They had been together for over eight years now.

Daisy was a school teacher and the closest thing to a real-life fairy that Claire had ever met. She was ethereal. With long, curly, strawberry blonde hair, blue eyes, a sweet nature and the face of a pixie, Daisy was impossible not to like. Although Claire did regularly tell her that it was for this very reason she was easy to hate (only out of jealousy, though). Daisy was due to marry in October later that year. Her fiancée, a lawyer called Joanne, was the more serious of the two. From her neat and professional, clean-cut outfits to her severe platinum blonde bob, Joanne was the opposite of Claire in many ways. Except for the one thing that really counted, the heart.

Today Claire was meeting Anna and Daisy at the Kingston foreshore, which was the start of her friends' normal catch-up walking route around the lake that they did every Saturday morning. Daisy would bring her socially anxious cavoodle Leia along, and they would talk about their respective weeks, whinge about the Canberra cold and fawn over other people's dogs. The circuit normally took them about an hour, followed by another hour at a coffee shop. Claire had gladly joined in on their Saturday catch-ups and had made a point of keeping that day clear every week with Ainsley.

It was these kinds of moments she had missed the most when living away from home and travelling overseas; just laughing over silly things with Anna and Daisy. There was something special about her friendship with these two. Claire was not sure if it was just because they had stayed in touch for so many years, or if it was because they had all grown up in Canberra, but whatever it was, it was always very easy to be around them. Claire would miss them when she left again.

"Sorry, I'm a bit late!" Claire apologised, joining her friends on the footpath they were about to trudge. "Dad fixed the television in my room last night and I stayed up way too late watching some freaky SBS German soap opera."

"Don't stress, we only just got here," Daisy said, frowning down at her cavoodle. "Leia had a bit of a tantrum about leaving bed this morning; I've never known a dog with so many emotional issues. It's exhausting."

"Aw, poor little fluffy princess!" Claire doted, leaning down and putting out her hand. Leia leant against Daisy's leg and stared up at Claire shyly. They went through this process every Saturday; Leia and Claire had met many times before, but it always took her a little while to warm up to any humans outside of Daisy or Joanne.

"Oh, for Pete's sake, Leia," Daisy breathed in exasperation. "You know Claire, hurry up and get over it."

"Oh, she's okay, the poor darling," Claire cooed, as Leia timidly shuffled over to sniff her hand and have a pat. "It must be very stressful, being so adorable."

"Don't encourage her," Daisy said, eyeing off her sulky ball of white and brown fluff. "She's incorrigible. It is like living with a dramatic teenager. Our household has enough estrogen as it is."

"No argument there," Anna quipped dryly, also leaning down to put her hand out to the timid Leia, who was now ever so slightly wagging her tail. "Okay, the dog has been placated; shall we start this supposed exercise? I've got to go into work this afternoon."

"On a weekend?" Daisy exclaimed. "Sacrilege!"

"It's okay – it's just for a few hours," Anna said quickly, turning to Claire. "Speaking of work, how is it going back at the Bookshop?"

"Well," Claire laughed, "we cannot call it that at the moment. Ainsley is at war with the new bakery across the road. I think it is a bit of a baked-goods struggle, so she is keen to highlight that we do more than just sell books."

"Crikey, café politics hey?"

Claire nodded solemnly, "It's a bloody business."

The trio took off down the path, Leia sticking nervously beside Daisy's leg, with morning runners and bike riders overtaking them as they walked. It was like the entire city was trying to make use of the last bit of semi-sociable weather before winter truly took hold and only the most seasoned of Canberra joggers could be seen battling through the bitter morning frost.

"Right, Daisy," Anna said, moving out of the way of a woman running past with her large bullmastiff trotting beside her. Poor Leia seemed to shrink even further behind Daisy's shadow.

"Honestly, dog," Daisy muttered. "But yes, what's up Anna?"

"Wedding plans. Explain."

"Ahh, Anna! You and your flowery dialogue!" Claire teased. "We barely ever get a word in around you…Good point though, what's happening? When is the hens' night?"

"Let's get sloshed, I need a good excuse," Anna agreed. "And to celebrate your nuptials, of course."

"Are we going to get sashes?" Claire gasped, doing a little jump on the spot, her curly hair bouncing about her face.

"Duh. Of course we are," Anna replied, pulling her long, dark hair into a ponytail behind her as they walked. "And they are going to be disgusting. And pink."

"Excellent! Let's go full tacky!"

"Diamantes, penis straws; the whole shebang."

"You had me at sashes, lost me at straws," Daisy interrupted, smiling at Claire and Anna's back and forth.

"Daisy's more interested in a shebang, after all." Anna shot her a sly glance, receiving a laugh and a shove from Daisy in return.

"Seriously, though, I'm thinking a girls' weekend in Sydney." Daisy's eyes lit up with excitement. "We can book a lovely apartment somewhere, get my sisters and girlfriends from work to come along if they want to."

"That sounds great!" Claire said excitedly. "And I can visit my sister at the same time, keep her off my back." *That, and she would love to see Lyn and the boys, of course.*

"Settled," Anna said. "I can handle the logistics; you just send me a list of people you don't hate."

"You are so organised, Anna," Claire sighed. "Any chance you could sort my mess of a life out while you are at it?"

"You wouldn't be impressed with the results, trust me," Anna murmured. Claire snorted.

"You are the most adult person I know. I doubt that," Daisy said, untangling Leia's lead from around her leg.

"Last night I fell asleep on top of half a block of peppermint chocolate and woke up with some in my hair," Claire confessed, running her fingers through the back of her head warily.

"See?" Anna pointed at Claire. "A hopeless case. I only work with Caramello types." Anna's phone vibrated and she quickly checked the message, her face expressionless.

"David all good?" Claire asked, stretching her arms out as she walked like the woman twenty metres in front of them. She looked particularly fit, so Claire had only been mimicking her movements. Who knows…fitness by symbiosis.

"It's just work," Anna said, sending a quick reply and putting her phone back in her pocket.

"They want you to work today and they are annoying you in your spare few hours on a weekend?" Daisy growled, agitated on Anna's behalf. "You should tell them where to go; they have been working you ridiculous hours lately. Every time I call you, you seem to be stuck at the office."

"It's just a busy time for us at the moment." Anna shrugged. "I'm fine, I promise."

"And David? I feel bad, I haven't even seen him since that first welcome home dinner we did when I got back a month or so ago," Claire said, keeping an eye on the fit older lady in front of her, who had started doing lunges as she walked – Claire attempted a few as well. Anna and Daisy tactfully ignored her plagiarised stretching.

"He's fine. Just busy as well," Anna said, not going into any further detail. Her phone vibrated again, but this time she ignored it.

"And are you two okay?" Claire asked. She wasn't sure why she did. Anna was hardly known for being outspoken on any real topic, always having been the kind of person to use only a few words and then half of them again. Today she was more reserved, though, even for her. *It might have been the long hours she was doing,* she thought. *Real adulting looks like bloody hard work.*

"We are our normal selves in our normal, old, eight-year relationship." Anna pulled her long ponytail over to her other shoulder, changing the topic. "Enough of my monologue, though, what's happening with you? What about that Argentinean?"

"Ahh, yes, Miko...the beautiful Miko," Claire purred, a shiver running down her spine. "Oh God, don't mention Miko, I am so sex-starved right now."

"Yes, what's happening there?" Daisy asked, perking up at the mention of a love interest.

"Nothing," Claire gave up on her lunges. "I left him in a clay hut of a homestay along the Mekong Delta, no doubt whispering sweet nothings into another backpacker's ear."

"Why don't you ask him to come visit?" Daisy asked, ever the romantic optimist. "You never know!"

"Oh yes, I can see how that would go down: *'Miko, of all the places in Australia you should visit, come to Canberra to make sweet love to me in my parents' granny flat – while my father potters about the backyard, installing TV aerials.'*"

"There are worse ways to spend one's Sunday," Anna reasoned. "He could be living in a hut along a dirty river."

"Hey! I'll have you know the Mekong Delta is a beautiful, peaceful place...besides, that was nothing more than just a physical attraction.

He was lovely, but his English was poor – my Spanish has improved, but ninety per cent of what I know is still just asking for directions to a toilet, swear words and a few things I learnt off Miko. Which I'm fairly certain are not fit to be said within earshot of anyone under the age of sixteen…"

"Okay, the Argentinean is out then." Anna shrugged. "We need to find you a man here."

"…or a woman," Daisy interrupted.

"Or, yes, a woman," Anna corrected herself, "to ride out your next six months in Australia, knock you up, and then chain you to Canberra so you can never leave Daisy or me again."

"Well in that case, maybe a man after all. But yes, I agree with Anna – we don't want you to go! The past six weeks have been so lovely having you home!" Daisy declared, just as Leia got a fright at the sight of her own shadow and let out a yelp. "Honestly, dog, don't embarrass me, just for today."

"Ladies, ladies, I'm flattered!" Claire gushed. "But I haven't been back that long. You will be sick of me before too much time. Now, should we do some actual running or is that too far outside the realm of our Saturday walks? I need the exercise; my butt is growing and not in a J.Lo kind of way."

Anna, ever the scientist, peered around behind Claire as if to test her hypothesis. She shrugged in a non-committal way, her face expressionless. Claire hissed at her.

"I go to yoga early most mornings if you want to join me?" Daisy asked. "It's supposedly like exercise but feels like you aren't doing anything; that's why I like it. Some days the yogi gives you a head massage after as well. I think it's supposed to be a prayer, but I like to think of it as a free head massage."

"Ooh, you are selling it to me! Yes, that sounds fabulous. I'm in." Claire made a mental note to wash her hair. "What about you, Anna?

Wanna let some hippy get all up in your temples?"

"Maybe...I'll let you know, just send me the address."

The three of them continued to walk around the lake, talking nonsense, with Claire demonstrating some strange interpretations of other people's exercises along the way. They came to a stop at a coffee shop at the end of their walk, where Anna excused herself and left early without staying for breakfast. Daisy and Claire both tried to convince her to stay, that the work could wait until later that day – it was a Saturday, let the buildings build them bloody selves. Anna just laughed, gave them both a hug and Leia a quick pat before disappearing down the road and out of sight.

Neither Daisy nor Claire, however, were that committed to their work on a weekend and were more than happy to sit down at the hipster waterfront café and order big breakfasts that they didn't deserve after what was a less than strenuous walk. It was lovely spending some alone time with Daisy, she had an infectious energy about her that made you feel like you were really special and she only had time for you and your feelings. Claire supposed that special skill is what would make her such a fantastic primary school teacher. *It would be hard to feel neglected,* she reflected, *with Daisy's radiant smile beaming down at you all day.*

Claire was a bit worried about how hard Anna was working herself; she even looked thinner and seemed tired and more withdrawn. She supposed one did not get to be an engineer without some long nights and hard work involved, but resolved to call David and meet up for coffee. He was a good friend of hers as well, and at this rate she would hardly be able to pin both of them down together.

CHAPTER 3

Rusty Frank and His Floppy Side Mirrors

Claire had spent her Sunday doing a combination of serving coffee and spying on the new bakery across the road at Ainsley's behest. Her disgruntled boss had sent her over on a reconnaissance mission to meet the owner and to 'get a feel' for the place.

"I'm not clever enough to act natural," she begged Ainsley. "It will be creepy!"

"Nonsense! There is nothing creepy about it. You are just having a look around the building because you work across the road. What could be more normal?" Ainsley continued wiping down the table in front of her innocently.

"You want me to steal a menu? They haven't even properly opened yet!"

"It's hardly stealing if they leave them lying about the place…"

Claire sighed and dutifully trudged across the road, where the bakery was in the process of being fitted out with furniture. Removalists walked in and out, carrying chairs and tables from a truck parked outside, in through the two chocked-open front doors. Claire hovered awkwardly in front of the open doors, peering inside to try and see if any stray menus were laid out on the empty countertops.

"Won't be fully finished for a few more days, sorry."

Claire yelped and spun around. A tall man in his mid-thirties was standing behind her, holding two chairs stacked upon one another.

"Oh, no worries!" Claire all but shouted. "Just having a look at the…ahh…chairs…"

"Yeah, don't get too excited, I spent too much on the ovens so had to squeeze the purse a bit when it comes to the furniture." He indicated to the tables being carried in from the truck. "These bad boys are an IKEA special. You work around here?"

"Yeah, just across the street," Claire said, pointing to the Bookshop Café. She was certain she saw a head pop down behind the register. This must be the mysterious owner who had Ainsley in such a mood. The way she had been going on, she expected somebody far younger; not this polite man who had a few years on Claire.

"Yeah, cool," he said, his interest suddenly perking up. "Is that with Ainsley? I met her the other day."

"Yup, she's the boss lady."

"Nice," he said, looking over at their café across the road. "I like her, she's got spunk."

Claire laughed, "I've never really thought about it that way, but yeah, she is a pretty funky lady."

"Hey, sorry I'm so rude, my name is Brian." He put down the chairs and held out his hand. "Nice to meet another Bookshop Café employee."

"Yeah, nice to meet you too," Claire said, shaking his hand. She decided that she liked this Brian character – he seemed friendly enough and not at all the arrogant child Ainsley had made him out to be. They stood in silence for a moment. Claire wondered if she should just ask him what he intended to sell so she could at least come back to Ainsley with some form of gossip. She had a feeling Ainsley wanted to know something other than the different forms of sourdough they would be selling, so she decided to dive in with another tactic.

"Well, your place is looking great, IKEA or not!" she said. "Was the décor your idea, or maybe your business partner's...or wife's?"

"Don't have either, unfortunately. Would have helped with the wallet if I did though!" His eyes wandered back to the chairs being unloaded inside. "No, it's always been a bit of a dream of mine to have a bakery around here and I wanted to keep it simple with an industrial feel, you know."

"Hmm, I do. Well, I hope you do really well here, it's a lovely area," Claire said.

"Thanks, Claire. If you need anything from this side of the road just give us a yell, okay?"

"Yeah, will do Brian, good luck with the tables."

Claire walked back over to the Bookshop, and Ainsley met her at the door, holding a tray of coffees in one hand and opening the door with the other.

"Well? Any intel? Did you find any menus?" she demanded, glancing back over to Brian across the road.

"Here, let me take that," Claire said, glancing over at the exasperated-looking couple at the far corner of the room as they eyeballed their caffeine, heading in the wrong direction. She took the tray from her distracted boss and handed the impatient duo their coffees. Claire took her time turning back to Ainsley. Let her squirm for a bit.

"He's single," she said, finally.

Ainsley jumped, looking somewhat guilty.

"Single, what do I care about that?"

"And he asked after you."

"He did?" Ainsley's eyes went wide. "Not that I care, what did he say?"

"That you were spunky."

"Spunky?!"

"Yup, spunky."

"And what did you say?"

"That you thought he was sexy."

Ainsley made a strangled noise, somewhere between a choke and a gasp.

"No, you didn't!"

"No, I didn't." Claire laughed. "But you do."

"I think nothing of the sort," Ainsley replied coolly, suddenly very interested in clearing tables. Claire just smiled wryly and went about cleaning the coffee machine before the midday rush.

* * *

Claire finished work early that afternoon and cycled home to find her parents bickering in the kitchen over some sort of Tupperware container, filled with large quantities of a mystery casserole.

Dianna was clutching the container with a dogged intensity.

"She's your mother, Harvey! If Ben carried on the way you did..."

"Yes, *my* mother!" Harvey threw his hands in the air. "Therefore, I get to decide when we visit. It'll be almost dark by the time we get there..."

"We're going." Dianna glowered.

"Where're we going?" Claire piped up; she assumed she would be dragged along by her father.

"Oh! Claire! You're home. Excellent," her mother said, shoving the Tupperware container into her arms. "Could barely see you there under all those scarves. You do know winter hasn't even really begun yet, don't you?"

"I think I cut a fine figure," Claire declared, flinging a stray scarf end over one shoulder. "Poised. Dignified."

"...and far too tired from work to drive all the way out to Yass?"

Harvey's eyes were wide, as if trying to use telepathy to communicate with her.

"Ummm…"

"We can't leave her here, Harvey. Claire will be all alone," Dianna rebuked. "Besides, it will do her good to see Nan."

"Well, you see, you *could* actually leave me here, what with me being, you know, an adult…."

Dianna chose to ignore this and turned back to her husband, one hand on her hip as she poked a finger into his chest. She would have made a fabulous school principal in another life.

"Harvey, get in the car and stop this nonsense."

"Claire?" Turning her attention back to her daughter.

"Yes, oh wise and wonderful bringer of life?" Claire asked innocently.

"Take that to the car and your father too, we are having dinner at your nan's."

"I shall leave my scarves on then!"

The drive from Canberra to Claire's nan's house in Yass was only about an hour on the highway. Claire sat in the back seat of the car and felt strangely déjà vu about the whole scenario. Growing up, they had regularly spent Sundays at her nan and pop's property in Yass. Back then, however, she used to have to share the back seat of the car with her younger brother and older sister, which had always been a painful affair. An hour filled with elbows in ribs, hair-pulling and empty threats from Harvey about leaving them on the side of the road. They always behaved when they arrived, though; neither Claire nor any of her siblings had been game enough to put a toe out of line when it came to their nan.

Beatrice Baxter was a formidable woman. She had grown up on a cattle station in Western Australia and Claire had always strongly believed that she was not afraid of anything or anyone. Beatrice had met her late husband, Gerald Baxter, in the sixties when, as a young doctor, he was conducting a rural placement out in the Kimberley. The fearless Beatrice, who had spent her life around hard men and doing even harder work, said she had found herself intrigued by the polite young doctor from the east coast. The two had quickly fallen in love, much to the dismay of Beatrice's parents, who had always hoped for a suitor of the country boy variety; someone who would stay and help run the cattle station.

However, Beatrice was not the sort of woman to be easily swayed, especially in matters of the heart. As such, it was not long before they were married and Gerald had whisked her away to the other side of the country. Gerald's father, also a doctor, had a small private practice in Sydney, which Gerald would eventually take over. Beatrice, who initially found city life exciting, would soon yearn for the tranquil open spaces of her childhood. Therefore, the couple had bought a property in Yass in the mid-seventies with enough land for a few cows and horses. Claire's father, Harvey Baxter, had grown up in that house; although Claire's grandfather had passed away a few years ago, Beatrice still lived there to this day.

Turning off the highway, they followed a small dirt road along for several kilometres. Both sides of the road were fenced off, with cattle grazing quietly along the rolling green pastures. Her father had to stop and open a gate to the property and drive through quickly, as several cows were heading over to their car inquisitively; sometimes, when the grass was low, her nan would drive out around this time of the afternoon and throw a bale of hay to them. Harvey sped up the long driveway, towards the house on top of the hill a further kilometre up the road.

"It's such a long way away from the neighbours," her mother muttered in the front seat. "What if something were to happen?"

"Both you and I have been through this with Mum, Dee," Harvey said. "This is the closest we'll ever get her to a city. Besides, Mum is never short of company. The last time I was here I walked in on what must have been at least twelve white-haired ladies playing bridge."

"I suppose..." Dianna replied, not sounding entirely convinced. "It just worries me."

Reaching the house, they pulled into the circular driveway and Claire clambered out of the car. She was about to rush indoors and take advantage of the warm fire her nan always had lit, but took a moment to appreciate the house itself. She loved this house; it was truly beautiful, and every brick just screamed old-world charm. An old, stone shearer's cottage from the 1900s, it was the sort of house you see in all the paintings from the settlers' era that Claire's mother loved to obsess over.

The house itself, originally only a two-bedroom shack, had been renovated to include a wraparound veranda and an additional section at the back that doubled the house in size. They had used a similar stone, so it was difficult to tell the difference from the outside. Inside, however, there was a definite modern feel and some clever insulation; the renovations were a little more transparent, bringing warmth and light into the home. Claire could not blame her nan for not wanting to leave. It was a beautiful house with a beautiful view and no neighbours to complain about how loudly you chose to listen to Shania Twain when the feeling should naturally take you.

"Claire, don't forget that casserole!" Dianna instructed, waking Claire from her thoughts.

The light on the front porch came on and Beatrice Baxter sauntered out, looking every bit the country matriarch in her crisp, white, long-sleeved blouse, clean jeans and flat leather boots. For a lady in her seventies, Beatrice was still in fantastic shape and was probably fitter than Claire by a longshot. Claire made a mental note to do something about this – her pretend exercise aka the gossip-walks once a week around the lake weren't quite cutting it. The nightly Cadbury binges probably weren't helping either.

"Is that my wild, travelling grandchild I see?" Beatrice declared loudly. "Still in Australia, not lost in a Patagonian rainforest or carried off by pygmies?"

"It is I!" Claire laughed, running up the steps to the porch to give her nan a hug. "Your wild, albeit clearly favourite, grandchild. Still in the country, forest-less, pygmy-less...slowly going mad."

"Excellent." Beatrice smiled, giving her a brief but strong hug. "Glad to hear your mother and father are doing what parents do best, frustrating their children."

"I won't even touch that one," Harvey said, kissing Beatrice on the cheek. "How are you, Mum?"

"Surprised!" she huffed. "I didn't expect to see you lot here today."

"I thought I had better drag your son out here to get out of the house before his tinkering sends it down around our ears." Dianna gave Beatrice a hug. "Good to see you, Mum. Sorry it's been a few weeks."

"Harvey, what is this about tinkering? Why are you worrying your poor wife?" Beatrice glanced at him sharply.

"Not tinkering, Mother, I've been doing little renovations. Now that I'm working part-time."

"Nothing worse than idle hands, Harvey." Beatrice walked through the front door and into the house.

"They are not idle, Mum! I'm really busy..."

"Harvey, don't argue with your elders," Beatrice snapped. "Honestly, anyone would think I brought you up in the city."

"Sorry, Mum," Harvey apologised, audibly gritting his teeth. He rolled his eyes at Claire, who just giggled. She loved spending time with her nan. As a child, she had been slightly scared of her, but the older she got the more she appreciated her sass.

Claire sat down at the dining room table and commenced the long process of removing all her layers and scarves. As predicted, Beatrice already had the fireplace going and the room was a beautiful, toasty-warm haven. Her nan pulled some mugs out of a cupboard and starting making everyone tea. Her mother told Beatrice about a new exhibition she was working on at the gallery and Beatrice listened with interest; Claire had always found it a little funny how similar they were in many ways. Maybe it was true what they say about your partners. Claire was not going to be the one to point this out to her father, though; the poor man didn't deserve it.

Claire settled into her chair, the room warm and familiar. She let herself switch off and enjoy the exchange between her nan and parents. It was moments like this that she had missed when she was away.

"Now, I'm glad you've come over tonight," Beatrice said seriously, steering the conversation away from exhibitions. "I've been thinking a lot this week about making some changes around here."

"Why, what's the matter?" Dianna's voice ringing with concern.

"Nothing, I just think it's time. I want to start distributing some of Gerald's personal effects among the family," Beatrice said seriously.

"Oh…Mum, are you sure?" Harvey asked warily, no doubt thinking of their already cluttered house filled with his wife's collectables.

"Not everything, obviously, just a few key items I have no use for here and want to keep within the family. I know your father would have wanted it that way."

"If you're sure…" Harvey mumbled, uncertain.

"Of course, Beatrice!" Dianna interrupted, shooting Harvey a dangerous look. "This is your decision. Just tell us how we can help."

"Well, firstly, I want to give that piano Gerald used to love to play to Lynette and her family. I think it will be good for the children to have so they can learn growing up." Beatrice pointed to the beautiful instrument Claire could just see peeking through the other room.

"I'm sure she would love that, we'll arrange to get it to Sydney… that shouldn't be too difficult," Dianna said slowly. Claire could almost see the logistical cogs turning in her mother's head. She never stopped working, that woman.

"For Ben, I want to give him that old motorbike in the shed. I still use it, every now and then, but it would be far more fun for a young man to use than this old lady."

Claire's mother inhaled sharply. "I don't know about a motorbike, Beatrice…he's so young."

"Nonsense! He will be fine. Boys need their fast toys; otherwise, they will get themselves in trouble in other ways. I know he used to ride it with Gerald around the property when he was younger, and he still gets on it every time he visits, so I'm confident he knows what he's doing."

Dianna didn't look all that convinced, but didn't argue any further; she would no doubt bring it up with Harvey on the drive home. Claire made a mental note to put headphones in when it was time to go.

"Now, for you Claire," Beatrice said, turning to her.

"Oh, Nan," Claire said quickly, finding her voice. "You don't have to give me anything, there's not much I need. Lynette is the responsible one with the kids and the big house and everything… she's in a position to collect things."

"Don't be ridiculous, child." Beatrice dismissed her protests. "I have thought about it and I think you are best suited for Frank."

"Frank?" Claire asked, confused. *Who's Frank?*

"No way!" Harvey exclaimed, raising his eyebrows. "You still have Frank? I haven't seen him in years!"

"Fifteen, to be exact. He's down in the back shed and coated in over a decade's worth of dust."

"Wow." Harvey's eyes glowed with excitement. "There you go."

"Hold on, who is going to clue me in here?" Claire asked, imagining a bony, ancient cow locked in an old shed somewhere. "Who is Frank?"

"What kind of condition is he in?" Harvey asked eagerly, ignoring Claire's question.

"I had a look the other day. He has not been touched since your father locked him up so will probably need a lot of work."

"Hmm…" Harvey nodded thoughtfully, scratching his chin.

"Oh no, I know that look." Dianna pointed at Harvey accusingly. "It's the face of a new project. God help us."

"It's what Dad would have wanted, Dee," Claire's father replied innocently.

"Don't try and turn that on me…"

"Excuse me, ahem!" Claire looked between them impatiently. "Will somebody please tell me who this Frank character is?" *Parents, honestly, no respect for their late twenties burden children whatsoever.*

"Why don't I show you?" Beatrice said, with a twinkle in her eye.

"Yes, how about you lot go and do that, and I will heat up dinner?" Not waiting for a response, Dianna got up from the table and walked straight to the kitchen. Her mother had quickly disengaged at the mention of another project for Harvey.

"Follow me, dears," Beatrice led both Claire and her father out the back door of the house and into the backyard. The sun was slowly slipping beyond the horizon, but there was still enough light to illuminate their way across the yard and down towards a series of sheds away from the house. Claire had a feeling that even in the darkness her nan could find her way confidently across the yard, knowing every inch of the property intimately.

Coming up to a large shed, Beatrice led them though a side door and switched on the light.

"Follow me, just mind the implements."

Claire followed behind her closely, interested to see who or what this mystery Frank was. Her mind began conjuring all sorts of exciting things. *Maybe Frank was a creepy sentient doll that one member from the family must take responsibility for keeping under control, so he didn't unleash his evil on the world?* Claire didn't know why her mind went there, it was possible she had spent too long in the sun these past few years – and she also needed to stop watching bad nineties horror films with Harvey when bored of an evening. Claire did not have to wonder for long. Once she had walked around the lawnmower, there he was.

"Claire, this is Frank," Beatrice introduced. "He's a little rustier than he used to be."

Wedged between a shed pole, several barrels of hay and an old John Deer ride-on lawnmower was what looked to be a very dusty, very old, very forlorn-looking Volkswagen Kombi van. He was as orange as a tangerine, with what looked like a once-white pop-top roof.

"Gerald bought him fresh off the ship in 1968 when we were living in Western Australia," Beatrice explained, watching Claire's face closely. "I think he is one of the first bay-window campers, that year…at least in Australia. We drove him from my parents' to Sydney, back then, when I first left home."

Claire could not believe it. This was absolutely the last thing she had expected. She didn't know what to say; she just continued to stare at Frank's dusty face peeking out from among all the junk hidden in her pop's old shed.

Harvey whistled. "Wow, talk about bringing back a few memories!"

He moved in to take a closer look. "I remember holidays camping in Frank. Back then everyone had one. They were just your average family camper."

Harvey walked around to its side – squeezing between the hay bales – and pulled open the sliding door, which acquiesced, albeit with the low groaning of unoiled metal. Disturbed dust swirled in the air about his head and Harvey coughed.

Claire, finally having regained apparent consciousness from the shock, could not believe her nan would want to give something like this up! A Kombi van – they were classics! Surely something like this was far too special to just give away?

"Nan, are you sure?" Claire asked anxiously. "These are basically vintage now, you could get a bit of money for it if you sold it. I could even help you put an ad online if you wanted."

"No, Claire, my mind is quite made up. I need to start letting go." Beatrice shook her head firmly. "Gerald has been gone for over five years now, and at first I couldn't bear to part with anything but time has gone on and now…I want the things he loved to be loved again. I want them to be used, by the people he used to love."

Beatrice put her hand on the dusty side mirror, turning it back into place gently.

"It would feel like a part of him is still alive, in a way."

Claire didn't know what to say, she just put her hand on her nan's and squeezed it tightly. Beatrice Baxter had always been a strong, impenetrable woman and it was rare that she showed any emotional vulnerability, especially to Claire or her siblings.

"Anyway," Beatrice said, clearing her throat. "It's decided. You will take this rusting box, your sister the piano and your brother will get that old dirt bike off my hands. I might finally be able to make some room in these sheds."

"Wow, Nan, I don't know what to say." Claire reached out and ran her hand along the dusty side of the van. "It's beautiful…I love it so much already. I've always loved these…they are so special."

Claire could barely hear her thoughts over the loud pounding of her heart; she couldn't believe that something so beautiful could be hers…just like that. It didn't feel real.

"Well don't say thank you, just yet…it's going to need a fair bit of work. Gerald just parked it in the shed about fifteen years ago and Frank's been here ever since. God knows if the engine hasn't rusted to a fine powder."

"Hey, are you guys in here?" Dianna pushed the door to the shed open and sneezed as dust swirled in the air above her.

"Over here, Mum!" Claire cried out, excitement suddenly bubbling in her chest. She couldn't wrap her head around it. She, Claire Baxter, the backyard-dwelling twenty-six-year-old with no possessions and a scarily depleted savings account was now the owner of a beautiful, historic, classic car.

"Oh, my," Dianna said, taking in the van in front of her. "Well, this should keep you and your father busy."

"He's beautiful," Claire whispered.

"…and rusty," Beatrice added, ever the pragmatist.

"Hey, Claire!" Harvey called, overexcitedly; he had climbed inside the back of Frank. Claire could barely see him through the dirty windscreen, it had that much grime and dust covering it.

"Come check out the interior! Crikey, it's exactly as I remember!"

Claire ran around the side, squeezed past the hay bales and stood facing the open side door into the inside of the van.

Frank was a true child of the sixties. A wood-vinyl cabinet with a small sink ran down the length of his interior, and what once must have been bright orange curtains – now faded and covered in what looked suspiciously like mould – covered the side and back windows. The floor had old wooden floorboards, and Claire's father was sitting on what looked to be a brown-and-orange upholstered seat.

"See! It folds down into the old rock and roll style bed, so you can take him camping but then also make it a seat if you want to," Harvey explained. "Check this out!"

He reached out and pulled down a little pop-up table secured against the cupboard under the sink.

"See! You can have your breakfast here but then pack it back down and pull out the bed if you want." He ran his hands over the dusty table surface. "This is so strange, it's so familiar."

Claire climbed in the back and sat next to him; she still felt in shock and was happy to let Harvey simply fall into his memories while she took stock of the whole situation. When she had climbed into her parents' car this afternoon, the most she had hoped for was maybe a cup of tea after a long day on her feet. She would never have thought she would be coming away with a car of her own. Her very first car, in fact; there had never been the need to have one when she was travelling the past few years. A car was a privilege of the settled, someone with a home address that a car can be registered to.

"What colour is even under all that dust?" Claire heard Dianna ask from outside. "It looks like a reddish-brown right now."

"Orange – there is a specific term for it, but I can't remember off the top of my head," Beatrice replied. "Maybe Brilliant Orange? I remember when Gerald first bought him, he was gleaming…Gosh, that was over fifty years ago now…I'd say we are both looking a little worse for wear, these days."

"…and see this here," Harvey said, pulling Claire's attention away from the conversation outside as he stood up and undid some clips along the roof. "Check this out."

With both hands over this head, Harvey pushed the roof up, and after a few groans and what felt like an avalanche of dust on his and Claire's heads, the roof extended out so they could stand up comfortably inside.

"A pop-top, great for camping," he explained, cleaning the dirt off his glasses with the inside of his shirt. "Sorry about the dust storm."

Claire just shrugged her shoulders and remained frozen in the back seat; Harvey jumped out and squeezed his way around the back of the car. The sounds of metal groaning ensued, a bump and then a soft curse.

"Engine still here!" Harvey called out. "So strange they put them at the back of the vehicle. Much different these days."

"Right, well, dinner is getting cold," Claire heard her mother say. "Let's head back and sort out how we are going to move all this stuff."

"I'll meet you back at the house," Claire called out from the back of the van. "I want to just have more of a look."

"I knew she'd like it," Claire heard Beatrice mutter smugly. "That child is half-gypsy. They love a house on wheels."

Her parents and nan left, with much excited chatter on her father's part. Soon it was just Claire, sitting in the back of Frank, half a kilo of dust in her hair and a fast-beating heart. She was so excited, so full of possibilities. A camper! She could do it up, get the interior redone, paint it and have him serviceable. You never know, this might even be one way to get out of her parents' house. These vans were worth some money now, but Claire did not think she could sell Frank, not after what her nan said. He was a part of the family – a very neglected part, but nonetheless, not something you could simply put on Gumtree and forget about.

Claire tried to calm the excitement of her stray thoughts and climbed out of the Kombi, pulling the side door shut with a hard slam. She patted his side as she left the shed, turning to look at him before she turned the lights out.

"See you soon, Rusty Frank," Claire whispered.

He didn't reply, but it was only their first meeting after all.

CHAPTER 4

Mr Long Black, Extra Hot

"I can't believe your nan just gave you a Kombi van," Daisy whispered, effortlessly stretching her legs over her head. "That is so freaking awesome!"

"I know!" Claire attempted to do the same but in a far less graceful manner, flailing about unsuccessfully. "I have never been this in love. Frank and I are destined to be. It has been written, he is my one true love..."

"Now, inhale deeply and when you exhale, increase the stretch."

"...the Clyde to my Bonnie, the Hillary to my Bill."

"Feel the stretch through the back of your legs, your left foot should be on a 90-degree angle."

"Not sure if that is the best comparison..." Daisy murmured under her breath.

"Huh? Hillary? It's a classic love story!"

"No way! He was a total sleaze."

"Yes, well, maybe...possibly, but iconic all the same."

"If this stretch feels too much, you can lower your weight onto your knee and do the same again."

"Still, cheating presidents aside, it is possibly the coolest gift I have ever heard of. Maybe I should invite your nan to the wedding? She sounds all over the gift department." Daisy easily mimicked the instructor in front of her; Claire grunted at the effort. Bloody show-off, how did her body do that so easily?

"I don't know, Beatrice is a bit of a badass. There is a strong possibility Jo might make a run for it..."

Daisy snorted, stretching her hands up in the air as instructed by the now less-than-zen yoga instructor, who was glaring over at the whispering pair. Claire smiled an apology and went back to also attempting to stretch her hands up in the air. She was supposed to be breathing in at the same time, or was it out? There was a lot going on during this yoga business. Wasn't it supposed to be relaxing? Nobody else seemed to be having the same issues; Claire looked about the room at the other participants. They seemed very comfortable with this morning's practice, flowing through the movements easily, with an air of routine. Claire envied them.

As she gazed around at the other people stretching limbs here and there, Claire's eyes stopped on one particular person. Across the other side of the room, effortlessly following the steps, was what Claire could only imagine to be yoga Ken in loose-fitting shorts and a white singlet. He was very attractive, and had short, neat blond hair and a very muscular body that seemed almost out of place in the dimly lit room full of middle-aged woman and a hopeless twenty-six-year-old with far less flexibility.

He caught her staring and gave her an easy smile back. Embarrassed about being caught out in her admiration, Claire attempted to pretend to be stretching her neck by turning it side to side, her curly hair shadowing her face.

"So, what are you going to do with it?" Daisy whispered, earning her a warning look from the yogi.

"I think I'll try and get him going," she muttered back. "Dad is so excited to help. That man needs to go back to work."

"Maybe he's just excited at the prospect of doing something with you; you were gone for so many years. I bet he's just trying to make up for lost time."

"Perhaps." Claire hadn't really thought about it like that before. She and her father had a good relationship. They weren't best friends, but who was with their dad? Growing up, she had always been very self-sufficient; it was Lynette and even Ben who had seemed to take up most of her parents' time. Claire hadn't felt like she had missed out or anything, though – did he maybe feel that way?

"Will you sell it, do you think? You could get a decent amount for it…enough for your next overseas jaunt, I'm sure."

"I can't, would break Nan's heart." Claire shook her head. "And that woman can be scary."

"Now stand up and reach for the sky."

"I'm sure she would understand though, if it meant doing something you loved."

"Hmm, maybe, but it's more than that. It's a big project, but I'm excited to do something with him more than just sell…we shall see." Claire was reaching for the sky as instructed, but when you were only a short lass, 'the ceiling fan' was probably a more apt metaphor. She stretched her arms and tried for both.

"Well, if he's going by my wedding, I'll pay you in free wine for an extra wedding car…"

"Okay, LADIES…" The yoga instructor raised her voice pointedly. *"And gentlemen. Now we are going to move back to our knees."*

"It's a deal!" Claire whispered back excitedly. "If he's going, of course…I can't promise just yet."

After a few more murmured conversations and another bunch of convoluted stretches followed by a significant period of time just lying on the mat (this was the part Claire really connected with), Daisy and Claire rolled up their mats and Claire went to pick up her shoes from the foyer.

When she was out there, trying to shimmy her shoes back on while wrapping herself in scarves at the same time, she bumped into the broad-shouldered stranger whose hip thrusters she had been enjoying so much earlier.

"Good class," he said, smiling at her as he put on a sweater over his singlet. "Going to feel some of those tomorrow, though."

"Isn't that the opposite of why we come to yoga?" she replied, her mouth slightly dry at the sight of his shirt riding up and exposing the solid, flat plane of his stomach. Christ, Anna was right; she was starting to miss that Argentinean.

"I suppose." He flung his bag over his shoulder and held the door open for her. "After you."

"Thanks, but I'll probably be here for a while," she said, pointing to the pile of jumpers and scarves still at her feet.

He raised an eyebrow at her and shrugged. "Have a nice day."

"You too, see you next time."

"Yeah, I know you will," he said, with a wink. Claire felt her face colour – her neck stretch hadn't been all that subtle after all. He left, and Daisy came out of the yoga studio behind her.

"Who was that you were talking too?" she asked curiously, hopping on one leg as she put on her shoes. "He's bloody gorgeous and I'm about as straight as your hair."

"No idea. But I know one thing." Claire sighed. "I seriously need some sort of love in my life soon, otherwise all this sexual frustration is going to lead to something embarrassing. Like an addiction to midday television romances."

"Well, my hens' night is coming up, that can be one of the challenges!"

"I can't knock back any serious offers at this stage." Claire smiled wryly. "You are on." That's if her desperation hadn't manifested into embarrassing online dating profiles by then.

Daisy squealed in excitement. "Fabulous!"

Claire and Daisy walked out of the yoga studio and into the bright morning sun. Canberra was unique, in that you could never really tell the temperature by looking through the window. If a photo was taken right now, it would show a beautiful, sunny morning; one would never know it almost felt below freezing.

"Hey, have you seen Anna at all this week?" Daisy asked, suddenly a little more serious.

"No, why, what's up?" Claire replied, tilting her head with concern at the tone in Daisy's voice.

"Oh, it's nothing, really…" she said. "I just have this feeling something is a little off. She's been a little reserved lately…"

"Anna, reserved? Surely not!"

Daisy laughed. "Very funny. I'm serious though. I can sense it, something is different with her lately and I can't put my finger on it. She won't talk to me though, I know her, and even if she is struggling with something, she wouldn't want to burden me ahead of the wedding."

"Hmm, it's a good thing you have a sad, single friend with no prospects of love or marriage ahead of her who can do a little digging…"

"Ha! You could have had all the weddings you liked, but you chose the wanderer's life. If we were in another time, I'd call you a drifter."

"Daisy!" Claire exclaimed. "And you, a school teacher, with such thoughts."

"Anyway, you still on for a lake walk this weekend?"

"You know it. I'm going to see if I can catch up with Anna before then, though," Claire decided. "I picked up on a bit of a strange vibe from her the other day as well. Hopefully, everything is okay."

Daisy shook her head, as if shaking away the thought. "Bah, we are probably just worrying for nothing. Meddling friends. It's Anna, the strongest person I know. I bet she is just being promoted or something and is now grappling with how to fit even more hours into her work week."

"Or maybe David has finally proposed and she doesn't want to take the spotlight off you?" Claire suggested.

"That would be a very Anna thing to do," Daisy agreed. "Just internalise something momentous to ensure it doesn't impact anyone else around her."

"Maybe," Claire agreed, kissing Daisy on the cheek. "Thanks for the stretch, I will definitely come back."

"Mmm, I'm sure you will," Daisy teased, giving her a wink. "I saw you enjoying the scenery."

Claire watched as Daisy climbed into her car and drove off down the street. Claire, on the other hand, climbed onto her bicycle and began the short ride home from the yoga studio. She found that she was very aware of cars now. Daisy's car, for example, was a small Honda sedan. Bright red, clean and practical; very much the opposite of Frank in many ways. She was excited to get home that afternoon, as Harvey had organised for Frank to be picked up from Yass and towed to their house. Her mother had been less than impressed with the idea of Frank taking over the carport, but as she generally parked out on the street most days anyway, Harvey said she had no right to complain.

As she was cycling and thinking of Frank, her father called. Claire pulled off onto the grass next to the sidewalk and answered her phone.

"Yo Harvs, what's cracking?"

"Harvs? Cracking? You are an odd one Claire," Harvey said, bemused. "Enough of that though, get home quick! The tow truck has just arrived, and Frank is here!"

"What!" Claire squeaked. "You said he wouldn't be here until later today!"

"Yes, well…" A guilty tone creeping into his voice. "I may have made a few phone calls this morning and I think they have come early just to get rid of me. How far off are you?"

"Just coming back through Manuka, so another ten?"

"Okay, no worries, see you…Oi! Hey mate! Stop! I gotta open the fence…"

The line went dead and Claire sprang into action, cursing her short legs as she cycled home as fast as they would take her. The more she thought about Frank and all the ideas she had for him, the more excited she became. She had some money saved up, left over from her last few jobs overseas and from working at the café. Maybe she could redirect it into Frank, just to get him back on his feet. Or wheels, whatever was the right terminology for a Kombi van that had fallen on hard times. How would that affect her future travel plans though? Not that Claire had any at this point…she still couldn't decide where she wanted to go next, the unfamiliar problem was continuing to eat at her. Everyone who knew her was aware this was her passion, her identity; it was how she was known. Anna was known as a being a kickass engineer, Daisy as the kind primary teacher, and Claire – Claire was the adventurer, the traveller, with an Instagram to die for (but not many followers; you needed to look more like Daisy to achieve that, and Claire's stomach was anything but flat).

Would it be wise to spend a lot of money on Frank, when she did not know where or what she wanted to do next? On the other hand, did she owe it to her nan and pop – carrying on his legacy? The whole thing was all a bit confusing, but Claire felt in her heart of hearts that was what she wanted to do, and Claire had always been the sort of person to listen to what her gut was telling her. Right now, it was saying focus on Frank, get him going. It was also saying that she was starving and also yoga planks hurt…but that was neither here nor there.

Claire arrived home, panting from her bicycle dash, to quite the commotion taking place outside her parents' home. A large truck, with Frank strapped to the back, was taking up half the street and attempting to reverse into their driveway, with a frantic-looking Harvey waving his arms around in what Claire assumed was an attempt to marshal the vehicle. The truck driver, to his credit, seemed to be more focused on ensuring he did not run Harvey over, waving his arms in turn, in what seemed to be the direction for her father to get out of the way. The loud beeping of the reversing truck, coupled with Harvey shouting, had attracted a few neighbours to come out onto their front lawns, curious as to what all the commotion was about.

Claire groaned and quickly wheeled her bicycle over, abandoning it on the front lawn and smiling apologetically to the evidently very frustrated tow-truck driver.

"That's it, that's it!" Harvey was yelling, standing far too close to the back of the reversing truck for Claire's peace of mind. "Just a little further and you can lower him down!"

"Hey, Dad!" Claire yelled. "Can you come over here?"

"Oh, Claire!" Harvey yelled back over the incessant truck beeping. "You're home! How cool is this!"

"It's awesome, Dad!" she shouted, "Can you come over here… I need to ask you something!"

"Okay…He looks like he's got this now." Harvey walked around the side of the truck and over to where Claire was standing, well out of range of the reversing wheels.

"What's up Claire-Bear!" His eyes were dancing with excitement behind his glasses. "I can't believe how quickly it has arrived; we are going to have our work cut out for us, you and me!"

"Oh, yay," Claire said, half-heartedly.

"He is going to need a lot of work, don't get me wrong…good thing I know a little about mechanics!"

"Oh, you do?" she asked with surprise.

"A little! Enough to get your mother and me by over the years. This will be a true test though." His eyes sparkled at the challenge; behind him, Dianna was shaking her head in exasperation.

"Do you think it's going to be expensive?" Claire asked. Frank looked a lot the worse for wear now that he was exposed to the cold hard light of day. From his deflated tyres to the rust she could see even at this distance, Claire suddenly had a vision of her bank account dwindling down to nothing and her parents' granny flat becoming even more permanent.

"It depends," Harvey said, hearing the concern in Claire's voice. "If you want him perfect, that will be a lot of work. An entire engine rebuild, rust removal, respray, new upholstery with original colours, material, etc...that's in the tens of thousands of dollars..."

Claire's eyes went wide.

"As in, tens...?" she spluttered, choking on the words.

"Oh, yeah," Harvey said, taking in her panicked stare. "But that's okay! We don't have to do all that, or at least not at first."

"Tens of...thousands..."

"Yes, but that's if you get it all professionally done by external providers. These classic car companies are like...like people who specialise in weddings," Harvey explained, patting her on the arm consolingly. "You tell them something is for a wedding; they suddenly add an extra zero on the end of their quote. Classic cars are much the same."

"Dad..." Claire's heart sank, all her daydreaming of cruising around in Frank, with his pop-top, bed and kitchen for camping fading quickly behind a sea of dollar signs. "I work at a café and live in your backyard...I don't think I can afford that."

"Don't stress, hun." He gave her an awkward half-hug. "We will do it together, it will be our project. We will focus only on what's necessary to get him going and just build up from there."

Claire nodded gratefully, trying to not feel sorry for herself. The scale of the work in front of them suddenly seemed momentous, and she had no experience with cars. Hell, Claire had never even owned one; she had never even changed a tyre let alone oil or whatever it is everyone harps on about doing.

"I have a good feeling about Frank; I think he's tougher than he looks." Harvey smiled. "Just like my favourite, middle child."

Claire laughed, "That's because I'm your only middle child."

"At least that's what your mother thinks. I'll have you know I was quite the looker in my day."

"Gross, Dad." Claire screwed up her face, punching his shoulder.

The truck suddenly stopped reversing and the truck driver climbed out of the cabin. Harvey ran over to shake his hand and together they walked over to the back of the truck, where the driver picked up a hand controller. He slowly lowered Frank onto their driveway and soon had him unhooked, shaking their hands again when he left. An efficient sort.

Both Claire and Harvey stood, hands on hips, staring at Frank. After much fussing, they decided to push him another ten metres until he was under their carport.

"Well, at least we know his handbrake works," Harvey said optimistically. "What do you reckon we do now?"

"Why ask me? I thought you were the mechanical expert!" Claire exclaimed. "I'm just the house layabout."

"Hey!" Harvey said sternly. "Don't steal your mother's favourite nickname for me, took me many years to earn that one."

"How about we…give him a wash?" Claire suggested. The wind on the drive from Yass had blown away a lot of the dust that had coated him in her pop's shed, but the dirt, grime and all the dust on the inside remained.

"That…is a genius idea!" Harvey cried exuberantly. "The perfect place to start!"

Claire laughed. "Dad, I think Mum's right, this early retirement is sending you bonkers."

"Pssh! It has just blessed me with the time to see how brilliant my children are."

"Do we even have car-washing stuff? Doesn't Mum normally just take hers to that drive-thru cleaner?"

"Hmm, good point…we don't. There is a Repco in Fyshwick though?"

Feeling slightly overwhelmed by the tasks ahead of them, Claire and Harvey went to Repco, where they bought a mountain of probably unnecessary cleaning products. Claire had no illusions about the fact that there was still a lot of work required to get Frank on the road, regardless of how clean he was – but this felt like an easy, comfortable place to start. Surely, anyone can wash a car. Even people like her, with their questionable mechanical expertise. Besides, just seeing how excited Harvey was to crack into working on Frank was adding to her own elation.

After returning with half a store's worth of vinyl wipes and many smelly things with ambiguous names like *Diamond this* and *Pine that*, they spent the rest of the afternoon cleaning Frank from badge to boot. On Harvey's recommendation, they started with the inside first. Claire began by cleaning the front two seats. They were brown and orange like the back seat; their vinyl was a little cracked from age, and the colour was very faded, but once she wiped them down, Claire was pretty happy with the result.

In the glovebox, she found an old Volkswagen manual from the sixties, Frank's car keys (thankfully, because neither Harvey nor Claire had thought to ask her nan for them, possibly because the concept of driving him seemed so far away). She also found a small polaroid photo of a young man and woman with their arms around each other, in front of what Claire could only assume was Frank in his younger years. She showed it to Harvey, who recognised it straight away.

"That's Mum and Dad, for sure," he said softly, looking at the picture and wiping his hands before picking it up. "I think Mum has a photo album somewhere with a bunch of pictures of them and Frank in it, I remember seeing it as a child."

He handed back the photo to her and went back to cleaning out the cupboards under Frank's sink. Claire stared at the happy couple; young and vibrant, staring back at her. Beatrice had long, curly brown hair that fell around her waist and was wearing a pair of wide-legged jeans. Gerald was a least a foot taller than her and had wavy brown hair as well, which finished about his ears. They both had huge smiles as they posed in front of their van, somewhere around five decades earlier. Claire put it back in the glove box, making a mental note to put it somewhere special later, and continued with her cleaning mission. After a solid two hours, they had finished cleaning the interior and Claire marvelled at the change they had already made. Harvey had taken out the mouldy curtains – they lay in a heap on the concrete next to the car – and had cleaned out the cupboards and seats until they gleamed. The whole car reeked of a lemon-scented surface spray, so much so it was giving Claire head spins when she climbed in the back for too long. Even that was preferable to the musty smell of neglect that had covered Frank before, though.

"Do you want a break, or should we crack on and clean the outside?" Harvey asked, wiping his grimy and sweaty brow with the back of his hand, which didn't make his face any cleaner, particularly.

"I reckon we crack on." Claire was tired, but invigorated by the change taking place before her eyes. "He is looking so good!"

"Alrighty, onwards it is." Harvey sighed wearily.

"Come on old man, we are only just getting started!"

Pulling Frank's pop-top back down and making sure all the windows were shut, Claire got out the new buckets they had just bought and filled them with water and a blue car cleaner. Harvey pulled the hose out from the side of the house.

"Would you like to do the honours?" He handed it to Claire. "Let's see what's underneath all that muck."

Claire took the hose and began to rinse Frank down, starting from the top. Streams of brown dirt began to waterfall down his sides; Claire upped the pressure, working her way down Frank's sides. As she went, the dirt began to dislodge, and his bright orange started to shine through from underneath.

"Would you look at that!" Harvey cheered, grabbing a sponge soaked in the car cleaner and wiping away at the vehicle's side. "There is a car underneath here after all!"

Claire laughed and worked her way quickly around the van. She wanted to get scrubbing as well. It took them about an hour to go over the whole van properly; rinsing, scrubbing and rinsing again until they were satisfied enough to turn the hose off and admire their handiwork. It was fair enough to say, she was well and truly in love.

Frank looked far less sad than he did when he'd been dropped off by the truck this morning. His tyres were still quite flat, he had surface rust along some of his edges and a few suspiciously large-looking rust bubbles at the bottom of his passenger door; but overall, the transformation revealed a car that, while neglected, was not a total wreck in the least. Harvey was the first one to say this, while they stood back admiring their hard day's work.

"You know, I actually thought he was going to be in much worse nick," he murmured, echoing Claire's own thoughts.

"I know, he's over fifty years old and he's still got it. Just a little bit of rust."

"Who doesn't at that age? Hmm." Harvey scratched his chin. "Do you think we would be pushing it if we tried to start him?"

"I don't know much about cars, but I reckon his battery would not have appreciated sitting in that engine bay for fifteen years straight." Claire pointed towards Frank's boot.

"Good point." Harvey said. "There wouldn't be much point even charging it. We should have got another one at Repco." Harvey checked his watch. "I've got to get dinner on before your mother gets home and sees that we've stolen her car space."

"I can go!" Claire said enthusiastically, still high after today's efforts. She wasn't ready to stop working on Frank just yet, not when he was looking so good.

Harvey took out the current battery and put it on the ground next to Frank. It was grimy and didn't look very good. Claire decided not to take it with her; she had enough problems without getting battery acid across the back seat of her father's car. After taking a few photos and swiping Harvey's car keys from inside, she was on her way back to Fyshwick Repco, feeling far better about things than she had earlier that day. So heartened was she by Frank's clean transformation that she did not even mind that she was looking somewhat dishevelled. As if someone had perhaps pushed her down a muddy hill. Her sweater and jeans were covered in dust, dirt and wet patches. Her hair –which, thanks to her curls, looked mad enough as it was – had been pushed back by a headband but was still somehow seeming to defy gravity, sticking up all over the place.

Claire bounced into the store and headed straight to the counter; she knew there was no point trying to locate which of the fifty or so car batteries that were lining the wall to her left would work for Frank. She would let the experts figure that out for her. The lady behind the counter, a short, middle-aged woman with bright purple hair, was at least polite enough to not mention her appearance.

"Hello, love, how can I help you?" she asked kindly.

"Hi! I am looking for a battery," Claire said, scrolling through the pictures on her phone. "It's for an old Volkswagen, a Kombi."

"What year, love?" the woman asked, going to her computer. "I can just look it up to see what matches here."

"1968, a manual."

The purple-haired lady tapped away on her computer, making a humming noise as she went. She was a very slow typist, using a single finger to type each, individual letter.

"This computer is so slow," she murmured cheerfully.

Claire thought that debatable, but she was happy to wait; nothing could ruin her good mood after today. She was a car owner – and not just any car, a historic car. A classic.

"Hey, Nance." An impatient male voice behind Claire interrupted her thoughts. "I'm in a rush, how long do you think you will be?"

"Not a moment dear," Nancy, with her purple hair, said cheerily.

"Well, can you chuck these filters on the account?" he responded in frustration. "I've got to run."

"No worries love," Nancy replied, unfazed as she continued to one-finger tap away at the computer.

Claire spun around and locked eyes with the abrupt individual behind her. He was tall; standing so close Claire had to snap her neck up to look at his short, messy, dark hair and annoyed eyes. His dark glower was enough to put a dampener on her good mood.

"Sorry to get in your road." Claire left more than a hint of sarcasm in her voice. Who was he to be annoyed at her? She had been there first; it was simple line etiquette. Totally un-Australian.

The rude stranger just stared at her for a moment, as if surprised to see someone in front of him. Let alone the very short, very dishevelled Claire. She expected him to direct his frustration at her, but he just held her gaze for a moment.

"You have a leaf in your hair," was all he said, before stomping off out of the store with what she could only assume were his 'filters'.

"What a grump," she muttered under her breath, turning back to Nancy – who it seemed had only just managed to figure out the online system.

"Okay love, looks like you are in luck." She beamed down at Claire, speaking in an overly cheerful voice, as if she were talking to a child. "We have one that should do just fine for a '68 VW. Just let me go get it for you."

Claire left the store with a new battery but all former excitement decidedly diminished. What a rollercoaster of a day. She didn't normally let rude strangers upset her mood, but she did feel somewhat deflated. Maybe she'd been living at home for too long. She had forgotten what it was like dealing with grumpy, unshowered backpackers stomping about the dorm room of her hostel after their laundry had been dumped on top of the washing machine instead of put in the dryer. Maybe she shouldn't take it so seriously.

Her phone rang. It was Anna.

"Hey girl," Claire answered. "What's up?"

"Gin," Anna replied. "Lots of gin."

"Your place?"

"Yes."

"Dress?"

"Don't care."

"You drive a hard bargain, my raven-haired friend! See you soon!"

✳   ✳   ✳

CHAPTER 5

Air-Cooled Autos Online

Claire's head felt as if it was about to explode. As it had turned out, it wasn't only Anna who had needed a booze-filled evening. After David had gone to bed early, the pair had spent the night in Anna's kitchen, drinking gin and eating their way through several different kinds of cheese. All that dairy and alcohol was starting to feel less than a great idea the next day, as Claire tried to ignore the intensely fragrant coffee fumes exuding from the workspace around her. As much as she was suffering today, she was glad she had over to Anna's regardless. Being able to spend time like that, getting drunk in Anna's kitchen, was one thing she had missed over the years. Even better, these days they did not have to steal any of Anna's mum's divorcee alcohol to do it.

Claire did end up broaching with Anna the fact that Daisy felt something was off with her. There had been a brief instant when it looked like Anna was going to say something, but then she seemed to change her mind. Claire had not been entirely convinced, but had completely forgotten the moment a few more gin and tonics later, when they were on Anna's couch watching the latest episode of *Billions* and arguing about whether Bobby Axelrod was attractive or not.

Now here she was, several hours later. Her morning so far had consisted of what Claire suspected was an under-the-influence bicycle ride from home to the Bookshop, a very unsympathetic Ainsley, and a few near-misses – with her traitorous sensitive stomach being overwhelmed by the smell of food, coffee and sobriety. Having seen how worse for wear she was, Ainsley had banished Claire to hide behind the coffee machine, while her boss worked the floor and the cash register.

"You will scare off the customers," Ainsley rebuked, ushering her behind the counter. "You look like you've been dragged through a park."

Claire kneeled below the coffee machine and rested her head against the cupboard. She silently cursed Anna and her gin-influencing ways.

"Everything okay down there?" a male customer asked.

"Yup," she groaned, "just…looking for the ol'…coffee beans."

"That makes two of us."

"I suppose you are after a coffee, then," Claire replied, her hangover immediately intensifying at the idea of being upright.

She braced herself against the counter and stood up, albeit unsteadily, from her crouched position on the floor. Her gaze directly locking with the bright blue eyes of the handsome blond man from her yoga class with Daisy.

"Oh…" Claire said, taken aback. "Hi there."

"Hi," he smiled, looking equally surprised. "Yoga, right?"

"Yup," she said, cursing Anna once again. "The ungraceful one."

"Again, that makes two of us."

Claire gripped the countertop in front of her, willing her body to momentarily cooperate.

"Can I…ugh…get you something?" she asked, with forced cheer, her wild-eyed smile probably coming across more manic than welcoming.

"A long black, thank you," he said, leaning against the counter. Claire was suddenly hyperaware of how horrendous she must look, like a body someone had fished out of the river. She quickly processed his payment, grabbed the tamper and went about her business, attempting to seem natural. But he was watching her every move, and his gaze made her already sluggish reflexes feel extra awkward and uncooperative.

"So, how long have you been going to that yoga studio?" he asked. "I hadn't seen you there before."

"Oh, that was my first time," Claire replied, inwardly groaning that she would have to make some sort of conversation in her current state. "My friend Daisy brought me along."

"I thought as much," he said. "I would have remembered you."

Claire's eyes snapped up to meet his. Was that a hint of flirtation? Surely not? Was he not wearing his glasses...couldn't he see the absolute mess of a human she looked like right now?

"It's the hair," she joked light-heartedly. "Most people gave up on the bowl cut in the nineties, but my curls persist on keeping the dream alive."

"Not so much," he laughed. "Well, hopefully I'll see you there again sometime soon. I go most days."

"You must be really fit," Claire replied without thinking, feeling the colour rush to her face immediately. *Bad Claire, think before you speak!*

"That is...what I mean is..." Claire felt her face burning; he just stood there with a smile, eyebrows raised.

"...yoga is hard," she finished somewhat lamely, mentally face palming. Behind him, Claire saw Ainsley visibly cringe at their conversation. Claire handed him his coffee silently, wishing the ground could open and swallow her and her wretched mouth.

"Thank you," he said, politely ignoring the embarrassed stain adorning her cheeks. "I'm Zac, by the way, what is your name?"

"Claire."

"Till next time, Claire."

As Zac left the store, Claire sank back down to her original crouching position on the floor. This time she was groaning from embarrassment as opposed to the bottle of Hendricks, which was still sweating its way through her every pore.

"Oh, dear," Ainsley leant over the counter to shake her head at her. "Was that just as hard to live through as it was to watch?"

Claire just groaned in response, hiding her head in her hands.

"He was bloody cute, too," Ainsley said. "God knows why he's interested, you look like a House of Horrors role player."

"Thanks, Ains," Claire said curtly, running her fingers through her hair in some last-minute attempts to tame her appearance. Too late for that anyway.

"Jesus, hopefully, he can't smell you either..."

"Here's to hoping."

"...like a bloody distillery..."

"Awesome. Good to know."

"How about you go home, Claire?" Ainsley said, finally taking pity on her. "It's quieted down now anyway, and besides, I think all your pitiful moaning is making people look around for creaky pipes."

Claire looked up from her curled position on the floor. "Are you sure?"

"Yeah, get out of here; I don't want to pay you when I can avoid it anyway."

"I'm so sorry Ains..."

"Pssh." She waved her hand in dismissal. "Don't be, I feel sorry for you."

"You are the world's best boss..."

"Oh, not for the hungover thing." Ainsley shook her head. "For that pitiful flirtation, it was almost unbearable."

Claire found herself groaning again. "Okay, that's it, I'm going. I will see you tomorrow."

"Be gone, my smelly, alcohol-ridden child. Make sure you peek into the bakery across the road on the way home."

"Will do," Claire promised. "I'd say nothing has changed from the last time, but I will have a look."

"That's my favourite little gin-soaked spy!" Ainsley clapped her hands. "Now get out of here."

As Claire pushed her bicycle across the road, she did an obligatory look through the open doors of the bakery. Brian was inside, and waved cheerfully at her as she passed. Claire smiled back, considering her duty finished.

* * *

That afternoon, Claire got home to find her parents' house empty, except for Frank. She gave him a good pat as she walked past the carport into the house, the battery she had bought yesterday sitting on the concrete next to him. She had been looking online at Kombi vans for sale and was pleased to see there were a lot out there – for sale and on the road – that looked in the same if not worse condition than Rusty Frank was in. Claire looked down at his very low tyres and decided that would be the next thing on her list for him. She kept thinking about restoration in terms of the interior, rust and tyres, as these were areas that made logical sense to her. As opposed to the mechanical/electrical-engineering side of things, which just felt like some sort of dark magic she did not understand.

As the house was empty, Claire raided her parents' fridge, made a sandwich and ran herself a bath. She hoped one of the expensive-looking bath bombs or oil-scented bath salts that her mother had hidden away in her ensuite would help draw out the toxins currently hurting her brain, stomach and apparent ability to act credibly sane in front of attractive, potential yoga suitors.

Once Claire was in her lavender-scented bath, forcing down a sandwich, her hangover did begin to subside. Claire picked up her phone and continued to google Kombi vans for sale in the Canberra area. There were a few around; there was also a man selling VW secondhand parts on Gumtree, which looked promising as well.

Claire went onto her Facebook, where she searched for classic car and Volkswagen groups around Canberra. One particular group popped up, called 'ACT Air-Cooled Autos Online'; it had several thousand followers, so Claire assumed it must be okay. She sent a join request and was given several questions to answer before they would accept her. How exclusive.

Do you live in Canberra?

Does your parents' granny flat count? *Yes.*

Do you own a historic air-cooled vehicle?

How about your grandparents' hand-me-down? *Yes.*

Claire happily ate her sandwich, soaking in the lavender scent – all that sweeter for knowing her mother would be furious that she had pinched it – when her phone vibrated. It was a notification of her acceptance into the group. After several minutes of scrolling through the previous posts, most of which just seemed to be people either asking mechanical questions or trying to sell their cars, Claire decided to quickly put up a post about Frank's wheels.

I'm a relatively new Volkswagen owner. Relatively as in, less than a week, with just about as much experience with cars in general. The van's tyres are in pretty bad nick. Can I just use any old tyre, or are they car specific? Sorry, I know this is probably a low-level, basic question and sadly I have more to come. See picture of Rusty Frank below, in all his carport glory.

Claire attached a photo she had taken of Frank yesterday, just after they had bathed him; looking at it gave her little thrill all over again.

A comment popped up. *Nice van.*

Then another one. *That's one of the Early Bays; she's worth holding onto, that one.*

Original only, otherwise it's not worth it. Find some online or at second-hand parts stores.

(*Cheers Gary Halden,* Claire thought, *but that sounds like a whole lot of effort.*)

Why get a classic car if you don't know anything about them? It seems like a pretty stupid move.

(*Thank you, Roy Finley, for making the internet just that little bit more of a condescending place.*)

Right-size tyre, hub compatible a George Williams replied, his profile picture a fat-looking labrador.

Finally, someone who was a little more helpful and wasn't car-shaming her. Holding her sandwich in one hand, Claire took another bite while typing an awkward single-handed reply with the other, being careful not to drop her phone into her fragrant bath.

Thanks, George. I haven't lived in Canberra long...

It was only partially a lie. She hadn't lived in Canberra long *this* time around.

So, would you have any idea where I might be able to pop in and get some? As she posted the reply, an incoming call came through. It was Anna.

"Are you alive?" Claire asked, exaggerating her groan through the phone. Her hangover was partially Anna's fault, so she needed her to feel slightly guilty about it.

"In theory," her friend responded. "In reality, I'm not too sure though...Holy damn, I felt horrendous all day. Work was a nightmare. Why did we drink on a school night?"

"Because you are a terrible influence," Claire accused. "And if we can't escape the mundane certainties of our everyday lives, what's it even all about?"

"Hey, Claire," Anna replied dryly. "Don't ever get involved with rehabilitation projects."

"Easy," Claire laughed. "What are you up to, anyway?"

"Well, I just had a phone call from Daisy. She wants to talk hens' party stuff."

"When? She's the bride, she's not supposed to worry about that stuff anyway. It's our job."

"I know, but then she made valid points about wanting family there, etc."

"Ahh yes, the sisters, etc." Daisy's sisters by all account were lovely but somewhat high maintenance; this was all secondhand knowledge, as most of them lived in Queensland now.

"Indeed, etc."

"Okay, well, should we meet up and plan stuff?"

"Yeah, she wants to convene at mine this afternoon because it is closer to all of us."

"This afternoon? Closer? Everywhere is close in Canberra!" Claire exclaimed.

"I said this," Anna replied wearily. "But it is as she wishes, and she is the one rocking white. You free in an hour or so?"

Claire groaned. "I had plans to die quietly in front of the couch, but okay. For Daisy."

"Sweet, I'll see you soon."

Claire sighed, draining the bathtub of bubbles and climbing out gingerly. So much for her relaxing afternoon. She had no desire, really, to return to the scene of the crime from the night before – but if it was for Daisy, return she would just have to do.

After getting dressed and calling an Uber, Claire threw herself into the back of a small Ford Focus driven by a very talkative Jamie in his early twenties, which took her to Anna's house. After several more than slightly impatient knocks on Claire's part,

David answered the door with a wry smile.

"Hey there," he said smugly. "Long time no see, feeling suitably fresh I imagine?"

"Bugger off," she said, punching his arm playfully. "I feel suitably terrible if you must know, no thanks to your girlfriend."

"You two were very entertaining last night. The others are just in the living room."

"Thanks, David."

Claire went through to the living room, where Anna was wrapped in a blanket on the couch, looking just as miserable as Claire. Daisy sat perched on the end of a nearby recliner; her golden blonde hair danced in the afternoon light piercing through the glass windows, making her look every bit a midsummer's night dream and she, Claire, like the nightmare.

"Claire! You made it!" Daisy exclaimed, jumping up from her chair and giving Claire a kiss on the cheek. "I wasn't too sure after seeing this one. You two did a number on each other last night."

"We didn't drink that much," Anna murmured. "We are just old people now. I spent half the morning in an out-of-body experience."

"At least you didn't have to try and make coffee." Claire threw herself down on the sofa next to Anna. "Not to mention Ainsley, who has officially lost the plot over her bakery beau by the way, being way more eccentric than a next-day alcoholic should have to bear."

"Oh, dear," Daisy sighed sympathetically. "That sounds rough."

"Oh!" Claire exclaimed. "It gets worse yet! Remember hot yoga guy?"

"The one you nearly snapped your neck perving on? Yeah."

"Well, he came in. Today. Of all days."

"To your café? The Bookshop?" Daisy asked, her eyes bulging in disbelief. "What are the chances of that?"

"I know!" Claire replied, groaning. "Well, Zac is his name and he has officially seen me at my worst. They say you aren't supposed to do that until at least a few weeks into a relationship. So, we're basically married now, it's no big deal." She shrugged casually.

"Can we talk hens' party now?" Anna whispered desperately from her blanket cocoon. "I would like to resume my nap on the bottom of the bathroom shower soon please."

"Okay!" Daisy replied excitedly. "Let's jump straight in! It's going to be soon!"

"Soon?" Claire asked.

Anna groaned softly, as if Daisy was going to suggest they all get in her car right that minute.

"Very soon!" Daisy replied. "And I need my two main ladies there with me, so no more writing yourself off for the next week or so because I want you to be able to do filthy shots with me like absolute teenagers."

"We can do that," Claire said.

"Yes, we can," Anna agreed weakly.

"Excellent! We are going to have a girls' Sydney weekend and it is going to be all the fun, ridiculous clichés. Jo isn't invited either, she can do her own thing with her friends."

"That sounds about right. Sydney it is," Anna replied, burrowing herself further into the couch.

Claire mentally reminded herself to talk to Ainsley about leave for a weekend. She felt a little bad, given today's antics and the weekend of the hens' night being the Bookshop's busiest time – but this was a big part of why she had come back to Canberra. To spend time with her family, which included Anna and Daisy.

Claire sat back and listened while Anna and Daisy discussed logistics, trying to subtly steal some of Anna's blanket. Her mind wandered back to the attractive yoga-goer Zac. She wondered if Ainsley was right. *Had he been flirting with her? Even in her less than desirable state?* Not that it particularly mattered; she would probably never see him again regardless, unless she decided to keep going back to yoga with Daisy. She had been saying she should improve her fitness for a while now. *So, going back would not just be for a cute boy but also for self-improvement reasons…and as a woman, she didn't need a man…but being healthy is important, right?*

With that settled – and with plans in her head to sign up for a month's membership at Daisy's yoga studio and not stalk the very delicious Zac – Claire managed to edge some of Anna's blanket over to herself and once again listened in to the hens' night discussion.

"…don't get me wrong, I am far from against strippers," Daisy was saying. "I just know Jo will get jealous, so maybe let's just get some dudes in to keep the other ladies happy. She won't care about that."

"This is why I love you," Anna stated. "Always thinking of the happiness of others. Hot men it is."

Claire laughed, nodding appreciatively. Hot men were turning into a bit of a theme. Claire was okay with this.

CHAPTER 6

Sydney Weekend Traffic and Other Bad Ideas

The days that followed the impromptu afternoon meeting about Daisy wanting to have her hens' night early flew by quickly for Claire, between Kombi maintenance with her dad and work – aka spying for Ainsley in her deep denial. Anna had driven herself and Claire to Sydney early on the Saturday morning so they could spend the day attempting to tan at Maroubra beach before meeting the other bridesmaids and girls attending the hens' night later that day. Anna had said the more sun they got, the less they would have to drink that night due to heat stroke, which was a logic Claire could not argue with.

After several hours of Anna stretching out on the sand in a small two-piece bikini, her golden skin drinking in the sunlight, while Claire hid under the umbrella to avoid the angry pink her own became with too much sun, the pair battled the inner-city Sydney traffic to the hens' party. Sometime later, they found themselves knocking on the door of the apartment Daisy had rented out for the whole weekend.

"Have you met any of these women?" Anna whispered to Claire; they could hear squealing on the other side of the door.

"How would I know anyone? I don't know people, I've been on Australia hiatus, remember?" she hissed back, juggling an armful of heavy grocery bags.

Suddenly, a very excited, very beautiful, Daisy lookalike answered the door with a scream.

"They are HERE!" she squealed, throwing herself into the shocked arms of a very confused-looking Anna, who responded by patting her back awkwardly.

"We have been SO excited to meet you girls!" Mini-Daisy exclaimed.

She ushered both Claire and Anna into the open-plan apartment, where a group of mostly golden-haired beauties were all bustling about the kitchen and living area. A large sign had been hung up on a giant glass wall that opened out to a balcony, saying, *Happy Hens,* and half-empty sparkling wine bottles were already scattered across the coffee table and kitchen bench.

"You made it!" squealed Daisy from the centre of all the chaos, her hair a sea of bouncing curls as another unknown blonde woman dutifully styled it with a straightener, a glass of bubbles in the other hand. A dangerous venture. Claire was impressed.

"Of course we're here." Anna dropped her bag onto the floor, disentangling herself from the attack hug.

"And we brought cheeses!" Claire chimed in, holding up two very heavy Woolworths bags. "'Tis the delicious stuff of lactose-intolerant nightmares."

This revelation brought a round of applause from the Daisy clones and the first of several '*woo*'s.

"Anna, Claire! Come meet the girls!" Daisy yelled from across the room; she tried to turn to look at them front on, but one of her cousins had firm hold of her head with that straightener.

"I'm Harriet!" said the original Daisy clone. "The younger sister."

"And this is Danielle and Brianna…my two other sisters, they are all bridesmaids with you," Daisy introduced, pointing with her wine glass to two other older looking blondes talking together intimately across the other side of the room. They nodded at Claire and Anna in almost frosty acknowledgement, none of the same warmth that naturally exuded from both Daisy and Harriet.

"And these ladies here are my first cousins…" Daisy continued. The list of blonde-haired beauties went on, all raising their wine glasses when Daisy got around to their name.

"I am SO excited for tonight!" Harriet all but screamed in Anna's face when Daisy finished. "It is going to be SO crazy!"

"Mmm," Anna replied neutrally, trying to subtly inch away from the excitable Harriet, whose face was now almost pressed against her own.

"Well, I guess I'll make the snacks," Claire said to no one in particular, as the introductions came to an end, and the rest of the room resumed their giggling and gossiping among themselves.

"I'll come and help you," Anna offered quickly, seemingly disturbed by all the female energy crowding the room. Claire didn't mind; having worked in hospitality across the world, a room full of excitable hens' goers didn't disturb her in the least.

As the afternoon wore on it became clear that Daisy and her gang of *wooing* sisters and cousins had no intention of going to dinner – they were hitting the bubbly hard. At one point Harriet declared eating to be 'cheating', and at yet another Claire had to go to Woolworths for another cheese run, as the girls were going through those wheels with a vengeance.

After a couple of slightly inappropriate games had been played – all involving phallic objects that a drunken Daisy kept declaring she found 'gross' and 'not all they were pumped up to be' – they finally headed out in one giant, blonde gaggle (Claire and Anna being the exceptions) to Tank nightclub in the city. After a few more hours of rounds, shots and cocktails, Claire wondered how any of them were going to even make it to midnight. Daisy's family were impressive drinkers, they just kept throwing them back and *woo*ing and dancing; all as energetic as Daisy herself.

Claire was struggling to keep up, but even she was doing a better job than Anna. Claire watched her friend go from happy to slurring her words to an absolute mess in about two hours flat. When she stood up at one point and grabbed the table in front of her to steady herself, Claire grabbed her arm.

"You okay?" she asked, watching Anna's eyes almost roll back into her head just from the mere act of standing.

"Need a bathroom," she murmured, before stumbling off towards the ladies'. Claire followed her; her friend wasn't in the best way. The line to the women's bathroom went out the door it was so busy. Anna looked at it and shook her head. She pushed the door to the disabled toilet open instead, locking it behind her and Claire.

"Good plan, I cannot deal with all the women in the other one."

"I need to tell you something," Anna said seriously, swaying dangerously on her feet.

"As long as you don't vomit on these shoes while you're at it. They are the only comfy heels I own," Claire joked, steadying her with one hand. Anna leant against the wall and sank to the floor, Claire crouched next to her, rubbing her back.

"Just kidding," Claire joked, trying to lighten Anna's dark mood. "These are your heels, so go crazy, the full exorcist."

"I'm sleeping with someone, Claire."

Claire continued rubbing Anna's back, hoping her shock did not register on her face. *So that explained why Anna had been acting even more distant than normal.* When she didn't say anything, Anna continued.

"He works in our building, for the firm…it was an accident at first, just a stupid drunk night out that ended back at his apartment."

"Are you okay?" Claire asked, knowing this probably sounded somewhat lame after the bombshell Anna had just dropped.

"If by okay you mean my life is in ruins, then yeah, I'm getting by." Anna groaned, rubbing her temples.

"Does David know?"

"Not a clue," Anna replied, almost bitterly. "I feel like a completely different person, I feel like our dynamic has totally changed…but he hasn't seemed to notice."

"I'm so sorry Anna…"

"Please…don't, Claire," Anna whispered. "I don't deserve that. I deserve to be yelled at, I hate what I'm doing, and I hate who I'm doing it with."

"Well, if you don't like the guy…"

"Well, this is the thing," Anna slurred. "I loathe him in the way that the whole situation makes me hate myself. That, and he can be so arrogant sometimes, which is insanely infuriating – but then he can also be incredibly sweet and…ahh…"

"And?" Claire asked, poking her in the ribs.

"And…Claire…. the sex, Claire." Anna put her face in her hands and groaned. "The sex is just insane."

"It's always better when it's forbidden," Claire mused, in all her drunken wisdom. "That's why so many people get done humping on park benches."

Anna did not seem to hear her. Now that she had started, it was as if months' worth of pent-up emotions were just pouring out in one big, garbled, drunk mess.

"I feel weirdly addicted to him. When I'm at home with David, I just feel sick in my stomach and want nothing more than to tell him to jump off a bridge, never talk to me again. I do, in fact, tell him this all the time, about once a week now. It always ends the same, though; I can't even be around him anymore. Just the smell of him is enough to send me over the edge."

Tears started streaming down her face and Claire immediately gave her a strong hug. She had never seen her friend like this before; this lost, vulnerable person. Anna was always the strong one, always the one who knew what to do.

"I am a trash human," she mumbled, wiping away tears – and her mascara in the process. Claire dutifully grabbed some paper handtowels and handed them to her to wipe her face.

"Don't be ridiculous!" Claire said. "You are the best, strongest person I know."

"David doesn't deserve any of this…" Anna blew her nose noisily.

"Pssh." Claire unravelled some toilet paper and dutifully handed it to Anna. "This is not about David; this is about you and your journey. Things happen, love happens, lust happens. It's messy and scary and never according to plan."

Anna continued to cry, holding herself against Claire.

"I know you love David, so you are thinking about him,' said Claire. "Do not get me wrong, I like the guy, but I don't *love* David. David is not my best friend – you are. So, he is not my top concern right now."

"I don't know what to do."

"That's okay, none of us ever really does."

"What do you think I should do?" She turned her make-up smudged face to Claire.

"Right now? I think you should stop crying before you get make-up all over this fabulous dress. I am a bloody barista; I can't afford to buy you another."

Anna laughed and wiped her eyes. "I won't tell you how much it cost, then."

"So…this other man…"

"Paul."

"Paul?" Claire cried in mock horror. "What kind of steamy, sex god name is Paul?"

Anna gave a sniffled laugh. "The kind that works in Accounting."

"Oh, god." Claire shook her head in disbelief. "You mean he's a finance guy as well? Honestly, Anna, you are terrible at this affair stuff."

"I wish that were true," she said softly. "The scary part is how much easier it's getting. The first time it happened I was physically ill for days after, I could not sleep, I was just wretched. Now, it is as if…it is as if I have separated things in my head. Like I have two lives, totally separated. It seems to keep the guilt at bay."

"Compartmentalising, I do that with my night-time Cadbury bingeing. Morning Claire is a different person, a *healthy* person."

"It's just all such a mess, Claire," Anna said, slumping further down against the wall, hugging her knees.

"Are you happy with David?" Claire asked, sitting down next to her.

"Happy? I suppose we're happy." Anna shrugged. "We are not unhappy, if that makes sense. We've been together for so long."

"Are you happy with Rafael?"

"Who?"

"My more appropriate name for Paul, the sex god."

"Ahh." Anna turned her head to one side. "Well…I don't think I want to be with him, if that makes sense."

"Does he want to be with you?"

"He says he does, but I'm not convinced; I always tell him it's just because he can't have me, you know."

"Well," Claire teased. "Sounds like he's definitely had you."

Anna laughed, a few more tears coming down in the process. Claire got her more handtowel.

"Look," Claire said. "I'm not going to tell you what to do – *you* need to figure that out. I am not going to judge you either; you are doing enough of that for the both of us. What I will say is you can't go on like this forever, Anna. I've never seen you this torn up."

"I know," Anna sighed. "It's a 24/7 job feeling like an absolutely horrendous human. I think I will literally drive myself mad with sleep deprivation."

"Whatever you decide to do, just keep me in the loop. It's always better having someone to talk to about these things than to bottle it up inside."

Anna sniffed. "Thanks Claire, I really appreciate it."

"And besides," Claire said. "As a twenty-six-year-old barista who lives with her parents, poor life decisions are literally my area of expertise."

Anna laughed, before wiping some stray tears off her chin. "Ugh...I think I need to go to bed."

"Want me to come with you?"

"No, no – the last thing I want to do is ruin Daisy's night. I'll just sneak out of here and get a cab; I can only imagine what I must look like right now."

"You look great. Like a beautiful, misty-eyed panda."

"Oh God, my mascara!" Anna exclaimed, catching sight of her reflection in the mirror.

"You sure you are okay to get home?"

"Yeah," Anna said sadly. "There's nothing like reflecting on your secret love affair in a nightclub's disabled toilet to really sober a girl up."

Claire helped sneak Anna out of the club and into the street, where she hailed a taxi. Giving Anna a hug, she put her in the cab and waved it goodbye. Feeling exhausted from their conversation, Claire drew took a deep breath and walked straight back into the nightclub, pushing her way through the now heavy crowd to find the table Daisy and her other hens were sitting at. She felt emotionally drained and worried about Anna all in one; she secretly wished she could go back to the hotel with her friend, get a burger and fall asleep, but knew she had to push on for Daisy's sake. Daisy would understand, but she could hardly tell her. It was up to her to represent their friendship trio now.

Claire could hear them before she saw them, there was so much *wooing*. She decided to divert to the bar and give herself some renewed Dutch courage in the form of something horrendously poisonous, to try and catch up with the other girls.

Politely moving through the crowd, Claire squeezed between two men and leant against the bar. The bartender in her corner was very busy, but she was happy to sit patiently and try to digest the information Anna had just thrown at her. Anna was having an affair, with an accountant named Paul, who by all accounts was more of a Rafael in the bedroom. Anna had not told David this small piece of news, but in a way she also felt hurt that he had not noticed. What a bloody dilemma. They had been together over eight years, which must be a long time for any relationship; maybe things had become stale between the two? Surely it would be hard to keep the romance alive after eight years? Maybe this was just a break for Anna, something to get out of her system before she went back to David and put it behind her?

Claire put her elbow on the bar and rubbed her temples. What a night. Surely things couldn't get any more dramatic than this?

"Well, this seems like a bit of a stretch..." a male voice behind her said.

Claire, trying to focus her tipsy mind away from Anna and towards the source of the words murmured so close to her ears, turned around – and once again found her gaze locked directly with Mr Long Black, Extra Hot.

"...bumping into you again." He smiled down at her warmly. "Get it?"

"Did you...did you just make a yoga pun?" she asked, slightly breathless.

"Enjoy that, did you?" he asked, placing a hand on the bar next to her. Claire suddenly felt herself very close to him. Ainsley was right, he smelt delicious. Like expensive aftershave and clean linen. Claire's mouth went dry.

"Not as much as I enjoyed that move," she giggled, her previous numerous gin cocktails loosening her tongue. "But crikey, it's effective. You smell really good; did you know that?"

He burst out laughing. "Sorry, I didn't mean to come across like that."

"Oh, what?" she joked sweetly "Do you just seductively loom over any old stranger you meet at a bar?"

"Only the really, really short ones. It's good for my ego."

"I have a feeling you don't need any help in that department," she quipped, her eyes dancing up at him. Who knew linen scent would be such a turn-on? Probably too many years sleeping on dodgy hostel sheets. Nurture versus nature and all that.

"Oof, hurtful," he joked, holding a hand to his chest. Claire's gaze followed his hands; she wondered if he worked in finance as well. He seemed like a Rafael type.

"Can I help you?" the bartender interrupted, yelling over the music.

"Ooh, yes please!" Claire shouted back, leaning across the bar. "Can I have...What are you having?" She quickly turned back to Zac.

"Aren't I supposed to be the one buying you a drink?"

"Gin? Tonic?"

"Sounds good."

"...and tequila!"

"...what..."

"Two gin and tonics and two tequila shots please. Oh! And another vodka martini for the bride-to-be."

"I don't know whether to thank you or not," he laughed, rubbing his chin. "I haven't had a tequila shot in a long time."

"I need some to catch up with that group of girls over there." Claire pointed to the rowdy table that now featured one of the cousins grinding on Daisy while she sat in her chair, snorting with laughter, a large drink stain across her sash.

"Blimey, should have ordered more than one." His eyebrows raised as he followed her gaze.

"Do you want to join us?" she asked impulsively. He just smelt so bloody good.

Zac hesitated, and at that moment the bartender set down two shots and two drinks in front of her. Claire quickly paid and passed the tequila to Zac.

"*Salute*," he said, clinking her glass. Claire threw hers down and quickly sipped at her drink.

"I'm just catching up with some mates...they are outside at the moment..." he said, slowly, as if calculating something. "I can come inside and find you later, though?"

"Yeah, if you want," she replied nonchalantly, not particularly all that fazed at that moment, as the alcohol set in. She swayed a little, clutching at the bar in what she hoped seemed like a totally casual way that didn't reveal her for the lightweight she absolutely was.

"I do want," he replied, grabbing her arm and steadying her. Claire was once again really close to him; his gaze seemed to sear into hers and she felt butterflies take hold in her stomach.

"Me too," was all she managed, but it was enough.

He released her and she smiled at him, trying to walk away casually although her legs felt like jelly. She cursed Anna's high heels, comfort aside.

Back at Daisy's table, things were in full swing. Row upon row of empty cocktail glasses were strewn across the surface and Daisy was in full cackle mode, half-dancing off her seat and half-sitting. When she saw Claire, she called her over.

"Oi! There you are!" she yelled, half-hugging her from her position on the stool. "I am having THE BEST time. Where did you go, where is Anna?" She stood on her tiptoes, looking around the crowded room for her.

"Anna wasn't feeling crash hot, so I stuck her in a cab. She texted me before – she is back safe and snug in the hotel room. Probably on my side of the bed, sneaky bitch."

"Already? She's supposed to be the tough one!" Daisy exclaimed, her nose scrunching in disappointment.

"I know!" Claire nodded in agreeance; Daisy had no idea.

Claire handed her the martini and then inserted herself into the group of girls, getting among the conversation. One good thing about having travelled so much in her lifetime was that Claire was generally able to strike up a rapport with anyone. It was her one superpower and not a particularly exciting one at that. After about another half an hour of half-sitting/half-dancing on her chair, Daisy announced to the table that it was time to dance and ushered all the girls up and onto the dancefloor. By this point, Claire had consumed several more cocktails pushed onto her by her new best friends, and was more than pleased by Daisy's decision-making.

Her head was spinning, as was she as she twirled her way around the dancefloor, moving with the heaving crowd and laughing with Daisy and the other girls. It was shaping up to be one of those great nights where everything was just hilarious and – apart from the bathroom incident earlier – not particularly dramatic. Claire was happily dancing next to one of the aforementioned cousins when she felt a hand slip around her waist and she was pulled up against a rock-solid chest. Claire knew it was Zac before she had time to look up – that expensive, clean linen smell once again. She shivered with desire and did not pull away, leaning into his body as she stood on tiptoe to whisper into his ear over the music.

"You found me," she said.

"I did," he replied, his arms drawing her closer against him. "My friends have just left, thought I'd drop in, see if you were still here."

Claire smiled, her night just that little bit better. Beside her, Daisy let out a giant "*WOOHOO!*" at the sight of Zac, and Claire laughed along with her and the rhythm of the music around her.

Zac, as it turned out, was a fantastic dancer, and he seemed to move her body naturally around the dancefloor, making even Claire – the goofiest dancer in the world – feel light as a feather. It was not long before their bodies were so close that it only took a mere tilt of Zac's head to lean in for a kiss. It was electric; Claire let the music and desire pulse through her, kissing him back passionately.

At the end of the night, when they were kicked off the dancefloor and ushered out of the nightclub, it seemed the most natural thing in the world to go with Zac back to his friend's apartment to spend the rest of the early hours of the morning. As it turned out – as she would tell Anna on the car ride home the next day – maybe he worked in finance after all.

CHAPTER 7

Rusty Frank and His Broken Accelerator Pedal

It had been a whole week since Daisy's hens' weekend and Claire had still not heard a word from Zac. Despite being problematically hungover, she had been excited about her improbable run-in and a consequential one-night stand with the hot coffee-drinking yoga-guy. He had been sweet and considerate when she had wanted him to be, and then not so much at all when she had wanted that. They had swapped numbers before she had left to go meet Anna and drive back to Canberra, so while Claire had not sent him anything, she hadn't received anything from him either. While she knew that in this day and age of Tinder and casual dating a text back wasn't always guaranteed, it irked her in this instance. Claire knew this was probably just because she was lonely, sex-starved and living in her parents' backyard, as opposed to flitting off on another adventure like she had been doing up until a few months ago.

Therefore, whether it was out of physical desperation or curiosity, Claire found herself drafting a follow-up text the following weekend. She mulled over it for a while, changing the words around, shortening it, then adding more for some attempted humour, only to take them out once again. In the end, she stuck with what she hoped was a simple, upbeat message that didn't sound as desperate as she felt.

Hey there dance partner, I hope you pulled up okay the other day. Thanks for an awesome night xo

As soon as she hit send, Claire practically hurled her phone across the living room in self-disgust.

The drive back from Sydney had been a sombre affair. Claire, being initially very excited about her antics the night before –and potentially still drunk – had chattered away for the first half an hour of the drive, before finally succumbing to her hangover. Anna, on the other hand, having at first been quiet and somewhat awkward about her secret reveal in the cold light of the next day, eventually opened up on the subject completely. The following three hours were then spent with a sickly Claire listening to a very talkative Anna letting out every stray thought she had had over the past three months that she had not, up until now, been able to share with someone else. Claire had mostly just groaned encouragingly as a response.

She didn't know what her friend could do, or should do for that matter; she just hoped that she made a decision about her predicament soon. If there was one lesson Claire had learnt during her short twenty-six years, it was that these things – that is, secrets with the potential for any sort of emotional disaster – would find their way to the surface sooner or later.

Then there was the other surprise...Zac. What were the chances he was going to be at the same club as Daisy and her hens' party? What were the chances he would have remembered her? And what, what on earth, were the chances of them ending up having amazing, drunken, messy, steamy, toe-curlingly good sex? Claire knew she was not unattractive, but Zac was something else. He seemed put together, successful, and he smelt good; something a decade of backpacking didn't throw you into connection with. He made her nervous.

In an attempt to distract herself from her message to Zac, Claire decided to take Harvey's car and go visit her nan in Yass. She wanted to thank her for Frank once again and to give her an update on all the work she and Harvey had been doing on him. It was nice being able to spend time with her while she was still in Australia. Since her last visit, and all her talk about her pop, Claire was suddenly very aware of her nan's age. Visits like this, just the two of them, would not be able to happen forever. The drive also gave Claire some time alone to process the previous weekend and all its surprises.

Beatrice Baxter had been wrapped to see her when Claire finally arrived in Yass, still determinedly ignoring her phone. Well, *wrapped* as in she had raised her eyebrows when Claire just waltzed in through her front door and poured herself a cup of tea.

"Now how is that van going? Has your father made himself useful?" Beatrice had asked her, once they were settled in at her table, both sipping from her nan's handmade ceramic mugs.

"He's killing it, Nan." Claire couldn't help but stick up for Harvey. "Frank is starting to look good."

"Hmmph, he never was much of a handyman your father. Much better with books."

"Well, that doesn't appear to be dampening his enthusiasm." Claire laughed. "He has started wearing this old pair of overalls around whenever he is tinkering with Frank; Mum has been teasing him constantly about it."

"Your father is a lot like my Gerald in that regard, he was always undoubtedly enthusiastic." Beatrix pointed a finger accusingly at Claire at the same time. "You seem to have inherited a bit of that yourself."

"Ooh, I hope so." She smiled.

Beatrice stood up from the couch and went over to the bookshelf. Pulling out a number of large volumes, she brought them back over to the couch. Opening one, several old polaroid photos fell out. Claire picked them up; they were of her nan and her grandfather holding a baby, who she assumed was her father, in front of a Christmas tree.

"I have an album here that might interest you," Beatrice said. "It's from the trip we did, Western Australia to Sydney, in Frank in the late sixties. We had just gotten married and flying was expensive in those days."

Scanning quickly through a few of the volumes, it didn't take her long until she picked one up and made a small victorious noise.

"Hmm." She nodded thoughtfully, flipping through the pages of a dark blue photo album. "This is the one."

She passed it over to Claire, the yellowing pages open on several polaroids which had been glued into the album decades earlier. On one particular page, Gerald was smiling happily at the camera in the front seat of Frank. He had a hat on and what looked like a sandwich in one hand. In another photo, Gerald posed in front of Frank next to what looked to be a giant cactus.

"This is so awesome, Nan." Claire flicked through the pages with interest.

"We were so young, back then," she replied wistfully. "By God, I was in love with your grandfather. Looking back at that haircut, though, maybe I'd spent too much time on the farm."

Claire flipped through some more pages of the photo album. It showed the young couple camping on the side of the road, in front of Frank around different parts of Australia, standing in front of surfboards on beaches and napping in the back of Frank's camper with the roof popped.

"We took about three months, I think, to travel across Australia. We could have done it in a matter of weeks, but we were in that honeymoon phase, everything was a wonder. I remember at one point we found this beautiful spot to park on the side of a beach in Agnes Water in Queensland, we stayed there for almost two weeks. It was glorious."

Beatrice's eyes went a little misty and she dabbed her handkerchief at the corner of her eyes; Claire pretended not to notice so she did not embarrass her nan, who was a very proud woman.

"That sounds wonderful, what an incredible way to see the country."

"His parents weren't all that happy about it when we arrived, I can tell you that."

"Really?"

"Oh yes, I was quite the bad influence on Gerald, according to his parents," Beatrice said with a wry smile. "They had these grand plans for him and the daughter of one of his father's friends, another Sydney local. Not a wild cattleman's daughter from Western Australia, leading their son astray and never happy in the city. Our marriage was quite the scandal in the Baxter family, at the time."

"Nan, you vixen!" Claire winked. She wished she had a romantic story like theirs; all of hers just involved alcohol and brief affairs.

Beatrice smiled a little smugly. "By the time we made it to his parents' in that van, he had a rough beard and I was already pregnant. We had already been married in Western Australia, there was no way my parents would have let me leave had that not been the case, but this was all terrifyingly new to his parents. Gerald had wanted it to be a surprise."

"Wow." Claire was impressed. "Your love life was so much more exciting than mine is."

Claire continued to flick through the book, fascinated with all the photos of her grandparents and Rusty Frank from so many years before.

"Hey, Nan, I've never really asked before, but do you still have family in Western Australia?" Claire asked, looking up from her inspection of the photo album.

"Oh, only a few since my parents passed. I think you would have a couple of second cousins, but I would need to call and check that they haven't moved on recently."

"That's so cool, I had no idea."

"Why don't you keep the album, Claire? You can see some before and afters of the van. I think it should stay with Frank; they are his memories as well after all."

"Are you sure, Nan? I don't want to take any more of your stuff…"

"Hush!" Beatrice silenced her with a cutting glance. "Don't be ridiculous, you are helping me out. Don't say another word."

"Thanks, Nan," she said, holding the album close to her chest. "It means a lot."

As Claire continued to flick through the pages of the photo album and over the images of beautiful, rugged places across Australia she had never seen, an idea formed. She had Frank, and an album full of the places he had been – it felt like a bit of a map. A map to the past, to all the places her grandparents had been before they began their life in Sydney, a life that led to her father and then to her. Could she retrace their steps?

They had been young, in love and on their way to a new life completely involved with each other. Claire was at the other end of her journey, she was less young, decidedly not in love, and her future was a blank canvas – but something resonated with her about this idea. She felt as though something had just clicked into place, the thing that she had been missing. The feeling of uncertainty, of being without a plan had suddenly dissipated and Claire knew what she had to do. She had been on this path before she had even known what it was. She had to finish restoring Frank with her father, and then she would take her time, retracing her grandparents' trip in reverse.

She didn't know what she would do when she got to Western Australia – maybe keep going and complete the lap? The details were less important. Claire felt reinvigorated, she once again knew where she was going and who she was; her previous passion for travel hadn't disappeared, it had just got a bit closer to home.

Inspired, she drove home that morning from Yass thinking with excitement about all the things she would need to do to Frank to get him ready for her big trip across Australia. She and Harvey had made some small improvements, but they were going to need to up their game if he was going to be registration-ready in less than four months.

When she came home, as if he was already in on her plans, Claire saw her father with his head stuck in Frank's engine bay.

"Hey, Dad," she greeted his protruding lower half. "Whatcha doing?"

"Claire!" he cried out in fright, bumping his head. Harvey cursed, backing out of the engine bay and rubbing his head. "You almost killed me!"

"Baby boomers, so dramatic," she mumbled, leaning over to have a look at what he had been doing.

"I've just been checking the fuel lines," he said proudly. "They actually look pretty good. I've put in your new battery too. Everything actually looks pretty good in there, from my perspective anyway... and with the help of YouTube."

"You reckon it's time we tried to fire him up?" she asked, her eyes lighting up with excitement.

"I think it's as good a time as any!" Harvey agreed. "We just need to fill him up with some fuel; there's been no leaks since we added oil the other day, so that's a good sign."

"I'll go grab the jerry from the shed!" Claire raced off, her excitement taking over as she imagined cruising in Frank down beautiful coastlines, her hair (which for the sake of her daydream had magically grown several inches and had a perfect blow-dry) blowing in the wind through the van's open window.

Grabbing the twenty-litre jerry can, usually reserved for Harvey's mowing, Claire dragged it back to where her father stood rubbing his hands together in excitement.

"Fill him up, baby!" he cried, doing a little victory dance, with his hands in the air.

"What's going on out here?" Dianna asked, opening the side kitchen door out to the carport.

"We are going to try and start Frank, Mum!" Claire said excitedly, hoisting the jerry can up into her arms. "It will be his first attempt in almost fifteen years!"

"A moment of truth!" Harvey opened the fuel cap on Frank's side.

"Okay," Dianna sighed. "Just wait one moment; I'm grabbing the fire extinguisher from the kitchen."

"No faith," Harvey whispered to Claire, shaking his head sadly.

"Oh, I have every faith." Somehow Dianna heard him from all the way inside. She came out of the side door with a small hand-held red extinguisher. "Every faith in this van's ability to get set on fire and burn the house down with it."

Claire finished filling up the fuel and replaced the fuel cap. Harvey handed the keys over with a big grin.

"Here you go, middle child, you can do the honours," he said. "As the new official owner of Frank, it is only fitting. I will watch the engine to see how it goes."

Claire took the keys, suddenly feeling a little nervous. This felt like an important moment in her and Frank's future, a test to see how far away her new dream of cruising across Australia really was.

"I'll stay with your father." Claire's mother held up the extinguisher in her hand. "Poised for action."

"Frank will be fine, Dee," Harvey replied confidently. "Claire and I have been working on him for over a week now."

Dianna made a noise, which Claire suspected might not have been agreement. She took the keys and jumped into Frank's front seat. Winding down her window, she called out to her parents at the back.

"You guys ready?" she yelled, patting Frank's side.

"Crank it!" Harvey yelled back.

Claire put her foot on the clutch and inserted the keys; turning the keys slightly, she noticed the radio in the dashboard suddenly come to life. A chorus of static filled the quiet afternoon air.

"We've got radio!" she yelled. Harvey whooped in the background.

Claire could hear a ticking noise, was that from the engine? Turning the keys even further, the engine suddenly kicked into action, revving slowly.

"Pump the accelerator!" Harvey cried. "We need to get some of the fuel into the lines; it's been dry for years."

Claire pumped the accelerator and kept her hand on the ignition. She could hear the engine; it sounded clunky, as if it was trying to catch something, or was almost there but couldn't quite get into a rhythm. Frank vibrated and a strong smell of petrol filled the air.

"That's enough for now Claire, turn him off!" Harvey called from the back. Claire turned the key back the other way, feeling slightly dejected. She had really thought he was going to spring to life. Her mood only lasted a moment though, as a very excited Harvey wrenched open the front door and gave another victory cry.

"He lives!" Harvey yelled, doing his best Dr Frankenstein. "That was awesome!"

"Almost, anyway." Claire tried to hide her disappointment from her elated father. "Just felt like he couldn't quite get there?"

"What are you on about, child?" He stared at her incredulously. "That was far and above what I was expecting for a first go! Your mother's car makes more of a complaint getting going in winter."

"You reckon?" Claire said, her chest refilling with hope. Ever since her lightbulb to road-trip Australia that morning, Claire had probably invested far too much emotionally in the idea already. It was Frank's first time trying to start, after all.

"Absolutely!" Harvey reaffirmed. "You should have seen his engine, woke up straight away after all this time. Incredible."

"Your father's right, Claire," Dianna said, surprisingly agreeing with Harvey. "I didn't even expect the first key turn to do anything. That was a very good sign."

"Yeah…see?" Harvey gazed at his wife in disbelief at being agreed with. "Nothing to be down about at all. I think we let him sit for a while and try again in about half an hour, then make sure you pump the fuel lines a bit more. We've stirred him up a bit; let's see what he does now we've got some fuel in those lines."

The trio went inside while they waited, Harvey chattering away excitedly about their first attempt at starting Frank. The more he recalled it, the better the story became. Ask him in a week's time and Frank would have taken off out of the carport at the mere suggestion. Dianna made everyone a cup of tea, and they all sat around the table listening to Harvey's excited ramble.

"I think we will have Frank going before you know it, Claire," Harvey finished proudly. "What do you think you will want to do with him?"

"Claire's going to be off again soon, Harvey," Dianna reminded her husband. "She won't be in Australia for long, will you Claire?"

Claire considered her response. If they had asked her a few weeks ago, her response would have been a resounding 'Yes!' But now…

"I actually had an idea after visiting Nan's this morning," she told them, sipping her tea. "She gave me a photo album, from when her and Pop drove from Western Australia to Sydney."

"I remember those photos!" Harvey said. "Dad used to pull the album out when visitors came around and he'd put them through all the family photos."

"She gave me the album actually; I'll go grab it."

Claire went and got the photo album from the passenger seat of her mother's car and joined her parents back at the kitchen table, laying the album open in-between them.

"I thought if maybe we could get Frank going, to a point where he is reliable and registered, I might try and do a bit of an Australian road trip," she said, rushing the words out quickly. "I just feel like I've seen so much of the outside world but not much at all of Australia. Some of the photos in here are so beautiful, at the places they stopped and camped and saw along the way."

Claire stirred her tea a little awkwardly during her parents' silence. "I thought it might be nice...might be nice to retrace their steps, back to Western Australia? I've never been there, but Nan says I have cousins there. Might be nice to meet them."

Neither Harvey nor Dianna said anything at first; they both seem to be considering her words. After a few moments, Claire realised Dianna, her mother of all people, had tears in her eyes.

"Mum!" Claire cried out in surprise. "Are you okay? What's wrong?" It was shocking to see her mum cry. Harvey was the emotional parent who became a mess during graduations; Dianna the stoic sensible one.

"It's just...it's...." Dianna wiped her eyes quickly with her hand. "It will just be so nice to have you close by."

"Western Australia is hardly far away..." Harvey said, putting his arm around his wife.

"Oh, well, you know what I mean." She laughed, embarrassed. "Your father and I have just missed you a lot over the years, Claire; it has been so nice having you home. I'm just glad to hear you will be in the country longer than five minutes this time."

Claire felt taken aback at her mother's comments. Maybe she should have visited back home more often these past couple of years;

she hasn't realised that her travels would have had any real effect on her parents. Children are a selfish lot.

"Sorry, Mum," she said quietly. "I didn't realise you felt that way."

"Ignore your silly mother!" Dianna said, trying to laugh off her outburst. "I think that sounds like a wonderful idea, Claire – and what a great way of seeing Australia. Your father and I have been talking about doing something similar when I finally do retire."

"*When* being the operative word," Harvey muttered. "Besides! We can fly and meet you places in the meantime, if you get stuck, or even just for a weekend!"

"Of course," Claire agreed, now factoring visiting parents into her road-trip plan. It was not how any of her normal travel plans went, but nothing ever went to plan anyway. She made a silent promise to work a bit harder at keeping in contact with her parents when she went away.

"Well!" Harvey said, getting to his feet. "Shall we give him one more try for the day?"

Climbing back into Frank's front seat, with her parents again positioned at the back of the van, Claire once more tried turning the key. Again, Frank made the ticking noise – until she turned the key the full way and put her foot flat on the accelerator. To everyone's surprise, Frank sprang to life! His engine roared as Claire revved the accelerator, shaking the whole vehicle as it blew out over a decade's worth of cobwebs. Claire gave out a strangled cry of excitement; she heard her father cheering in the background.

"He lives!" she cried, truly getting excited this time and slapping Frank's driver's-side door with her hand hanging out the window.

"Go, Claire! See if you can get him moving!" Harvey yelled, running up to the open driver's-side window. Claire put the long gear stick into what looked to be first, gently easing her foot off the clutch and all the while keeping a steady pressure on the accelerator.

Slowly, like an old man getting out of a chair with fifteen years of stuck joints, Frank ambled forward. Even Dianna was cheering in the background now, waving the fire extinguisher in victory. Claire slowly eased Frank up the driveway.

"Get in!" she yelled at Harvey, who quickly ran around the front and into the passenger seat, slamming the door shut.

"Where are we going?" he asked.

"I don't know!" she replied. "I'm just so pumped that he's moving!"

"Let's do a lap of the street," Harvey suggested, pointing for Claire to go left. She turned slowly, having to keep her hands wide on the massive steering wheel.

"I feel like I'm driving a bus!"

"You kind of are. How is he feeling?"

Claire turned and started slowly moving up the road, waving at her mother who stood at the end of the driveway, watching them go. She beeped Frank's horn.

"Good." Claire picked up a bit of speed and the revs went higher, so she changed into second gear, the engine making a bit of a clunking noise as it got into a rhythm. "Just need to shake out his cobwebs a bit I think."

"Okay, turn up here," Harvey said, pointing at a side street. "We will do a lap and go the back-way home. Good thing we got that new battery the other day."

Claire slowed down to turn into the next street; she went to change gears back to first, but felt the engine suddenly die on her as she put her foot on the clutch.

"Uh oh..." she said, steering Frank to the side of the road. She turned the key off and tried starting him again – but nothing, just the initial ticking noise.

"Try pumping the accelerator again," Harvey suggested. "But not too much, we don't want to flood him."

"It's okay buddy, that was my fault," Claire purred, patting Frank's dashboard as she once again tried unsuccessfully to start him. Pumping the accelerator, she suddenly felt the metal beneath her foot give way and lie flat against the floorboard.

"Uh oh..." Claire murmured, looking over at her father in horror. "I think we've got another problem."

"What's up?" Harvey said. "It's okay; it's all flat ground, so we can just push him home...good thing we didn't get too far!"

"It's not that," Claire said, pulling the handbrake on. "I think his pedal just snapped."

"Snapped?" Harvey asked curiously, getting out of the car and walking around to the driver's side. Claire jumped out as well and inspected the accelerator pedal in front of her. The link that pushed the pedal had snapped, leaving a piece of metal protruding off to the side. That gave resistance when she pushed on it, but the pedal itself just lay flat next to it.

"Well, the things you see in old cars, hey!" Harvey said positively. "Not much point trying to start him now, let's get pushing."

Using their happiness over Frank's progress as fuel, Claire and Harvey put him in neutral and pushed the van up the street. It took them about twenty minutes, and with the help of a nice neighbour who came out to assist, they had him back in his home under the carport.

Claire and her father went back inside to clean themselves up. *Now that I'm planning on doing a proper road trip in Frank*, Claire mused, *we should probably get him looked at.*

"Maybe it's time we take Frank to a professional," Harvey said, echoing Claire's thoughts.

"I know," she said. "I just hope it doesn't cost me my firstborn."

"It's okay – I've got one of those, so am happy to help with any trades."

Claire laughed; Lynette would have something to say on that matter. Her sister was a force to be reckoned with; she was a lot like her nan, actually, the more Claire thought on it.

"We will figure something out." Harvey put his arms around her shoulders. "I have been calling some local mechanics for advice; I reckon one of those will be able to fix Frank in his sleep."

Harvey gave Claire a kiss on the head and went off to make some phone calls, while she finished washing her hands. She looked at Frank as she did so, from the kitchen window, imagining all the things they would see together. In the background, she could hear Harvey on the phone.

"Yes, a '68, I've done a fair bit to it myself of course…Tomorrow? I think I can manage that, it's not that far…I'll see what we can do."

Claire picked up the photo album from the kitchen table and held it against her chest. Australia was a big place; it was time to do some research.

CHAPTER 8

Barry's Tyrepower and Mechanics

Utilising a bit of wood, rubber-banded to a thong, to work as a temporary accelerator pedal, Claire and Harvey managed to get Frank going once again. Harvey had found a local mechanic, only about three kilometres from their house, that was happy to work on classic cars. The real reason they were so happy to find a mechanic nearby – apart from the fact they weren't sure Frank would make it any further in his current state – was that Claire and her father were pretty certain the car wasn't legally allowed anywhere near a road.

"You know, we could just get a tow truck…" Claire suggested for the tenth time that morning, cursing the fact that her mother, as the normal voice of reason, had gone into work early.

"Nonsense! We can do this!" Harvey said with determination.

"I'm more concerned that we *shouldn't* do this in the first place…"

"I'm pretty sure if you are just taking it to the mechanic's, you don't need a registration," Harvey explained, nodding his head confidently.

Therefore, it was Harvey who would get Frank started and slowly crawl him the short distance to the mechanic's up the road in Manuka – as Claire blatantly refused to. He had just volunteered to take the hit to his licence if some stray local cops did happen to be driving by, when Claire felt her phone vibrate in her pocket.

She had been single long enough now not to be overly upset when a man did not reply to a message; it was part and parcel of modern dating. Therefore, she was surprised, albeit pleasantly, when she received a message from Zac following her thank you of the previous day. *Hey, sorry for the late reply. How was the rest of your weekend?*

Claire considered how to respond. It was bizarre, how you could go from being the most intimate you can be with another human being to becoming paralysed at the idea of sending them a follow-up text.

Hey, weekend was good although felt those tequila shots the next day. My poor liver didn't deserve that. You? She sent, immediately throwing her phone down on her lap as if it had been set on fire. Liver jokes, really Claire?

It was only a moment before Zac replied again. The message tone made her stomach churn with nerves.

Pretty much the same...Much on throughout the week? You should come around for dinner. Would like to show you I am good for more than just a post-nightclub kebab.

Claire raised an eyebrow; well, he was being more than communicative now. After the fun she'd had on Saturday night, there was no way Claire would say no to that.

You're on. I'm curious to see what kind of kebab you rustle up in the kitchen though. Let me know what night works.

Tonight? I'll send you the address.

Deal. I'll bring wine.

Claire closed her phone, letting his reply to her wine offer sit on unread for a while. After the antics she had got up to on Saturday night, she could hardly claim playing hard to get, but there was nothing wrong with being slightly less easy to get, surely? *Who was she kidding?* Claire thought, abashed. After her previous dry spell, she was feeling exceptionally easy to get.

"Here we go..." Harvey said, using both hands to turn Frank into a large concrete driveway in front of a massive green shed. Cars lined the sides of the driveway, some old and some new. She could see men working on cars through the building's wide-open doors.

Pulling up in the carpark outside, Harvey and Claire were about to walk in to the shed when a friendly, older gentleman all but ran over to them, a big grin on his face.

"Ahh, this must be Frank!" he said in a faintly Italian accent, "and you must be Harvey. I'm Barry."

"The Barry of Barry's Tyrepower and Mechanics?" Claire asked with a smile, pointing to the sign printed in large letters across the top of the shed.

"The only one!" he replied, taking both her hands in one of his and squeezing them in greeting. Claire didn't quite know what to do, so she just continued to smile in what she hoped was a polite manner, although probably more like slightly deranged; was she supposed to squeeze back? Claire just continued to smile madly until he dropped her hands and took to shaking her father's hand instead. Releasing his grip, Barry quickly walked around Frank, putting his hand over the rust bubble on the van's passenger door, before moving on and opening the engine bay in the back. Claire walked with him, unsure if she was supposed to be making comments or just letting him become acquainted on his own.

Harvey had no such qualms; opening the driver's-side door he called Barry over to have a look at the broken accelerator pedal. Barry's eyebrows raised at the sight of their makeshift pedal, but he didn't say anything more.

"So, what state do you want to get him to, what are you looking to have done?" He directed this comment at Harvey, who glanced at Claire beside him.

"Well, that is really up to Claire at this stage as he is her car."

Barry turned his big smile towards her. Before she even had a chance to open her mouth, he suddenly yelled out to a man who was working on a vehicle in the shed, his head half-buried under a car bonnet.

"Hey, George!" Barry bellowed through the open doors. "Come over here for a second, mate!"

George looked up when Barry called his name; his brow was creased in concentration and he seemed to frown at being interrupted. Picking up a rag, he walked over to the trio standing in the driveway, not saying a word as he dutifully wiped the offending grease from what looked to be an old-model vintage Volkswagen Beetle off his hands. *At least they are used to working with the Germans,* Claire thought. *Vehicles, that is.*

"Harvey, Claire, this is George, he will be working on Frank for you. I figure as he will be doing the work he might as well hear what you would like to have done," Barry said, slapping George on the back. "From there, we can talk quotes after he's had a look."

A shrill phone rang from inside and Barry sighed. "'Scuse me, I will be back later. George will get you sorted."

Claire frowned. This mechanic looked very familiar, she just couldn't pick from where. He was tall, with short brown hair, dark brown eyes and a seemingly permanent crease between his eyebrows. His nose was distinctively large as well. Tucking his rag into his back pocket, George walked over and shook Harvey's hand, then hers. His hand was large and calloused; her hand felt like a child's in comparison.

"Hi, I'm George," he said quietly, his voice soft but deep, before looking over at Frank. "And who do we have here?"

He directed the question at Claire, who paused for a moment before responding. How did she know his face? In the scheme of things, it wasn't particularly distinctive – how many tall, short-haired brunette males could Canberra contain? Hundreds? Thousands, even?

"This is Frank." Claire continued racking her brain. "He's a 1968-model Volkswagen bus."

"Is he running at the moment?"

"Kind of…he starts, and we can get him a few kilometres unless there are stop lights or any period of pausing…then he likes to shut down."

"What are you looking to have done?"

"Well," Claire said, feeling somewhat out of her element but deciding to own it anyway. "I don't particularly care about aesthetics, that doesn't matter. I just want him reliable and I want him roadworthy."

"Historic or regular?"

"Just normal old, everyday registration."

"Okay," he said, his eyes squinting as he took in Frank's exterior. "I will have a look over him and see where we are at."

It was the squinting that did it, and the ensuing frown. He was the impatient man from Repco, when she had been buying the battery for Frank. Claire suddenly bristled as she made the connection – of course fate would throw the world's most sour mechanic at her. Where did cheery Barry go when you needed him?

"Okay, just follow me inside and I'll take down some of your details. Once I've had a chance to do an assessment on the car, I'll give you a call."

Claire took one last look at Frank, as if trying to calculate even with her zero years of experience in mechanics the potential dollar figure she would soon be dealing with. Sighing, she followed her father and George into the large shed, walking past several cars being worked on by other mechanics, who all nodded to George as he passed. At the back corner was a small office space, which contained a desk and a couple of chairs. He indicated for both Harvey and Claire to sit down while he leant up against the wall, letting them squeeze past, his shoulders almost taking up half the room. Harvey pressed himself against the other side of the wall as he went past, before sitting down on a chair. Claire did the same.

George picked up a clipboard and started quickly scribbling down details on a piece of paper. The man always seemed to be in a hurry.

"Number," George directed at her sharply.

"Um....04 665 34 470." Not a man of many words, this one.

"Email?"

"claire.baxter@femail.com.au."

He raised an eyebrow; Claire found herself irritated even by this. She wondered what he had a problem with now.

"Need it again?" Only a hint of sarcasm.

"No, I got it."

"Cool," she replied coldly, watching as he ran his fingers briefly through his hair. She spotted a smudge of dirt on his chin that she hadn't noticed before. The top of her head wouldn't even reach his chin...probably more in line with his shoulders. She found herself sizing him up as he was scribbling, wondering if he really was that tall or if his apparent humongous, impatient, Repco-line ego just made him seem that way. Normally a fairly easygoing person, Claire was unsure why her one, brief experience with this man had encouraged such strong feelings of dislike, but decided to just take enjoyment from the fact he looked ridiculous squeezed into that tiny office, like a bull in a dollhouse.

"Well, that's everything from me," he said, ripping off a piece of paper at the bottom of his clipboard. "All my details are on there, if you need to get in touch. I'll have some spare time to have a look at him and do up a quote in the next day or so."

"Thanks so much, George," Harvey said warmly, shaking his hand. The corners of George's mouth lifted into what would be the first sign of a smile Claire had seen out of him. Trust this man to have limits on that, as well.

"No worries." He shook Harvey's hand.

"Yeah, thank you for your...help." Claire hoped her voice remained neutral. George locked eyes with her, his gaze stirring up her emotions once again. Claire didn't know what was wrong with her, why couldn't she stand the sight of this man? She broke eye contact, shaking his hand quickly.

"You're welcome," he said quietly.

Saying their goodbyes, Claire's mostly to Frank, she and Harvey began the several-kilometre walk home from the mechanic's. Claire continued to glower about George with his big nose and lack of manners.

"Well, what did you think?" Harvey asked cheerfully, a spring in his step as he strolled along the path next to her.

"I think that I can order us an Uber instead of doing this walk..."

"Nonsense, Claire-Bear! How can I get to spend time with you if I'm chatting away to a driver, desperate for a good rating?"

"Well, anyway..." Claire considered her words. "I thought Barry seemed nice."

"Oh yes! I remembered him once we saw him, from the ads. It's a bit like meeting a celebrity when you meet someone you've seen on the television."

"That's one word for it." Claire laughed.

"And George? He seemed like a nice, quiet lad." Harvey wasn't quite echoing her thoughts. "I was a bit concerned about him walking around that garage with all those suspended cars though, surely someone that tall has to come to work wearing a helmet in a place like that?"

"Probably has a thick skull, like those Neanderthals."

"He was a bloody beanstalk," Harvey continued. "And those shoulders, bet he plays rugby."

"About as large as his nose," Claire added meanly. Harvey raised an eyebrow at her, but didn't say anymore.

As they walked, Claire's phone vibrated.

It was another message, from Zac.

Can't wait for tonight…

She drew in a deep breath, the pit of her stomach doing strange things at the sight of those four little words. *Neither can I,* she thought, which was probably why the rest of the day went by agonisingly slowly.

* * *

By the time she had made her way over to the apartment address Zac had sent her, Claire was beyond hungry for their dinner. Food would be nice as well.

Claire was not surprised to find that Zac lived in a brand-new, minimally furnished apartment on the Kingston Foreshore. In many ways, the man was a bit of a cliché of the type of guy she would normally avoid – the type of man who seemed better placed to be called Rafael and work in Accounting. The organised sort, who probably had shares in something sensible.

When she arrived at the bottom of his apartment building via a very nice Uber driver called Sam, a couple had already opened the door to the foyer, so she just snuck in behind them. Following them into the elevator, Claire made the wild guess that the '3' in front of the house address he sent her meant level 3. The elevator felt painfully slow as she stood in silence, staring blankly at the wall, feeling very much like a one-night stand with her oversized bag filled with toiletries and spare underwear (not that the others would know that) and a bottle of wine in hand. She had decided on a simple summer dress, paired with a denim jacket and warm tights. It was her fanciest albeit comfiest outfit, without having to raid Anna's closet. When the elevator finally arrived at level 3, Claire gave the couple a parting smile and quickly shuffled out, looking for Zac's apartment number. She briefly considered the fact she could have just texted him and waited downstairs, but she had come this far already.

Ringing the doorbell, Claire tried to ignore the butterflies that were swooping around in her stomach. She was a little nervous; she didn't have the courage of a raucous group of blondes and an afternoon of day drinking to back her up this time. She knew she shouldn't be, considering the man had literally seen all there was to see the previous weekend – a couple of times in fact – but this didn't stop her nerves peaking as she waited for him to answer the door. Wiping her hands on her skirt, Claire plastered on a big smile, hoping the poppyseed muffin she had foolishly scoffed down on the ride over had finally disappeared from her teeth.

Zac answered the door, looking even more delicious than she remembered. Claire felt her knees wobble a little at the gorgeous blond sight of him in a tight blue sweater, the very same shade as his eyes. Was he doing that on purpose? It wasn't fair, some people had all the luck with genetics.

"You're early!" he cried, opening the door wide and leaning in to kiss her on the cheek. Claire felt her stomach flip at the unexpected touch. "I'm almost finished, thanks for coming over."

"Thanks for having me," she responded, her voice squeaking slightly. As she walked in, Claire caught the smell of something delicious wafting through the whole apartment. "That smells incredible, much better than kebabs; you came through with your promise."

"As did you." He nodded to the bottle of wine Claire was juggling as she took off her jacket. "Here, let me take that, I'll pour you a glass."

Claire took a seat at the stool next to the kitchen island, where Zac was bustling around pouring her a glass of shiraz as well as madly taking things off the stovetop and throwing in chopped-up green things at the same time. The whole process looked very adult; Claire was impressed. When she made dinner, it was an upmarket occasion adding cheese on top of some Vegemite toast. All this sauté vegetable business was on another level.

"Hope you like stir-fry," he said as she sipped her shiraz, watching him buzz about.

Daisy had told her to take a riesling or something white instead, so that she didn't end up looking like a twelve-year-old with an addiction to grape Zooper Doopers, but Claire figured there wasn't much mystery as to why she was here, so she might as well as enjoy the wine she brought at the same time.

"It looks great," she replied, making a mental note to do something about her lack of culinary abilities. "Do you cook most of the time?"

"Not always, just when I want to impress nice girls from yoga." He gave her a wink. Claire laughed, briefly wondering how often that was, but choosing to squash the thought.

"Very charitable."

"I like to think so."

Pulling out two bowls, Zac hummed to himself as he filled them with cooked rice and a huge serving of stir-fry from the saucepan on the stove.

He paused mid-serve. "This is probably a bad time to ask if you are vegetarian…"

"A terrible time," she agreed. "That chicken has already met its maker."

"I hope you are joking," he said, his blue eyes suddenly going wide.

"I am," she laughed. "Although you should know better, especially from the yoga crowd."

"Guess my cover as yoga Casanova has been blown, bugger."

Passing her a fork, Zac beckoned her over to his balcony where a table and chairs overlooked Lake Burley Griffin. Below them, cyclists and runners were still out exercising as the last of the sun disappeared. It was a beautiful view. Claire much preferred to be watching them from her comfortable elevated vantage point, with a hot man and a hot dinner, rather than from down below in the cold. The air was still cold on the balcony, but it seemed to crackle with electricity.

"This is a lovely apartment." Claire voiced her thoughts. "Great view, do you spend much time out here?"

"Most of my meals, except when it is too cold…"

"Right? Canberra in winter is ridiculous! I grew up here but spent too much time away."

"I'm from Sydney," Zac said, nodding. "Even just three hours away, it's a different type of cold there. I'm not built for it either."

"Oh, I didn't know you were from Sydney," Claire said, surprised. "What are you doing here then? Working?"

"The only reason why anyone seems to be," he replied. "I'm a media advisor for the Minister of Health. Or at least, one of them."

"Really?" Claire replied, even more surprised. She had assumed maybe he worked in finance, judging by Anna's review of accountants in bed.

Zac laughed. "Didn't expect me to work, or…?"

"I don't know," Claire replied. "I guess I just assumed you spent your days getting coffee, doing yoga and being harassed into dancing with girls at hens' parties."

"You just described my retirement plan."

Claire sipped her wine and took a moment to subtly study Zac's face. A political staffer? I suppose that did explain the clean-cut persona. Claire had never had any friends before who worked in that kind of area; her transient lifestyle and years of homeless travelling tended to keep the ambitious, political types far from reach.

"Do you like it?" she asked, genuinely curious. Zac shrugged, swallowing a mouthful of food.

"Most days. Some days can be painful though." He took a sip of wine.

"So, what do you do?"

"Try and keep the Minister out of trouble, mainly."

"And how does that work out for you?" Claire asked, sipping wine also.

"Okay, most of the time I guess," he laughed. "Otherwise I wouldn't be in Canberra for much longer."

Below them, laughter rang out from a couple of women walking along the path next to the lake. It reminded her of Daisy and Anna and their Saturday morning walks. Claire smiled at the thought, mentally reminding herself to catch up with both soon.

"How about you?" Zac asked.

"Hmm?" she said, briefly lost in her own thoughts.

"What is it you do when you're not working at the café?"

"Oh, there is no mystery to me," Claire said. "I am but a curly-haired, humble barista, desperately trying to save enough money to be free of Canberra's cold."

Zac laughed, raising his eyebrows. "If you say so."

Claire put her fork down and took a few more sips of her wine. The food had been delicious, and while it was nice talking to Zac, that wasn't why she had bothered to put on mascara that afternoon.

"You finished?" he asked, indicating her plate.

"Not quite…" she said, holding his gaze. Surely that was unsubtle enough for him to take the hint.

Zac smiled. "Me neither."

Setting down his fork, Zac grabbed her hand and drew her back inside. Claire closed her eyes as his arms circled her waist and his lips found her neck. She let out a soft moan as she felt his arms tighten around her.

Claire sighed. She should eat out more often.

CHAPTER 9

Wedding Blues, Pinks and Purples

"Can you pass me those scissors?" Anna asked, wrapping a ribbon around the tiny satin sachet of seeds. "I need it to tie this bow and then finish myself off afterwards."

Claire passed her the scissors, putting the finishing touches on her own small bow. "What a fantastic idea this is. I love it!"

"Of course you do." Anna hacked at her ribbon. "It's sappy even by your standards."

"Don't forget to add the little note inside," Claire reminded her cheerfully.

Anna cursed, picking up a small piece of paper and reading it aloud. "*Seeds are small, but they will grow into something beautiful, just like our love. Nurture these seeds and watch them flourish as a reminder of our happy day...love Daisy & Jo.*" Anna threw the note into the bag haphazardly. "Honestly, engaged people."

"I think it's genius," Claire said, popping a note into another small satin bag before filling it with seeds. "Thoughtful, environmentally friendly and cheap. She's a wedding inspiration."

"True." Anna agreed. "I think I've done about thirty so far...how are you going?"

"About the same. We're about halfway there."

"Did Daisy say what time she was going to come back?"

"Nope," Claire responded, groaning as the seeds she was piling into the satin bag spilled across the table. "Woolworths is just up the road, so she won't be far with snacks. Do you have somewhere to be?"

"No, no...it's fine." Anna suddenly went quiet.

The unsaid accountant's name hung in the air. Claire had been strategically leaving Anna to process the fact she had opened up about having an affair with a co-worker on the night of Daisy's hens' party several weeks ago. Anna, an intensely private and reserved person, had been sure not to give Claire any openings over the past few weeks as the air settled. Claire figured it was about time she checked in to see how the whole thing was going.

"No more...*work*.... you have to pop back in the office to finish up?"

"All finished for the day."

"No late night...*finance*...emergencies?"

"No."

"No?"

"None."

"Yeah, cool..." Claire casually filled several small satin bags with seeds. "So how about Paul, you still bonking him?"

"Claire!" Anna seethed, madly looking around Daisy's kitchen, as if she expected half of Canberra to pop out from behind the marble benchtop and judge her.

"Well?"

"I've...I've kind of just been avoiding him."

"Avoiding him? So, you are going to end it?" Claire pressed further.

"Not sure."

"Anna," Claire said, putting Daisy's 'thank you' gifts down and looking her friend directly in the eye. "You are going to have to give me better than two-word answers. I care about you and I want to talk about this. While Daisy is out of course. And before you ask – no, I didn't say anything to her."

"Oh, I know that," Anna nodded. "Daisy would be incapable of keeping that one quiet between us. I would have started receiving cryptic text messages before you had even finished telling her."

"You were really upset on the weekend…"

"Gin had a lot to do with that."

"Yes, but not everything," Claire argued. "I know you Anna, I know when something is wrong and this something is a huge kind of something!"

"Yes, well, my life is in turmoil, that's for sure," Anna said sadly. "Paul keeps messaging me, saying he misses me, asking what he has done. Now David seems to have finally clued onto a change in my mood, keeps asking what is wrong, is it him, etc."

"Oh, bugger." Claire wouldn't want to be in her shoes.

"Yeah, my life is a mess."

"That makes two of us," Claire said, tying another seed pouch with a length of purple ribbon.

"Things not going well with your Ken doll?"

"I wish you wouldn't call him that," Claire sighed. "It gives me confusing feelings towards the Barbie franchise. Can I have those scissors again?"

"Here you go." Anna passed them over. "Now spill."

"There's not too much to tell," Claire replied, trying to keep the smile off her face. "Besides, I don't want to depress you with the details of all the incredible, no-strings-attached sex I've been having."

"Subtle."

"Always." Claire gave a smug smile.

"So," Anna continued, frowning as she tried to open another satin pouch to fill it with seeds. "No strings attached?"

"None," Claire replied. "It is simple and lovely and not stressful at all."

"So, he's not your boyfriend?"

"Well, it's only been like three-and-a-bit weeks…"

"How often have you been seeing him?"

"Well, most nights…"

"Most nights? As in every night?" It was Anna's turn to push for information now, her face sceptical.

"Well…thereabout, except the other weekend when he went back to Sydney…The sex is very good you see."

"And neither of you have mentioned anything about what's happening?"

"Well, we both know what's happening. We hang out and the other thing I just mentioned."

"Hmm," Anna murmured sceptically.

"Don't get me wrong, I like the guy," Claire affirmed, putting her hands up in submission. "I like him a lot, mostly the physical side of things; but also having another someone to hang out with that isn't Mum or Dad at home has been lovely too. Now, stop trying to distract me. What is happening with the Paul situation?"

"Much the same."

"Although you are ignoring him?"

"Yes, for the most part."

"So, you've cut things off?" Claire knocked over a bag full of sunflower seeds with her elbow. "Shit!"

"No."

"You gotta help me out here Anna," Claire pleaded, scooping up the seeds and pouring them back into the satin bag. "I don't understand."

"I told you I don't want to talk about it, Claire." Anna ignored Claire's raised eyebrows, focusing on tying another bow.

"Well, too bad, because you are just going to have to."

"Why? It's my mess."

"Because I care about you An-"

"That's it!" Anna suddenly shouted, throwing her satin seed pouch down on the table. "I've had enough! I told you I don't want to talk about it!"

Claire froze, stunned at her response. Anna had never yelled at her before, or anyone else for that matter. She was always so calm. "Anna, I'm sor-"

"No! No, you are not! You are just bugging me like everyone else now…like David and bloody Paul. Everyone is bugging me. Wanting to know what I want, what I'm feeling – well I've had it! They're my feelings and I don't have to share them with YOU!"

"I'm just trying to help…" Claire begged her friend quietly, reaching out to grab her hand.

"Well, stop trying to help Claire because it's NOT helping!" Anna moved her arm away, standing up from the table and stomping over to the door.

"Tell Daisy I had to go," she snapped angrily, before slamming the kitchen door behind her.

Claire sat in stunned silence, not entirely sure what had just happened. Did she go too far in asking about her private life? They were best friends; Anna's crisis was Claire's business as well-intentioned emotional shoulder to cry on. Numbly, she began picking up the sunflower seeds that had scattered across the table in Anna's wake, putting them back into the pouches. A few minutes later, a sunny Daisy with an armful of grocery bags walked back in through the same door.

"Hey!" she said cheerfully. "Was that Anna's car I just passed down the street? Where did she go?"

"She had…she had to go to work for something."

"Oh," Daisy replied sadly. "That's a shame. She works too hard, that girl."

"Yup," Claire agreed softly.

Daisy and Claire finished the rest of the wedding gifts, with Claire managing to hold a conversation although her mind kept drifting back to her fight with Anna. Had it been her fault, had she been too harsh on Anna? Had she pushed her too hard? The last thing she had wanted to do was upset her friend. Worry clawed at her stricken emotions as she internalised their entire conversation.

After she left Daisy's and was walking her bike home, Claire decided to call Zac. While they generally messaged throughout the day and saw each other in the evenings, it wasn't very often if ever that they spoke on the phone. Somehow that felt more intimate, like crossing an unspoken boundary, but after the day Claire had just had she didn't care anymore. She felt like speaking to a friendly voice. Claire picked up her phone and called his mobile number, half-expecting him not to answer.

"Hey," he answered, sounding slightly surprised. "What's up?"

"Hey," she said breathlessly, her phone against her shoulder and ear as she wheeled her bike along the path furiously. "Sorry to call, just needed a rant. What are you doing?"

"I'm at work. You have actually called at a good time, however, as I was just debating whether to hurl my computer out of the window or not."

"Bad day?" she asked, relieved she wasn't the only one.

"Just a day, really." He sighed softly. Claire imagined him leaning back in his chair, putting a hand through his neat blond hair. "But enough about me, what's happening, why the rant?"

"Well, you are the only other person I have spoken to about this, because you are removed, but you know the friend I told you about? The one in the long-term relationship, seeing that guy from her work?"

"Ahh, yup, she made the drunken confession at that hens' party," he said quickly.

"That's the one. Well, I was just spending time with her, helping our other friend, the one that is about to get married, and we had a bit of a fight. Well, not a fight, but it was awkward and now I feel like a horrendous human, and as you are the only person I may have spilled the beans to, you are kind of it."

"Noted, get it all out."

"Strap yourself in." Claire breathed with sudden frustration over the phone, her worry about Anna turning into anger at her reaction. "So, I just don't understand her at the moment, the Anna I grew up with is not this indecisive, wishy-washy person. She's brave and forthright and honest. She doesn't have affairs, and if she was unhappy with something she would just fix it, not skulk around hiding it from her friends who love her while she drowns in this ocean of self-inflicted misery. As for David, I do not want to judge her for what she is doing and I truly don't like to think that I have, but it's like she can't even think of him as the same person…they used to be so in love."

"Things change, love changes," Zac said impassively.

"I understand that, but can a person change, or at least change that much? It's like she is acting like a totally different person."

"Maybe it's just a coping mechanism, with everything that is going on."

"That's what I think as well, but it doesn't change the fact that she's burying her head in the sand. The only person she is hurting is herself…and David, I suppose, but he doesn't know that."

"She will get there in her own time," Zac said quietly.

"I know, but it's so hard just sitting back and not getting frustrated."

"I get that, she is your friend."

"Well, I thought she was, but I don't think she wants me to be right now," Claire sulked.

"Everything will work out," he said, changing the subject. "Anyway, what are you going to do for the rest of the day?"

"Well, I was going to head straight home, but I might pop into the mechanic's and see how Frank is going."

"Nice, enjoy," he said, dropping his voice lower. "Coming over tonight? I promise to make you feel better…"

"I won't say no to that. See you later."

Hanging up the call, Claire jumped back on her bike and cycled to Barry's Tyrepower. She hadn't needed to go, but felt in need of a cheer up. She wanted to be reminded of the initial excitement she felt when she first thought of retracing her nan and pop's trip back to Western Australia. There had been plenty of drama with friends when she was travelling and living overseas, Claire was no stranger to that. Many of those friendships had been transactional, though; they were people she had met while working at the same bar, living in the same homestay or visiting the same hostel. There'd never been anything like that between her and Anna, they'd never had a fight before. Never a real one anyway, or of any real substance. The idea of something coming between them made her feel queasy, thrown off her axles.

Claire waved at Barry as she arrived; he was on the phone in his office. Waving back, he smiled and mouthed, 'Are you okay?'

"Just visiting!" she replied, pointing at Frank on the hoist at the other side of the room. Barry gave her the thumbs up and went back to his phone call. Claire walked over to Frank. It didn't seem right, his big tangerine bulk suspended in the air like some sort of square grapefruit. Stuck in limbo; Claire knew how he felt.

"You've got a good body there," George said. Claire squeaked in surprise, spinning around to see him standing there, examining

Frank. Claire felt herself craning her neck to look up at the mechanic. "Hardly any rust at all, only surface. Where was he living before you got him?"

"I thought that was a compliment for a moment," Claire breathed. "But it couldn't have been, I'm plenty rusty."

George didn't reply, simply raising what appeared to be a grease-smeared eyebrow.

No accounting for humour, in some, Claire thought.

"As for Frank, though, parked in a shed for fifteen years," Claire said, finding her voice again after her fright. "Before that, my pop had him and he took great care with him, I think there was a bit of sentiment still there for Nan. It was their first car together."

"You're lucky; people are spending a lot of money to buy Kombi vans in far, far worse condition right now," he said, watching her look under Frank's undercarriage.

"That's me, very lucky," Claire agreed but her voice said otherwise.

"You could get a tidy bit of money for him."

Claire shook her head. "He's not for sale."

George leant against one side of the hoist and Claire moved to the other, mirroring his stance.

"So," she asked, forcing a smile. "How is he doing, doc?"

"Well, as I said, you've got a tidy little van here. I haven't had to do as much as I expected." George wiped off some grease along Frank's wheel axle. "The engine is in good condition; you won't need to consider a rebuild for a few more years. I've replaced a few of the fuel lines, as one showed a hint of fraying and that is one fast-track way for these things to end up a bin-fire on the side of the road…"

Claire listened intently, very aware that this was probably the most she had ever heard him speak. His voice was deep and soft, and she found herself leaning towards him. It wasn't that he was hard to hear; his voice was just so melodic that it commanded attention without distraction or fuss. Claire wished she had a similar skill... would make handing out coffees a bit easier on the voice box.

"Your starter motor was looking pretty shabby, so I've reconditioned it and replaced it, the accelerator pedal was one of the trickier things as I didn't just want to do a dodge and make a short-term repair with the link. There is a Volkswagen spare parts store in Queanbeyan, so I went there and found the exact parts and replaced the whole accelerator pedal and linkages. I've driven him up and down our street – he's moving along really well. Apart from that, just the new air, oil, fuel-filter changes, as you would do with any normal car in need of a major service."

"You've gone to a lot of trouble, I appreciate it," Claire said with sincerity; he had done a lot of work in a short amount of time.

"Of course, it's not every day you see a classic like this, only one other owner before, with no modifications or changes made..." Their gaze met and Claire found herself holding her breath. "Completely original."

"Wow," she said, clearing her throat. "So, do you have much left to do now? Sounds like you have fixed all of my problems."

"Just checking the electrical really." He shrugged his wide shoulders. "I don't anticipate there will be many changes – just in case some wires are disconnected or fused together; but judging by what I have seen so far, I think your grandfather kept a pretty tight ship. Oh, and the last thing, I'm waiting on a new distributer as yours wasn't in the best condition. Will make starting him a bit easier, yours was on the way out."

"Awesome, thanks so much," she said, her heart refilling with hope at the idea that Frank would be ready to go by her deadline, with enough time for her to get him registered and hopefully smooth out a few kinks on the way; before she drove away from her parents and Harvey's enthusiastic mechanical help.

"So, what are you planning on doing with him, anyway?" George asked, his hands now folded across his chest.

"I want to do a bit of a road trip across Australia, actually," Claire said, feeling slightly vulnerable; George might tell her that it was a terrible idea, that she did not have the first clue about mechanics, let alone taking a historic car hundreds of kilometres into the unknown.

"I think…" he said, picking up on her uncertainty and looking at Claire with a smile, "that sounds like a pretty special way to welcome Frank back to life."

Claire smiled back gratefully, not expecting such a kind answer.

"A lot of people would just sell him and take the money," he continued gently. "I bet your grandad would be really proud. I know I would be."

Claire found herself tearing up at the sudden display of kindness from this man, who she had only just recently decided to dislike so intently. Her emotions were extra sensitive today from her fight with Anna, and this unexpected compassion from George the Grump just about put her over the edge.

"You," she said with a choked laugh, trying to subtly wipe away a few stray tears, "are full of surprises."

"I try," he said, putting a hand on his heart. "I also have a sister, so you know, I get regular training."

Claire laughed, resuming her walk around Frank, trying to restore the conversation to light-hearted banter. "So, any tips for my road trip then? I think I will need all the help I can get."

George shrugged, spinning one of Frank's back wheels. "You will be fine, just make sure you take lots of regular breaks. These old air-cooled cars like to overheat."

"Now that I can definitely do." Claire smiled. "More dedicated snacking time."

"Besides, I wouldn't be surprised if he works better by the end of your trip than the start. Old cars loved to be driven; the more you drive them, the happier they will be. Ignore them and they will have tantrums on the side of the road."

"Not unlike a woman, then."

"I choose not to respond to that one." George put his hands up defensively.

"Smart man." Claire nodded wisely.

George caught her eye and Claire felt herself holding her breath once again. He had such a piercing gaze, it was very disconcerting. Over the other side of the shed, someone yelled out his name and the frown she knew him for reappeared. He turned around and yelled something back; the small moment of civil exchange between them was over.

George turned back to her. "I'll message you when I'm done with him. It won't be long now."

Claire just nodded. She watched as he walked away, leaving just her and Frank. Claire hoped that when they were on the road, things wouldn't feel this lonely.

CHAPTER 10

Mr Long Black, Extra Strife

Claire's life over the next few weeks was consumed by whingeing about the Canberra cold, spending time with Zac and being decidedly ignored by Anna. Claire had not told Daisy, who was very preoccupied with the stress of her upcoming wedding, about her fight with Anna. There were times when she wanted to, but she did not know how to frame it without letting the proverbial accountant out of the bag. Anna had even stopped coming to their Saturday morning lake walk, citing work being too busy to Daisy; but Claire knew she was still just avoiding her.

She thought about simply turning up to Anna's apartment but was worried David would be there – and she even had less of an idea about what to say to him – so she just continued to message her absent friend every day and hope for a response. Even when Claire had been overseas, she and Anna and used to message constantly, at least once a fortnight. The past few weeks was probably the most time they had gone without speaking in their decades-long friendship. Thankfully for Claire, she had nights with Zac to look forward to for distraction. That was where she was when she decided it was about time to update her friends overseas on her Australian adventures; on Zac's couch, sipping a glass of wine and enjoying going through the many different trashy romantic comedies available on Netflix.

As she was watching one trailer – something about a woman getting married but her best friend was in love with her or something equally trope – Claire uploaded a photo of Frank in the mechanic's workshop to her Instagram. It was the first time she had posted anything on there in a while; she typed a caption saying *Rusty Frank! Watch this space…*

Humming to herself idly, she hashtagged *#Kombi, #Kombilife (almost), #VanLife (soon)* and *#Volkswagen.* Putting her phone away, she poured herself another glass of wine from the bottle sitting on the coffee table in front of her and switched to normal television. *The Bachelor* was on, and Claire settled herself in for some mindless entertainment while she waited for Zac to come back with their takeaway. She wondered what Anna was doing right now – if she was at home feeling conflicted with David, or out with Paul somewhere, hurting herself even more. Claire sipped her wine and picked up her phone once again; it had been vibrating sporadically as her online family expressed their feelings for the photo of Rusty Frank.

OMG, you have a van?

You're in Australia? Come back to Barcelona!

A Kombi that is sick Claire, can't wait to see it finished.

Claire smiled at the variety of lovely folk she had gathered as friends over the years. Her people, an eclectic mix of travellers and bartenders, easygoing folk for whom living in your parents' backyard was not embarrassing but simply a practical means of cheap accommodation.

A message popped up on her phone. For a brief moment her heart soared, thinking it was Anna finally replying to her, but it was from Zac.

On way back now, won't be long.

Claire texted back quickly. *Awesome, I'm so hungry. I'm two seconds away from gnawing at your table legs.*

Good, natural source of fibre.

She smiled; she was really starting to like Zac. He was very charming, put-together and more than enjoyable to look at. He was almost too perfect. To be fair, thinking back to the men she had pursued around the world, she never did normally go for the clean-cut type. From his haircut down to his cologne, everything about Zac was a magazine cut-out version of the modern male. Until recently, she'd had no intention of getting into a relationship during her short stay in Australia and therefore did not think that anything with Zac could be serious. The past few weeks had changed that, though, and whatever was happening between them was nice, really relaxed. Since that one hot and heavy night in Sydney, Claire had been regularly staying at Zac's apartment throughout the week before he went back to Sydney to see his family on weekends; selfishly, Claire was enjoying having a break from her parents' house. During the week they tended to just get takeaway, watch Netflix and catch up on their hunger for each other. Mostly they didn't go out; Zac said he enjoyed spending time with her one on one at home in his comfort zone. It was funny – could a one-night stand turned sexual convenience turn into something more? Not that she would even know what to do if it happened.

Claire's phone vibrated with another comment on her photo of Frank. She was getting more attention for him than one of her travel photos; not surprisingly, though – he was a handsome guy. She clicked on the likes, scrolling through and looking at the names as they popped up. A few names were unfamiliar, including a couple of car club pages that must have seen one of her hashtags. She scrolled through these mindlessly, clicking on one page called 'Kombi Life Daily', which had over 100 000 thousand followers. She went through their photos and liked them immediately; now that she was a Kombi person it was time to get invested in the community.

Going back to the list of likes, she noticed another name she didn't recognise. White teeth and blonde hair smiled out from the name 'Abbie Maree'. She wasn't a friend of Claire's, so she must have seen Frank through one of the hashtags as well. Claire idly clicked on her profile.

Abbie Maree had a lot of followers, over 45 000 to be exact. More than likely an influencer. Claire scrolled through the many photos of the beautiful Abbie on Sydney beaches in bikinis, drinking smoothies and posing in active wear. Her biography read '26yo Sydney beach bum, coffee lover and perfect pizza maker'.

In several photos, Abbie could be seen posing in front of what looked like a bright yellow Kombi van at a music festival. The van was in great nick, and Claire hoped Frank would get to that stage one day. She clicked on one of the photos to have a closer look at the Kombi; it was in beautiful condition but was a split-window – so, different to Frank anyway. So engrossed was Claire in admiring the van that she hadn't paid much attention to the people in the photo. Abbie stood with a crowd of other beautiful-looking people, leaning forward and giving the peace sign. The Instagram model looked stunning to be sure, but the real surprise for Claire, the one that made her pause in her tracks, was the handsome blond man smiling back at the camera.

His arms around the people on either side of him, he was wearing a loose-fitting white linen shirt and had gorgeous blue eyes and short blond hair. It was Zac.

"What are the goddamn chances," she muttered to herself, shaking her head. He didn't even have social media, something about his work for the Minister. Could the world be such a small place, that she would find a picture of Zac on her zoned-out social media trawling? Clicking out of the photo and back into Abbie's main profile, which was heavily inundated with selfies, Claire found another picture of Abbie with a blond-looking male. She clicked on the photo. It showed her standing on a beach with a very handsome-looking Zac, with his arm around her.

Claire felt her heart grow cold. Men and women were allowed to be friends. There was nothing unusual about that, surely. Claire wasn't entirely convinced in that instant, however. There was a familiarity between them, a casual intimacy that could not simply be unseen. Claire went back to Abbie's profile and frantically searched it for more photos of Zac. She found many more, each one more damning than the next, right up to a caption dated from the weekend before, literally reading, *My man, I love you more than I do an espresso martini. Which is a lot.*

Claire sat in disbelief. Did Zac have a girlfriend? In Sydney?

The door to the apartment opened and an exasperated Zac walked in, holding up the Malaysian takeaway bag. "Sorry that took so long, I think they forgot I was there."

He marched straight into the kitchen and started pulling out plates, putting them on the kitchen island next to the takeaway bag.

"I see you've gotten into the wine," he smiled at her. "Very good choice that."

Claire didn't respond, she was frozen in place with her phone glued to her hand, a photo of Abbie Maree burning at her with her perfectly white teeth. When she didn't respond, Zac frowned.

"You okay?" he asked, pulling out another wine glass from the kitchen cupboard and setting it in on the table. Claire still remained silent; she felt numb, unsure of what to say or what to do. Should she just make an excuse and leave? Confront him? They weren't together, but it still felt wrong. *She* still felt wrong, her heart racing.

"Do you have a girlfriend?" Her voice breaking as she said it.

Now it was Zac's turn to freeze, her question taking him unawares.

"Why would you...why would you ask that?" He spoke in a very deliberately casual manner. His tone was condemnation enough.

Claire felt her stomach turn.

"The why is not that important," Claire said softly, finding her voice. "And to be honest, I'm still trying to understand the odds of that one myself but...do you?"

Zac didn't say anything as he slowly unpacked the Malaysian from its plastic housing and placed it on the bench, leaning over the meal with his hands on both sides.

"Zac?" Claire asked softly. She suddenly felt very self-conscious in her track pants and hoodie combo; it was not necessarily confrontational attire. Abbie would not be caught dead in anything like this, if her Instagram was anything to go by. Feeling incredibly frumpy and unattractive, she smoothed her hands over her hoodie as if to try and flatten the six-month-old pregnancy belly the oversized jumper gave her. Claire wished she was wearing something slinky, or at least matching.

"It's...complicated," he eventually replied, his voice quiet, not moving an inch from the kitchen bench.

Claire felt a lump rising in her throat; she fiddled with the tag on her track pants, her mind racing. What should she do now? Throw stuff around? Leave quietly? Take the Malaysian with her?

Dammit, she was so hungry too.

"Abbie and I have been drifting apart for a while," Zac said finally, looking at her with his beautiful albeit guilty blue eyes. "I just don't know quite how to...end it...properly."

"Right." She nodded dumbly, unsure what to do or how to act. One thing she did know, though – the last photo she had seen of him with Abbie didn't look like a man struggling with relationship indecision.

"I like you Claire," he said softly, his eyes burrowing into hers from across the room, stirring emotions further within her. *He may be a bastard, but far out he was attractive...it just wasn't fair.* Claire looked away.

"I like you too, Zac." She cleared her throat. "But I should probably get home. Thanks for…for the fun."

Christ woman, Claire rebuked herself. *At least think of something more dramatic to say. Thanks for the fun? What was this, a merry-go-round?* Claire willed herself to stand up with her now slightly numb legs and pick up her overnight bag from the corner of the room. Zac's eyes followed her the whole time, but he didn't move from his position behind the bench, he now seemed slightly frozen in place as well.

Claire opened the door to his apartment and hesitated slightly. This was her one moment to deliver some sort of impressive exiting line. Something film-worthy, indignant and inspiring so she could sound like a badass when regurgitating the whole ugly scenario to her friends later. Her eyes lingered briefly on the food on the bench as her stomach growled. Oh, the Penang curry that could have been.

"Well…seeya," she finished lamely, closing the door behind her and walking numbly down the corridor to the elevator. She pressed the Ground button without thinking and felt the doors close behind her – and with them all chances of that dramatic exit. The cold, piercing Canberra wind struck her as soon as she got onto the street. Claire quickly ordered an Uber on her phone; she did not want to wait any longer than necessary in a place where Zac might be able to watch her loiter vulnerably. As she stood there, cars buzzing by, her teeth chattering in the cold and her stomach growling from hunger, Claire looked down at her phone at the profile of the person who'd been a stranger only moments before. How quickly things change.

A silver Ford Focus pulled up and Claire climbed in clumsily, frantic to get back to her little flat in her parents' backyard, away from Zac and the Malaysian curry that could have been. A disappointment on both counts.

"Having a good night?" the Uber driver asked, giving her a smile from the front seat. Normally Claire would have sat next to him, but this time she chose the back seat. She didn't feel like talking. She wanted to wallow in her own self-pity and obsess over a stranger's social media profile.

"Could be worse," she replied, looking back up at Zac's apartment building as they drove away, back to her parents' house. It could have been worse – she might never have known. Or would it have even made a difference? They weren't destined for forever, but it would have been wrong all the same. Claire didn't know how to feel, she just knew in that moment she wanted to get as far away from his apartment as she could.

CHAPTER 11

Wallowing and Other Productive Things

Claire lay in her bed, staring at the ceiling of the former hospice for her sick grandfather. Now, an emotional one for his lovesick granddaughter. She had slept through the whole morning, completely drained from the night before. After getting up to steal some quick leftover dinner from the house, she had skulked back to her room and lain in bed watching TV and overthinking the night before. The cold Canberra winter had decided that it wasn't enough to freeze everyone to death, it had to drown them too, and began bucketing down rain, as if Claire were in some moody foreshadowing sitcom. She couldn't help but resonate with the bleakness of it all as she stared sullenly through the blinds, making a conscious decision not to leave her bed again for the rest of the day. There was far too much obsessing she could do in one spot, lamenting on the miserable weather and even more miserable men.

Had I been in love with Zac? Claire wondered, staring at the ceiling as rain pounded against the tiles. *Of course not,* she reproached herself, *we had only known each other for over a month.* Was she hurt by finding out she was the far less attractive, mid-week sidepiece to a blonde goddess she had never met but was now obsessed with stalking on social media? Absolutely. The whole thing had shaken her in a way she did not expect, it had completely blindsided her. Not the affair, but the feeling it had brought on. She was not someone's priority but their convenience. She was the fun travel girl who never stuck around long enough in any one location to become serious with someone. All her love interests had an expiry date. It was an easy way to live, a good way to safeguard your heart, when you had resolved to never truly hand it over – because what would be the point, when you were only going to be there another few months, few weeks, few days…

Claire had never really been emotionally available for a relationship, to truly fall in love. She wondered if that kind of lifestyle was apparent, or if she came off as transient. Not there for a relationship but for a bit of short-term fun, a dalliance. Claire had always said she wasn't worried if she got married or not; she had never really looked for a partner, because of her chosen lifestyle. Something was changing in her though, something she had been experiencing even before she had returned to Australia. A yearning for home, for familiarity, for old friends. It had started off as niggling sentiment, a small thing, barely recognisable and therefore easy to ignore. But ever since she had settled into her old home and reconnected with her old friends – and become excited about new adventures closer to home – this feeling had been getting worse. While Claire had not been in love with Zac, the small routine they had created, the cosy warmth she had felt spending nights curled in his arms, had sent that yearning into overdrive. As in all things, however, she did not realise this until it was gone.

She had called Daisy the night before, in tears, after she'd got home from Zac's apartment, and told her the whole, horrendous Instagram-fuelled story. She probably would not have, had she not been so upset, as Daisy's wedding was getting so close and Claire did not want to throw any emotional spanners into the works to upset the bride to be. As expected though, Daisy had been wonderfully sympathetic. She had cursed Zac and his yoga zen of lies. She had said he was a trash human and deserved only bad luck and terrible haircuts for the rest of his terrible, girlfriend-cheating years. Daisy said she had been busy with Joanne's parents in town; otherwise, she would have come straight over. Claire had quickly sobered up, remembering the wedding, and told her not to worry. She would be fine, she was tough, she didn't love him, and wasting tears on someone who couldn't even bother to buy extra cutlery for his apartment because he only thought about himself was just wasted salt, in her mind.

She needed to focus on restoring Frank above all else and then begin her road trip around Australia. No more men and their distracting ways, with their sensible apartments, handsome jawlines and beautiful, festival-glitter-loving surprise model girlfriends. Claire needed to focus on her new goal; the rest was just unnecessary noise. She googled travel blogs for people who had completed similar trips to hers to see what kind of set-up she would need in Frank. He already had a sink cabinet and other cabinets lining one side of his interior; they were wood, however, and even though initially she had thought they were fine, upon further investigation some of the panels seemed to have rotted due to the mildew that had developed after years of neglect in her pop's back shed.

Claire found herself back on Air-Cooled Autos Online, scrolling through their page and reading posts people made about their respective air-cooled Volkswagen vehicles. She wondered if it was worth ripping out the cabinets and starting afresh, and if it would it be expensive. Claire had no idea. Could she ask George? Maybe the next time she swung by the garage.

She typed a post, attaching a few photos of Frank's interior.

Hi fellow car lovers, just a quick one. I'm going to be taking my van on an Aussie road trip and am starting to think about interior set-ups. The current one has some rotted wood and I'm wondering if I should try to salvage that or just rip it out and throw in new cabinets. Do I have to get them custom-made, or can you buy them stock standard? I don't want to spend too much money, although I know that is impossible with old cars, so just seeing what you all think. I appreciate your help.

The three little dots appeared under her post as someone began responding almost instantly. This is why she loved this group chat; these people did not seem to have much to do during the day apart from commenting on other members' posts about their cars. She thought the passion that people felt for their classic car was sweet; if a little overzealous at times, given the many notifications of different posts she would get in one day.

Do you have a photo of the rot? Michael Lang asked.

Nothing up close on me, sorry, he's at the mechanic's right now. It's pretty bad in some of the panels though.

Michael Lang's advice was blunt. *I would rip out and start afresh personally. It will cost you a bit though, depending on how you do it.*

I had a cabinetmaker custom-make mine. This from Rex Baker.

Susan Hamilton responded. *Go to CustomizedKombis.com You can order them on there brand new; just have to get them installed.*

Michael Lang replied on Susan Hamilton's comment. *Yeah. If you have a casual 3k to burn on overpriced stuff they are just marking up because they can!*

Peter Hudson posted next. *I've got a handmade kitchen cabinet I'll sell you out of my Land Rover.*

Claire read all the comments with only idle interest, her sadness taking over even her motivation to restore Frank. She must be in a state of exceptional wallowing today. Claire's phone vibrated as she received a private message on Facebook; she clicked on it, curious. It was from George Williams, with the labrador for the profile picture.

Don't replace all of Frank's cabinets.

Claire was confused. When had she said his name was Frank in her post? She had posted on the site a few times before, and this profile had commented then as well. Maybe she just couldn't remember mentioning it.

It's just a few of the wooden side panels that have rotted, the frame is fine.

It was at that moment that a lightbulb went on for Claire; of course, George Williams was mechanic George. What were the chances? Apart from being a small community for air-cooled auto-related people…therefore probably a pretty high chance. Canberra wasn't all that big after all.

Holy Jesus. How have I never put two and two together before?

A bit easier for me. I recognised you a while ago. Larson is the good-looking one between us, so he gets the profile picture.

Claire clicked onto his profile and opened up the picture further. He wasn't exaggerating – Larson looked like an exceptionally good boy, if a little on the pudgy side; Claire related to that, Christmas had been hard on everyone's diets. Larson even smiled as if he knew a photo was being taken. Claire couldn't help but smile also; maybe she could convince Harvey to get a dog for her last few months in Canberra?

So, the side panels hey. How easy is it to fix those?

Not sure, I'm pretty amateur with woodwork. A mate of mine, one of my housemates, is a cabinetmaker. I can get him to have a look for you?

Thanks so much for offering but I realistically probably can't afford it right now anyway. Just Frank's restoration alone will have eaten through a large chunk of my savings when I finally settle the bill. Kitchen cabinets are nice to have, not a need to have; I just have to focus on getting him on the road.

It's not a problem. He owes me anyway so probably would only cost you materials.

Oh wow, really? Claire was taken aback by his offer. *You don't have to do that though? I appreciate it so much.*

George started typing but then seemed to change his mind, the three little dots disappearing. A few seconds later, they appeared again.

I like Frank; you don't meet originals like that anymore. I would like to see him kept whole.

Claire's ragged emotions were not prepared for kindness today, her treacherous eyes welling with tears she did not want to spill. She put her phone down, making a mental note to thank him later.

The rain outside had cleared up ever so slightly now, drawing down into more of a light drizzle. Claire tucked herself under the blankets and left the Air-Cooled Autos page, finding herself once again back on the Instagram of one Abbie Maree.

She really was beautiful looking, Claire thought. In all the very traditional, blonde, fit, symmetrical-faced kinds of ways. They made a very handsome couple; it was like looking at an advertisement for successful youth. The beachy model with the cool and collected clean-cut Ralph Lauren-wearing, university rugby-playing public servant.

It was just as she was obsessing over every detail of every photo containing both Zac and Abbie that the door to Claire's granny flat was flung open. In stumbled a somewhat drenched, very dishevelled-looking Anna. Claire held back a scream of surprise as she took in her friend with her soaking wet hair, a bottle of wine in one hand and a bottle of gin in the other.

Claire stared at her with her mouth open, unsure of what to say, worried the exact wrong thing would tumble from her mouth and Anna would flee once again…her friendship lost forever. She didn't need to worry, though, as for once it was Anna who did the talking.

"Before you forgive me for being an absolute cow in just a few moments' time, I would like to point out that I have always been this way and, really, it's your fault for being friends with me," Anna declared from behind her soaking wall of dark hair.

Claire watched her take off her jacket and shake the water onto the vinyl floor.

"See how obnoxious I am?" she continued, walking over to Claire's small kitchenette and taking out two coffee mugs, which she proceeded to fill with riesling. "I just storm in here after weeks of ghosting you, and rant a little to try and distract you from the fact that I'm plying you with alcohol to try and make the forgiveness process a little easier."

"Well," Claire said, finally finding her voice and walking over to the small bathroom to find a towel to give to her. "At least you came prepared."

"I know what a girl needs when her heart is being torn asunder," Anna said, handing Claire the mug and draping the towel across her shoulders. "Which is exactly why I have a small gin problem currently."

"Did Daisy call you?" Claire asked her, going back to her bed and sitting up against the pillows. Anna nodded.

"I got a very stern phone call last night, telling me to sort whatever weirdness was going on between us two." Anna proceeded to wrap her hair in Claire's blue towel and then climb into bed next to her.

"I've really missed you, Anna," Claire sniffed, her self-pity once again washing over her. "I've felt like a total idiot about our fight. It's really none of my business whatever is happening in your life."

"No, I'm the idiot." Anna took a long drink from Claire's mother's National Library mug. "I am so lost, Claire."

"Well, that makes two of us."

"I'll drink to that," Anna said, clinking her mug of gin against Claire's. They both continued to drink in silence. Claire racked her brain, trying to think of something to say to break the heavy stillness between them. The last thing she wanted was to make Anna feel awkward and have her leave; in her desperation, though, Claire's brain seemed to have completely broken.

"Remember when we were in high school," Anna reminisced, breaking the silence for her and leaning back against Claire's bedhead, "and we both seemed to know exactly what we wanted?"

"Oh yeah," Claire nodded. "I was going to travel the world, every inch of it, and experience all that this big old green Earth had to offer."

"Well, to be a fair, you did a lot of that."

"Yeah, but that dream was just surface deep. I have travelled a lot, yes, but what happens when all that travel ends? What do I want, what do I want to do? I never got any further than just plain old 'seeing the world', seeing all the things my parents never did outside of their comfy world here in Canberra."

"Nobody knows what they want to do. It's a farce."

"You did, you became an engineer. You always wanted to be an engineer." Claire poked her in the shoulder. "Setting the bar way too high. I have a Cert Three in hospitality. They might as well have printed the bloody thing on a napkin."

"Yeah, well, my life didn't turn out the way I wanted it to in high school either." Anna sighed, grimacing as she took a long drink.

"So..." Claire asked tentatively. "How goes the old...love conundrum?"

"Essentially, not a whole lot of positive change. David has been away with work, so I've barely seen him, which has made the whole thing a bit easier."

"And lover boy?"

"Paul...Paul is getting a bit more impatient." Anna rubbed her shoulders defensively. "He says he doesn't want to do this anymore; he says that we should be together."

"Well, that's good for Paul, but how do you feel about all this?"

"Weird," Anna admitted. "I feel like the world's worst human saying this, but I was kind of able to separate both lives before. David was never spoken of; he has been the taboo topic in this whole torrid affair. I strongly avoid all mention of him, and Paul does the same."

"What's changed, do you think?"

"Oh, it's Paul alright," Anna said dryly. "He's really ramped it up a notch. He says he wants to be together – for real, though. He keeps asking what I want, am I going to leave David, what are we doing… all that emotional kind of stuff."

"Jesus." Claire's eyebrows all but hit the ceiling. "Isn't it us women who generally get blamed for being the emotive ones?"

"Apparently not. He wants to make a real go of it."

"As in, be a couple?" Claire tried to keep her face impassive, willing her rebellious expressions to be still. *That is a big change,* Claire's worried mind processed. *A lot of big changes happening very quickly.*

"Yeah," Anna replied, scrunching up her face. "He's even talking about marriage. I keep leaving whenever he brings it up, though."

"Wow." Claire sat up straight, no hiding her shock this time. "Marriage as in, aisle and dress and…"

"…and no long-term boyfriend of mine throwing a spanner in the works."

"Bloody hell," Claire whispered, shocked. "That is a turn of events."

"You're telling me."

"So, what are you going to do?"

"Right now? I'm going to keep day drinking with you and try to forget about my moral bankruptcy." Anna clinked her National Library mug against Claire's.

"Very funny. No, with your man issues?"

"Honestly," Anna shrugged, "I have no idea. I feel so emotionally drained by the whole thing, I'm finding it hard to even get out of bed some days, let alone make a decision like that. I keep playing over in my mind how much it would hurt David."

"Do you still love him?" Claire asked cautiously, not wanting to overstep the mark with Anna once again.

"Oh, yes." Anna nodded. "Not in the way that I used to, I think; more in the way that I love someone who's been a big part of my life for so many years. All the urgent passion is gone, but I suppose that is just time and familiarity."

"Or maybe you just prefer the accountancy types." Claire herself could barely count; she didn't need that kind of negativity in life.

"Maybe, maybe I do."

"Men," Claire lamented softly.

Anna's head snapped up and she studied Claire's face closely.

"Christ, you must think me a horrible hypocrite," she said suddenly.

"Huh? Why?"

"Well, here you are hurting from Zac cheating on his girlfriend with you, and I'm sitting here spouting off about my affair!" Anna cried out, mortification crossing her face.

"Pssh," Claire waved her hand. "They are totally different circumstances."

"How?" Anna asked. "He is a cheating twat, as am I. You are like a non-complicit Paul."

"Minus the marriage proposals." Claire winked, tipping her wine mug towards Anna.

"Still…" Anna trailed off, a worried expression on her face. "If it is making you feel worse having me here, please let me know and I will go."

"Stop being stupid, woman!" Claire cried, throwing her arms around Anna's neck and giving her a big hug. "You and Daisy are two of the best friends I have in the world. I'd want you here, even if you were sleeping with a thousand accountants."

"Jesus," Anna said, hugging her back. "You give me way too much credit, and that sounds like possibly the world's most boring orgy."

After devouring the bottle of wine and briefly sneaking into her parents' house to steal Dianna's diet tonic water, both Claire and Anna continued to rapidly down their drinks and rant about their respective distrust of the men of the world. The sun was well and truly down by the time they were back in Claire's bed, giggling like schoolchildren as all awkwardness over their fight from weeks before disappeared. They also spent an incredibly long period of time stalking Abbie Maree's Instagram, analysing in depth every one of her photos and looking for nonexistent flaws in the frustratingly flawless woman's physique.

"It's just bizarre," Anna said, nonplussed. "You are beautiful and special and wonderful Claire, don't get me wrong…but this woman is a super model…"

"I know! Like, even I'd rather sleep with her than myself. I'm too lazy to shave past my knees most of the time. She looks far more put-together, like she would even wax her legs…her whole legs."

"I bet if we scrolled for long enough, we would find her advertising teeth whitening."

"Do you reckon she knows?" Claire asked. "Perhaps, maybe, they have an arrangement?"

"If that were so, why wouldn't he just tell you when you confronted him about it?" Anna grimaced apologetically.

"Maybe he didn't think I would believe him, maybe he felt too insecure about being caught out?" Claire momentarily felt a small glimmer of hope. Perhaps she had judged him too quickly?

"I don't know, Claire – that feels like a stretch. He still kept her from you, regardless of what his arrangement with her was."

Claire conceded this made sense. She sighed, her shoulders falling slightly.

"Ugh, I know you are right," Claire said begrudgingly. "The sex was just so good, Anna…"

"How good?"

"Okay, well, not the craziest night of this here young gal's life… but he was just so attractive. So nice to look at."

"I can't judge on that account. Paul has these muscles literally on top of the muscles on his shoulders. I don't know what they're called but they are fun to look at."

Claire moaned, flopping her head onto Anna's shoulders. "Why do I always seem to attract these handsome, unavailable types?"

"I think you just attract all types, by being a genuinely good person," Anna said casually, running her fingers through her long black hair as it slowly dried. "Us horrible, cheating types like to surround ourselves with all you respectable folk. It makes us feel less shitty about ourselves, in the aura of your goodness."

Claire snorted. "What a load of shite."

"I mean it! You are very beautiful. If I was just attracted to you, I wouldn't have to deal with my Paul and David problems."

"I suppose I am quite the catch," Claire agreed. "Late twenties, living in a fibro shack in my parents' backyard that the council isn't technically allowed to know about. Just basically exactly what most men are looking for."

"How is Frank going, anyway?" Anna asked, changing the subject. "I was hoping to see him here when I came by."

"Oh no, he's still at the doctor's. He has a few more tweaks to go before he is ready for registration."

Claire told Anna all about Frank and his slow transformation, as well as her plans for taking him around Australia. She had had a fair bit to drink by this point, as had Anna, so the concept seemed extremely exciting all over again.

"Wow, Claire," Anna slurred, slumped on top of the sheets in

Claire's bed. "That sounds fantastic. You will be doing your own Aussie *Into the Wild*."

"Yeah," Claire replied with a yawn, "except I'll live off servo chips and pizza pockets so no sneaky plant can poison me."

"Smart."

"Bloody oath," Claire replied. "You know I've been to that bus, the Magic Bus? In Alaska."

"That's awesome," Anna replied, her eyes drifting closed. Claire felt her own starting to go as well.

Next to her in the bed, Claire's phone vibrated. It was George.

You should come around to the shop tomorrow; I think Frank is almost good to go.

Claire's heart soared; she quickly typed a reply.

Already? Fantastic!

I can go with you to get it registered if you like, might make things a bit easier.

I'll be there bright and early!

Assuming your dad will want to tag along, best bring him as well.

Never assumed I had a choice, will do. Claire's fingers worked furiously at the keyboard on her phone as she typed.

"Who are you talking to?" Anna asked, peering over her shoulder with a yawn.

"Just the mechanic who's working on Frank."

"Is he cute?" she asked, squinting at the photo of the overweight labrador from George's Messenger profile picture.

"No way," Claire replied quickly.

"That was defensive."

"He's a bit of a grump to be honest."

"Well, he seems very interested in helping you out with Frank."

"It's his job!" Claire explained, giving Anna a small shove. Anna always had a sense about these things, but she had missed the mark this time. She wasn't interested in George, he was grumpy and far too tall and did things like…like be too quiet. Besides, she could never date someone like him, he would barely fit in her flat.

"Not to go to Roads and Transport to help you get registered – that is above and beyond the mechanic's oath to serve."

"So suspicious," Claire teased, rolling her eyes.

"Mark my words," Anna yawned. "Mr Mechanic is digging what you're putting down."

"Jesus," Claire laughed. "Just go to sleep already."

At that moment, Claire's phone vibrated again, a message popping up on her home screen.

Oh, spoke to my mate also. He'll pop by throughout the week to check out the cabinets.

Beside her, Anna made a small triumphant noise, which Claire pointedly ignored, typing what she thought was a very professional message in response.

That is wonderful George, thank you so much for your mechanical help. Will touch base tomorrow re invoice.

"There, see?" she said to Anna, hitting send. "Purely professional."

"Hmmph," Anna replied. "I remember those days."

Claire punched her friend on the arm, before putting her phone down and taking another sip of her drink. Anna punched her back playfully and then leant her head against Claire's shoulder. The rain continued to pound on the rooftiles above and the Canberra cold continued to seep in through the crack under her door, but Claire didn't mind it so much anymore.

CHAPTER 12

Rusty Frank Gets Registered

Claire could not have been happier – her slight hangover be damned – when Harvey drove her to Barry's Tyrepower the next day. Frank's mechanical work had been completed and he was ready for registration, Anna and she were back to their normal friendship, and even the Canberra winter had decided to ease back a little and open up its skies for a lovely, sunny day. Claire hummed to herself cheerfully in the passenger seat next to her father, as he muttered under his breath about the different steps they would need to sort out to get the registration completed.

"…transfer to Claire's first and the roadworthy…" he murmured. "Surely those rust spots only surface…"

"Oi, Father-type." Claire whistled, interrupting the inner dialogue that was leaking out. "It will be fine; Barry said over the phone the other day that he is roadworthy. Quit your stressing."

"Me?" He feigned shock. "I'm not stressed, this is your car and your road trip, I am but an uninvested observer."

"Uh-huh," she said sceptically. "How many flights have you booked?"

"Two, actually! Can you believe your mother has already put in leave for it? I didn't think she would be as excited as I was to take time off work."

"I don't even know where I'll be yet, Dad," she laughed. "Where have you booked flights to?"

"Well, I figure you will be in the general vicinity if you go for the three months like you planned...we've booked Brisbane and Broome."

"Nice! I'll make sure I meet you guys wherever you are; you can buy me breakfast."

"Sounds like a deal."

"I'll need it, too," Claire mused. "Depending on how well Frank goes, I'm thinking of extending the trip."

"Oh, yeah?" Harvey asked, interested. "By how long?"

"Well, the original plan was just to go to Western Australia where Nan used to live, but I've done the maths and if I live off dry noodles and stolen roadside fruit, I should be able to have enough fuel to get me around an entire lap. It will just be slow going. I figure I can always do odd jobs along the way if need be."

"So, about...six months?"

"I don't know." Claire tilted her head to the side. "Maybe longer. Maybe a year or even two if I find a spot to make a little money for fuel and keep going. I think I could see all of Australia pretty intimately in about a year or two."

"Wow...that's a big decision!" Harvey said, looking over at Claire with a serious expression on his face. "Do you think Frank would be up for it?"

"Hmm, that is the biggest worry," Claire agreed. "Repair costs if he broke down. Classic cars ain't cheap."

"You may have to just take it very slow, if that's the case," Harvey said seriously. "Lots of breaks, keep that engine cool. Wouldn't hurt for you to learn some basic mechanics as well."

They pulled up at Barry's Tyrepower and Mechanics and Claire felt the excitement well up inside her; she all but bounced out of the car when she saw him. Sitting in the carpark out front of the shed sat Frank, gleaming like a ripe tangerine. Someone had given him another wash, to get rid of all the grime from the workshop. As she bounded over to the van, George and Barry walked out of the large open roller doors. Barry had a large, happy smile on his face; following behind him, George was more reserved, his face impassive. Claire felt herself bristling against it. *Would it kill him to smile?* She'd seen garden gnomes with more emotions.

"You ready to give him a go?" Barry asked, holding up Frank's keys.

Claire squealed, "So ready!"

"Well, here you go love," Barry said, throwing her the keys. Claire grabbed them, not needing to be told twice. Climbing into the front seat, she put the keys in, and with nervous fingers, her foot on the clutch, she turned him on. Frank's engine fired up straight away, no hesitation or slow turnover from the engine. As he rumbled underneath her happily, Claire revved the engine a few times, revelling in the loud, healthy roar each time she did. Excitement pumping through her veins, she put the gearshift into first and slowly eased off the clutch. Frank effortlessly jumped into motion straight away, with no hesitation. Harvey whooped as she drove past him, beeping Frank's horn in glee.

Despite not being registered, she did a lap of the neighbourhood, amazed at the difference a month with George had made. When she slowed down and put Frank in neutral, he idled healthily, not a hint of a stall. As she drove back to the mechanic's, with her window down, curly hair blowing in the wind, she imagined what it would feel like to be driving along the highway out of Canberra; a couple of changes of clothes, some bathers, a pair of thongs and a bed set up in the back, no idea when she would return. The feeling warmed the pit of her stomach, until it reached her head and she felt giddy with the pure notion of it. The freedom, the unknown. She wondered where she would wander, what sights she would find, what new friends she would make. Claire pulled Frank back into the carpark, a massive smile across her wind-flushed face.

"That was incredible," she breathed, reluctantly turning the engine off and sitting back in the seat.

"How'd he do?" Harvey asked, his eyes sparkling with the excitement as well.

"Like a bloody dream!" Claire said, bouncing in her seat. "It's almost like it's a totally different car to what we tried to start a month ago."

"Well, that's why these guys can charge what they do," Harvey replied shrewdly, glancing over at Barry. "Speaking of which, I'm going to go and get a look at this invoice to save you the initial heart attack."

"Oh God, break it to me softly when you do," Claire pleaded, her previous euphoria taking a steep dive.

"Will do, Claire-Bear."

Harvey walked over to Barry, who slapped him on the back and led into his office. Claire remained sitting in the front seat of Frank, reluctant to let go of the vision she had created for herself only moments beforehand.

"Happy?" asked George, walking up to her window and leaning against the roof. Claire noticed again with surprise how tall he was – she kept forgetting. Even when she was sitting up high like this, he loomed over her.

"I can't thank you enough," she said honestly, her hands stroking the leather steering wheel. "He is like a totally different car."

"Just doing my job." He gave her that elusive, disconcerting smile of his.

"No, really," she said. "I appreciate it so much. I've got big dreams

144

for me and Frank. I feel like they wouldn't have been a reality were it not for you."

"Well, in that case, thank away."

Claire laughed; he was smiling back at her. She wondered if there was any credence to what Anna had said – could he be interested in her, or could this just be the normal service for all his customers? Was she just reading too much into it because she'd recently split from Zac and needed the ego boost? She cleared her throat; she needed to stop with all these heavy thoughts, she was going to drive herself crazy. Besides, if she did all the worrying herself, what would her parents have left to do during the rest of their time with her?

"So where to from here?" she asked. "Do I just waltz into Roads and Transport and get some new number plates or something?"

"Pretty much. I can come with you if you like."

"You would?" she asked, feeling relieved for some reason. She had never had to register a car before, let alone a car that had been unregistered for fifteen years and was probably going to be older than the Roads and Transport service clerk.

"That I can do."

"That would be kind of amazing…. Dad is great, but I can tell even he is stressing about getting him registered. We were planning to go shortly; did you still want to come along?

"No worries at all, I'll just let Barry know."

He patted Frank's side and walked off to talk to Harvey and Barry. Claire knew she should go inside as well and deal with the payment for all this amazing labour George had done. She was just enjoying Frank so much right now. It was like she had left Canberra and slipped into another, far more freeing vision of the future.

Harvey came out soon enough, slipping a piece of paper into his pocket.

"You ready to go get Frank back on the road?" her father asked cheerfully, a small bounce in his step.

"Yup." Claire undid her seatbelt and opened the driver's-side door. "Just mentally preparing myself for the bill." She took a deep breath, steeling herself. "Alright Dad, hit me with it. What am I stung?"

Harvey shuffled awkwardly from one foot to another, pulling his keys out of his pocket.

"Not necessary, don't worry about it."

"Huh? Dad?" Claire asked sharply, suddenly her mother's daughter.

"Not to worry Claire, I've got it sorted."

"What do you mean you've got it sorted?" Claire's stomach dropped. What did he do?

"I've sorted it, I've paid your bill."

"You've done *WHAT*?" Claire jumped out of the seat and slammed Frank's door shut behind her. "Why would you do that? I said I would pay."

"It's nothing." He shook his head awkwardly.

"That's a lot of money!" Claire exclaimed, wringing her hands together. "Does Mum know about this?"

"It was her idea, actually."

"It was her *WHAT*?" Claire cried out in disbelief. "My mother, as in Dianna Baxter?"

"The one and very same, the old ball and chain."

"You two are ridiculous," she growled, throwing her hands in the air. "I'm so annoyed with you for that. You should be saving money for retirement, not spending money like that on your pesky children."

"Are you kidding, retirement? What am I going to do in retirement?" Harvey said defensively, his face hurt.

"Oh, I don't know…relax?" Claire retorted, sighing in frustration. "Have you seen what goes on in those retirement villages?"

Harvey shook his head. "No way in *hell* am I ending up in one of those; that's the least relaxing way to go that I can think of."

"Back to the point – at least let me go halves with you," she begged desperately, the guilt at such a gift overcoming any sort of appreciation she could show at that point in time.

"No, your mother and I are quite decided with this one." Harvey nodded firmly. "We've barely gotten to see you over the past few years, and being able to spend this time with you, working on and talking about Frank...it's been very special to me."

Claire didn't know what to say, so she just punched his shoulder.

"I guess you could say I've just turned into a big sook," he finished, watching her quietly process. "I have no doubt that if you needed to you would be fine, but still. Think of it as just free fuel money."

"Well," Claire began tearing up. "I don't know what to say, Dad. This is way too incredible."

"Just give me a hug and we'll call it square," he said uncomfortably, not enjoying the praise from Claire.

Claire ran up and wrapped her arms around him in a big, grateful hug. He smelt like coffee and soap; she took a moment to breathe in the familiar smell. They were a close family, but big hugs were generally saved for long term hellos and goodbyes.

"I love you, Dad," she said softly.

"Love you too, Claire-Bear," he replied, gruffly.

Letting him go, Claire looked around for George. He was waiting patiently by the roller doors, clearly not wanting to disturb an intimate moment. Claire indicated for him to come over, pointing at Harvey's car.

"We'll take Dad's car; you could get in the back if you wanted to come with us?"

"In the back I go," George said, squeezing into the messy and rubbish-filled back seat.

As they drove to Roads and Transport, Harvey and George chattered away across all subjects, including what each had for breakfast that day. George seemed very relaxed as he spoke to Harvey, a different man almost from the reserved grouch that seemed to inhabit his body whenever Claire was around – that is, until recently, when he had somehow learnt to smile. Claire listened happily, not feeling the need to interject at all.

"How often do you get out now?" George asked Harvey, leaning forward to talk through the middle front seat; it seemed they had somehow found their way to surfing.

"Oh, not much anymore," Harvey replied. "I'd be lucky if it was once a year at the moment!"

"That would drive me crazy." George shook his head. "I try to head somewhere once a fortnight at least. I only really go to Sydney to visit my sister – the beaches are so crowded there – but generally I like Kiama, Gerringong, Wollongong…even Jervis Bay."

"What's the surf like in Jervis?"

"Not bad, beautiful water. Few sharks hanging around though."

"They ever bother you?" Harvey eyes lit up with concern, he was such a dad.

"Nah, not me." George shook his head again. "I have heard of a guy getting his ankle nibbled on by a little cookie cutter though."

Pulling into Roads and Transport, Claire took her entourage inside, where she grabbed a ticket saying 101E. The trio waited patiently, George and Harvey chattering away about various shark stories they had heard that sounded frankly terrifying to Claire. When her number was called she headed over to the counter, with Harvey and George following like shadows; both seemed conscious of letting her be in control on this one. While she was happy to have a little extra money to go towards fuel for her trip, she was feeling bad that her parents had paid for the restoration of Frank. Because he had been given to her, she had felt that the act of paying to get him going again would kind of solidify her claim on him; as if she would deserve him more if she contributed financially. She knew that was not her parents' intention, however, and resolved to be less of a sook in the face of such a generous and kind gesture. Besides, registering a car was not cheap, so she might as well thank her lucky stars that was the only thing she had to pay today.

When the clerk saw Frank's age on the application, his eyebrows raised and almost immediately he asked to see some sort of mechanical note.

"Do you have the inspection certificate?" He frowned as he scanned the application, pulling up the large, seventies-inspired glasses that were attached to a string around his neck.

"Yup," said George, handing it to Claire, his entire purpose for coming along now filled. Claire momentarily pondered that he really didn't need to be here. Maybe he just wanted an excuse to get out of the garage for a while?

"Excellent," said the clerk, tapping away at his computer screen. After about another twenty minutes and a few more questions, Claire was handed her new number plates for Frank. Once they got out of the building, Claire threw her hands up in the air.

"Victory!" she shouted, waving the number plates around above her head. "At long last! Frank is back on the road and legally to boot!"

"Well done, Claire," Harvey said, hugging her. "You make me a very proud dad."

"Christ, Dad." Claire hugged him back briefly, unused to all this paternal attention. "You are becoming such a sap in your dotage."

"I've got some theft-proof screws back in the garage if you want to put those on straight away?" George pointed at her new ACT number plates.

"You wouldn't mind?" Claire asked, conscious that she was very much being looked after by everyone else today. "I will pay you for them of course."

"It's no problem." He shrugged. "We just have some lying around anyway."

"Thanks, George," Harvey said, beaming at him. "You have been an absolute legend."

George just shrugged his shoulders again as if to say it was nothing, clearly as uncomfortable with Harvey's heightened affectionate side as Claire was.

Clambering into the front seat of Harvey's car, with George once again squeezing his formidable size into the back seat, Claire opened a panicked message from Daisy.

Okay, so remember how I asked you if we could possibly borrow Frank as a wedding car?

How serendipitous! Claire typed back. *He is just about to get number plates put on in a few minutes, so that should be fine.*

Is there any chance you could ask your dad if he would like to come to the wedding and be one of the drivers? Daisy's stress levels were evident from the lack of her normal excessive use of emoji. *I know it's a weird ask but I will need you in the bridal party and I'm freaking out a little as Dad will be busy and Mum can't drive manual...*

"Harvs," Claire said, looking up at her father in the driver's seat next to her. "How do you feel about playing chauffeur for Daisy's wedding? Jeffrey is too busy playing the father of the bride and Tracey has gearshift issues."

"When is it again?" he asked, pushing his glasses up higher on his nose.

"Two weeks on Saturday."

"Ahh, sorry Claire, I've got to go to Sydney and babysit the grandkids for your sister that weekend. Tell Daisy I said sorry though."

"That's okay." Claire's mind raced as she thought of people she trusted enough to drive Frank. It would be one of his first longer trips, and she could hardly ask Anna to ask David…

Claire messaged Daisy. *Dad's a no-go.*

Daisy replied with several crying face emoji. Back in fine form. *Don't worry though, I will find someone.*

"What's the matter?" George asked.

"My friend Daisy is getting married in two weeks and Frank is going to be one of the wedding cars; just need a driver who can handle both old cars and manual gearshift," Claire explained absentmindedly, wondering if it would be weird to ask Ainsley… she would probably be busy working. Saturday was one of their busiest days.

"I can help, if you need."

"What?" Claire said, spinning around to look at George in the back seat, sitting with his knees extra high in the tight space of her father's car.

"I can drive Frank, it's no problem. I have most weekends off anyway," he replied nonchalantly, shrugging his shoulders.

"I couldn't ask you to do that," Claire said quickly, her heart suddenly beating a little faster. She hadn't expected him to offer, why would she have? It was an incredibly kind thing to do and Claire was quite determined to paint him as a grumpy sod.

"Well, you're not – technically it's your friend who's asking me," he pointed out. "Wouldn't be the first wedding car I'd driven; if it's a local thing, it's no problem."

"It's not." Claire bit her bottom lip. "It's like an hour out of town."

"That's hardly an issue, that's like getting to the local Woolworths from my sister's house in Sydney on a busy day. An hour is no problem." Their car hit a bump in the road and George put his arm up to block his head hitting the roof. He really was too big for the back of that car.

"Might be handy to have George around during one of Frank's first big trips as well," Harvey added cheerfully from the driver's seat, taking George's offer far better than Claire, who had gone into fret overdrive. It just felt too much to ask of him, and Claire found his personality confusing enough as it was; he made her nervous for some reason.

"Are you...are you sure?" she asked tentatively. "You've already done so much for me, I feel like I'm taking advantage of you."

"Hardly," George drawled. "Just a free weekend, will be nice to go for a cruise in a vintage van."

"Well, okay...if you're sure..." she said uncertainly, watching his expressionless face from the front seat. He, however, just continued to stare ahead out of the front windscreen. She gave up and texted Daisy back.

Okay, I have a driver...we just may need to supply him with some free booze or something as a thank you.

Amazing! Thank you! Tell him thank you so much, he has saved the day! Daisy's reply was followed by several flowers and wedding emoji. Claire imagined her blonde curls bouncing around in exuberance as she responded.

"Daisy said she will pay you in wedding alcohol and thank you very much."

Claire saw a small smile crack his blank face as he locked eyes with her in the rear-view mirror.

"Too easy."

Claire broke his gaze and focused instead on the number plates now resting in her hands. She ran her fingers over the embossed numbers and letters and felt a rush of excitement once again. These six little symbols felt like direction, like purpose. As she was enjoying imagining all the places they would go together, Claire tried not to think about the man taking up half of the vehicle in the back seat and why he was being so helpful, not to mention why she felt so conflicted about it.

CHAPTER 13

Bridesmaids, Make-up and Mini-bars

Daisy and Joanne had chosen Braidwood – a small, quaint country town about an hour-and-a-half outside of Canberra – for their wedding. The park in the centre of town was where they had stopped to have lunch on their first weekend away together; Daisy said it was the place where she'd realised Joanne was a keeper, when she had yelled at some birds during their impromptu picnic.

Claire had booked a room in the same bed and breakfast where the reception was taking place and where Daisy had a suite for the bridesmaids to get ready. She'd been given a lift to Braidwood by Daisy and her sisters that morning, as Anna was driving with David. Claire felt a little nervous about seeing David at the wedding; she had managed so far to avoid him as much as possible, but that would be a little hard to do when he would be literally sitting at the same table as her for the reception.

Set just outside of town, the wedding reception was taking place at the Cherry Tree Inn; a small bed and breakfast set on a couple of acres of land. Claire had fallen in love with it the moment she saw it. It was a two-storey building, with a wraparound veranda on both levels, painted a cheery, bright yellow with white trim; a bright green vine had twined its way up the side of the building and along parts of the veranda. At the back of this property was a large, rustic barn-style shed, where they would be partying the night away later. Claire was very happy about the logistics of this. She planned to make full use of a night of drinking, dancing and general frivolity in order to reset – to lift herself out of the slump that had been her emotional state since she found out she was actually her lover's secret lover.

It was in Daisy's spacious room that she, Anna and the other bridesmaids were currently crammed, as the clock hit 10 am and chaos started to descend on the wedding party. They were already several bottles of champagne and a couple of cheese platters down. Claire was sitting in a chair by the door, staring out across the open veranda to the garden, where the sun was shining down, and out to the barn beyond. Music, laughter, obligatory *woos* and a constant stream of chatter echoed about the room as she watched a group of men carrying long tables inside and stacking up chairs outside the shed. She continued observing them with interest as the chatter from Daisy and her sisters increased. Over the other side of the room, in front of a large dresser mirror, a make-up artist was doing the girls' faces, and on the other side of the bed was a woman curling and hair spraying as if her life depended on it.

"...friend of yours arrived yet Claire?" Daisy asked, sitting on the bed, sipping her champagne.

"Huh?" Claire jumped, coming out of her daydreaming haze.

"I said, has that mechanic friend of yours arrived yet? In the Kombi?"

"Ooh, I love Kombis!" one of Daisy's sisters exclaimed. "That's so cool."

"Yeah," Claire smiled, trying to hide her smugness. "Frank's pretty awesome."

"And hopefully that will make up number three of the classic wedding car party!" Daisy said; the closest to fretting that Claire had seen from her all day. "Things have been going so smoothly though, something is bound to pop up."

"Don't be ridiculous," Claire scoffed. "All will be well. George left about half an hour ago so he will be here within the hour. We have until 2 pm."

"This is true," Daisy conceded, taking another sip from her champagne flute. "I am just fussing unnecessarily."

"Who's next?" asked Nicole the make-up artist, her eyes locking on Claire's pale, make-up-less skin. As the Mediterranean goddess with curly black hair and beautiful tanned skin assessed her, Claire felt very aware of her translucency.

"How can you tell?" Claire joked, getting to her feet and sitting in the chair just emptied by one of Daisy's sisters. As if by the law of nature, her skin had decided to break out just in time for Daisy's wedding. "I hope you have enough concealer there to cover my entire face."

"Don't be ridiculous," Anna rebuked. "You are beautiful, you dolt."

Claire scrunched her nose and poked her tongue at her in response.

"We will have to use a different tone for you, I think," Nicole mused, peering closely at Claire's skin, having just dealt with Anna and then Daisy and her tanned sisters.

"I generally find just plain old sunscreen is my best match."

Nicole snorted. "Nonsense. You have lovely, pale skin."

"Embrace the moon tan Claire," Anna advised, having moved on to the hair station. The woman was now playing with her long, thick, straight hair, appearing slightly stressed about the sheer volume of it.

Claire looked down at her phone as Nicole rustled through her make-up bag, no doubt looking for a shade lighter than white. No messages yet from George; he must still be on the way. He had picked up Frank from her parents' house last night; apparently, he lived closer to Braidwood than she did, so it just made sense to drive straight there. She had offered to help cover his accommodation charges as well when he had agreed to help Daisy and Joanne out as a wedding car driver. He had declined, however, stating he would just drive home the same night or even sleep in the back of Frank if desperate.

Claire wished she had been able to drive up with him in Frank on his first out-of-Canberra trip since he had been restored, but Daisy had wanted to start hair and make-up early, and George had a quick job he had to take care of in the morning. Claire figured he was probably the best person to take Frank out in the first instance anyway; if he had a tantrum or broke down along the way, what better person to be there to fix him?

George had been very helpful to her. His friend – the cabinetmaker – had looked at Frank and figured out that the structure was fine; he just replaced a few of the panels and gave them a quick repaint, charging Claire only for the materials. He had also showed her the sink system, how that worked, and the best way to set up a small three-way connected fridge. Claire had found a secondhand mini-bar fridge on Gumtree for $100; he helped her install it the very same day.

Claire sent George a message, just making sure his trip was going okay.

I know you are probably driving, and you can't reply to this, but if you were broken down you could, so even if you don't reply it will make me feel better.

George replied almost instantly. *Don't curse us, you are just asking for trouble, sending messages like that.*

Oh no, what happened? Claire was suddenly worried.

Just stopped for a coffee, no stress required.

Phew, I did not want to have to be the person to tell Daisy her bridesmaids would have to get a taxi to the ceremony.

How is she going?

Nervous but no Bridezilla to be seen, I think she just wants the ceremony part to be over with.

Yeah, reception is the fun bit. Ceremony is the serious stuff.

If I was to get married, I think I would just throw a barbecue and see who turned up.

Practical, I like it.

How far off are you? Claire was feeling excited at the prospect of his arrival. Purely because of seeing Frank again, of course.

Probably in about forty. Do you guys need anything done when I get here? I am just a spare hand until my driving duties begin.

Claire looked over at Daisy, chewing at her perfectly manicured nails.

"Oi, Daisy. Do you need anything done between now and the ceremony? George, my mechanic friend, isn't doing anything else."

"Hmm," Daisy mumbled, thinking to herself. "My parents are setting up a few chairs at the park for the ceremony, but Dad is like, in his sixties. If he would help him that would be awesome, is that asking too much though? Tell him he doesn't have to worry; he's already helping us out anyway."

Claire messaged George back. *Daisy feels bad but says her dad is setting up for the ceremony at the park in town and could use some help? No pressure though.*

Sounds good. I like making myself useful, nothing worse than sitting around with strangers and nothing to do with your hands.

You are quickly becoming the best mechanic/wedding car driver/event hire I have ever met.

Live to serve.

With that, Claire put her phone down with a smile, focusing back on the ladies and champagne flowing around her.

* * *

The morning disappeared quickly, between hair and make-up and several bottles of giggle-inducing bubbles. By the time they were wriggling into their dresses, the whole lot of them were more than a little rowdy. For the bridesmaids, Daisy had picked flowy yellow chiffon printed with small white flowers. It was an interesting choice, but very Daisy in every way. Claire had no doubt that against her complexion it looked less 'summer goddess' and more 'nutritional jaundice', but she wouldn't have cared if Daisy had dressed her in a pair of pyjamas. She didn't know if it was the sparkling wine, the romance of the bed and breakfast or just the fact that one of her best friends was getting married, but Claire began to feel very emotional. She was an absolute sucker for a wedding, being notorious for crying even before the ceremony had started. Given she'd consumed a fair bit of alcohol, on top of a diet of grapes, biscuits and half a wheel of brie, this was no doubt going to be a heavily mascara-riddled affair.

Claire sniffed slightly, thinking back to when Daisy had first told her about the woman she was marrying. At that time, marriage had not been an option for them, as it hadn't yet been legalised in Australia. Daisy, her courageous, funny, sweet and kind friend, had always been so quiet on the subject. Even as her other friends got married around her, and after Joanne had proposed, the reality of being married had not seemed like something that would happen. Now here they were, years later, about to walk down the aisle together. Claire felt the moisture welling in her eyes and tipped her head back, willing the tears to stop before they ruined her mascara altogether.

"Oh, Jesus." Anna zipped up the back of her dress. "Really? Already? We aren't even at the park yet."

"Shut it," Claire ordered, as she wiped a stray tear off her perfectly made-up cheek.

"Daisy, you owe me ten bucks," Anna called out to Daisy, who was in the middle of stepping her legs into her wedding dress with the help of her sisters. "She didn't even make it to the ceremony."

"Dammit, Claire!" Daisy hopped about dangerously on one leg, two of her sisters steadying her as they tried to pull the dress up from underneath. "I'm a teacher; I'm not made of money you know."

"Oh, I'm sorry that I'm not a heartless monster!" Claire sniffled back.

"God knows how she is going to go for the rest of the afternoon. Does everyone have some spare tissues?" Anna asked the room.

"Yup, I have a bunch hidden in this pouch attached to the flowers," Daisy said. "Thought ahead."

"What time are we on?" Claire asked, looking back down at her phone. "Oh, gosh, we are getting picked up from here in like fifteen minutes...is everyone ready?"

A short while later, two wedding cars arrived to pick up the bridal party. A bright blue 1975 Beetle and a bright orange 1968 Kombi campervan. The ladies all waited on the veranda, watching them arrive. Claire's gaze automatically followed Frank, who had a white ribbon attached to his front. In the driver's seat was George, her mechanic-turned-black-market-cabinetmaker-dealer slash best-friend's-wedding-car-driver. His normally stern face had a small smile for her when she saw him, and he gave her a quick wink. Claire felt strangely unsettled; she gave him a little wave. Wedding jitters were contagious, apparently.

"Alright. Let's do this, ladies," Anna said seriously, striding out to the cars. Daisy went in the Beetle with her father, and all the bridesmaids piled into the back of Frank; except for Daisy's young sister, Harriet, who opted for the front. As she slid into the bucket seat next to him she glanced very appreciatively at George, who was looking much smarter than Claire was used to, dressed in a casual suit jacket and chino pants. His messy hair had been combed and he looked very different from his normal dirty face and work overalls. Claire suddenly felt very nervous watching his face in the rear-view mirror. *It must be the upcoming ceremony,* she told herself.

"All ready, ladies?" he asked calmly, turning around to face Claire and Anna in the back.

"Somewhere we can burn these dresses," Anna quipped dryly.

"I am if you are," Harriet replied sweetly. Claire raised her eyebrows; turns out Daisy's subtlety ran in the family. Claire saw him also raise his eyebrows slightly, before putting Frank into gear.

"Well," George said, "let's get going. As a warning, though, I just spent the best part of an hour getting swooped by a magpie while I was unloading chairs in the very spot. So prepare those bouquets as weapons."

"Oh, no." Claire bit her lip as she tried to suck in her body to give the bridesmaids next to her more room. "Is his still there?"

"Oh, he's there alright," he replied, following the Beetle and driving out of the Cherry Tree Inn property and onto the main road. "When more people turned up that seemed to spook him, though; when I left, he was just watching menacingly from a nearby tree. I think as long as we stay in packs, we should be okay."

"Bloody magpies," Anna grumbled.

"At least that means spring is coming!" Claire cried, rubbing her arms in excitement. "I'm not built for Canberra winters."

"No one is," George said, his brown eyes locking with hers in the rear-view mirror. "I can't wait to get back to the coast properly."

"Where are you from?" Harriet drawled, flipping her long, blonde hair over one shoulder as she studied George in the seat next to her. Anna nudged Claire with an elbow, nodding her head in the direction of the front seat. She pretended not to notice. It wasn't any of her business who Harriet chose to flirt with, and she decided to focus on taking in the looks from people walking down the main street of Braidwood as they rolled into the centre of town. After a few seconds of this, however, she couldn't help but look up again at mini-Daisy and her blatant appreciation of the driver Claire had brought along.

Poor George, Claire thought, *doing this favour and being sexually harassed at the same time.* As they rolled up to the park, Claire looked out the window and saw a large group of people standing over on the green grass, pointing as the cars approached.

George eased Frank into a parking spot right on the fringe of the park's green grass, just as Daisy's father turned off the Beetle's engine. Claire leant over Anna, pulled open Frank's door and climbed out; the other bridesmaids did the same and then rushed over to Daisy's vehicle. Claire lingered behind, leaning into Frank's passenger-seat window.

"I think you could probably just leave him here and come over," she said, as Harriet turned back to give George a wink and a wave from the front of the Beetle.

Claire didn't stay to see if he waved back. She walked over to Anna, who had just opened the back door of the Beetle and helped pull out a very pale-looking Daisy.

"Oh, boy," Daisy breathed nervously, as she stood up and smoothed her dress. "I can't believe this is finally happening, I can't believe it."

"This is happening alright!" Claire cried, straightening her own dress and glancing over at the park. She could see everyone stand up; they were peering over in anticipation, but Joanne herself at the end of the makeshift aisle was hidden from view.

"Come on, lady friend," Claire said with a smile, as Daisy's dad walked over to take her arm. "Get your shit together and let's get you hitched before Australia repeals any laws."

"Good point," Daisy laughed. "Well, you girls get in front and we will follow, I guess…"

Despite Daisy's previous concerns, the ceremony went off without a hitch. The previously marauding magpie was now simply watching with interest from a nearby tree, neither Anna nor Claire tripped in any sort of embarrassing fashion, and Frank started first go with no problems at the end when everyone was due to head back to the Cherry Tree Inn for the follow-on reception. Claire also only cried a little bit, without making any embarrassing sobbing noises… although it had been a close thing during their vows. However, a few warning looks from Anna had helped Claire pull her wayward emotions together. Weddings, they just got to her.

The inside of the very rustic-looking shed but been turned into nothing less than a magical, fairy wonderland. Several long tables, covered in beautiful green native flowers and candle tealights filled one side of the barn, while on the other side, room had been left for a dancefloor and a band. Fairly lights were strung up across the ceiling, reflecting a soft, glowing twinkling light. The whole effect was nothing less than stunning.

Claire, having been seated near Daisy's parents, was happily making good inroads into the free-flowing wine. Further along the table, on the other side of Daisy and Joanne, sat Anna and David. Claire felt decidedly unsure how to act around David. She didn't trust herself to be natural enough to not cause suspicion, so she was doing her best work to politely be engaged elsewhere whenever he was around. Anna seemed to prefer this course of action also; throughout the evening it was only very rarely that she was alone with him for too long. The whole business was very awkward, and Claire hoped that if she got drunk enough it might take the edge off. Anna seemed to be working off the same logic, too.

Across from her, and a couple of chairs down, sat Harriet and – conveniently for Harriet – Claire's very own mechanic, George. Claire had been very impressed with how easygoing and helpful he'd been; she was glad she had asked him to come along. Initially, he had just said he would head home after the ceremony, but Daisy was having absolutely none of that and insisted that he attend the reception. She could be very persuasive, that woman. For the second time that day, Claire couldn't help but notice just how different he was from the man in work overalls, and just how relaxed. And he seemed to take up so much space. Claire knew George was a large man, but it was more than that, it was like he just filled the space around him; even sitting at the table, he appeared to tower over all the people seated near him. If it hadn't been for the calmness of his manner, the situation could have looked a little ridiculous.

Claire wondered if she was only noticing this now, this presence, because she was at a wedding; and at weddings, any single man within a five-kilometre radius could be smelt out by desperate, newly single women like her. Claire shook her head as if trying to shake out the bizarre thoughts of George that were flitting around in it. Across from her, it seemed she was not the only single lady who had noticed him either, with Harriet fawning over George as he quietly ate his meal next to her. Claire found herself glancing over more than once, watching the two interact. George was being perfectly amicable, smiling politely at the beautiful Harriet as she batted her eyelids and flicked her long, blonde hair. Claire momentarily wished that she had beautiful long hair as well and not just her short, curly mop. Maybe if she did, Zac wouldn't be off gallivanting about Sydney in linen shirts with coffee-loving Instagram models. As she sipped her wine and silently cursed her lack of mane for the hundredth time, George leant in and said something to Harriet, at which she burst into laughter and grabbed his arm to steady herself. She was good, Harriet – putting on a good act for sure. Claire knew George wasn't all that funny. He was very serious, a lot of the time. Not funny.

"Well, Harriet seems to have found someone she thinks is interesting…" Daisy's mother, Tracey murmured next to her, nudging Claire with her elbow.

Yeah, she has, Claire thought a little bitterly, *and she's being downright un-bloody-subtle about it.*

"Hmm," she replied noncommittally.

"Do you know him?" Tracey asked, watching George and Harriet laugh.

"I do!" Jeffrey, Daisy's father said, leaning in on the table to join their conversation. "He helped me set up at the park today."

"Oooh, that was nice of him." Tracey smiled, her eyes glinting with the desperation of a woman pining for a grandchild.

"Yeah, nice lad," Jeffrey agreed. "Not very practised against swooping birds, though; never seen anyone try and use a plastic chair as a shield before."

Claire, who was midway through sipping her wine, snorted very ungraciously at the thought.

"Is he a friend of Joanne's?" Tracey asked her husband, with interest.

"Sorry, dear, he said he was here with Claire," Jeffrey said, pointing at the quiet Claire on Tracey's left.

Daisy's mother suddenly looked embarrassed; clearly, she worried that she had been verbalising her desire for a second daughter's wedding to the very wrong person.

"Is he now?" Tracey cried, her interest suddenly at fever pitch. "Well, hopefully you don't mind Harriet having a chat to him then dear…"

"No, no, no," Claire said quickly. "It's nothing like...like that, he is just a friend who kindly said he would drive Frank so I could focus on my bridesmaid duties."

Claire saw Tracey and Jeffrey exchange a look; she had had far too much wine to understand what had been said between them, however.

"He's a mechanic," Claire continued. "He put Frank back together piece by piece. He's very nice."

That look again, she was beginning to wonder if these two had telepathy.

"I'm sure he and Harriet would be lovely together," she added reassuringly.

Tracey raised an eyebrow in clear disbelief and then chose that moment to change the subject and ask Claire about where she had been travelling these past few years. For the next hour or so, while meals were being served, Claire answered the eager questions of both Tracey and Jeffrey, who wanted to get details on every country Claire had spent time in, and when. Across from her, Harriet continued to murmur into George's ear, eliciting a smile and the odd low, rumbling laugh. Claire forced herself to turn back to Tracey; it was just the wedding making her irrational. As the couple was about to cut the cake, she felt herself tearing up once again. She pulled out her now-soaked tissue and half-shoved it up her nose in anticipation. As she was doing so – hands covering her face, eyes wet, and mascara-covered tissue firmly thrust into her nostrils – a feeling drew her gaze back to George opposite her. Everyone else's eyes were on the happy couple as they cut through their three-tier flower-covered wedding cake – but not George's. They were locked on her face. His serious gaze now seemed intense rather than angry; his brown eyes were burning into hers so deeply it made her skin flush. Claire found herself holding her breath as their gaze held, only breaking when she looked down, suddenly acutely aware that she must seem like an absolute blubbering psychopath. When she looked back up, George was facing Daisy and Joanne, clapping along with the rest of the guests.

Claire removed the tissue and wiped her nose self-consciously, clapping loudly for Daisy as she fed Joanne a piece of the very expensive dessert that she and Anna had spent a whole day helping to decide upon only weeks before. She didn't look at George again for the rest of the speeches.

CHAPTER 14

A Mechanical Surprise

It did not take long for the wedding guests to consume enough free alcohol to gain the undeserved confidence to abandon their chairs and start flailing about on the dancefloor; each with varying degrees of success. Claire, with notably less success, was channelling her best Madonna for over an hour before she took a seat. Sweating profusely, she stretched out her arms in front of her in an attempt to dry the sweat patches on her flowing yellow bridesmaid's dress. She didn't have much success here either.

A large figure sat down in the vacated chair next to Claire as she was ungracefully fanning some air under her arms. Claire turned to see George watching Daisy and Joanne in front of them – they were still on the dancefloor, laughing and moving to the music.

"This has been a brilliant day," he said, taking a sip of his beer and watching the newlyweds dance like lunatics, his relaxed smile radiating calm contentment.

"Are you staying now?" she asked, indicating the drink in his hand, pretending that she didn't already know the answer to that question.

"Yeah, Daisy convinced me earlier, it has just gotten that bit too late. I brought some blankets, so will just camp out in Frank."

"You'll have to tell me how it goes." Claire tapped her wine glass against his and held it up in a quick salute.

"Probably far more luxurious than what my weekends normally consist of anyway." George shrugged.

"Paint me a picture," Claire commanded, leaning back in her chair. She felt warm, tipsy and full of love for both Daisy and Joanne. Weddings really did tend to get to her, and she was feeling especially sentimental. She felt very grateful to George, who had been wonderful help today. Claire sighed deeply; she felt very comfortable just pausing in place, listening to the cheerful music, watching the dancers revel and letting the groggy fog of too much wine and bubbles from earlier envelop her in a warm, contented blanket.

"Most weekends are excuses to get out and surf really," he explained, stretching out his long legs in front of him. "Which is getting a bit hard lately with all the weekend work Barry has on. He keeps taking on these vintage, hopeless cases you see…"

"Very funny. Now, are you from Canberra?" Claire asked, her mind trailing to Barry's Tyrepower. How did a coast-loving type end up in Canberra, if not for work?

"From Gerringong." He tipped his head. "Right on the water. It's only a few hours up the road, so not far … but you do feel it here, the lack of salt in the air."

"Are your family there?" she asked, continuing her interrogation.

"Mum and Dad still are. My sister Gail moved to Sydney to study."

"So many of my friends did that, it was like a migration." Claire nodded.

"I don't mind Canberra, though."

"It's funny, not many people seem to have grown up in Canberra, they all move there for work," she mused. "Except me, I lived there for all of my childhood."

"I just…just can't understand how it gets so ridiculously cold." He ran his hands through his now-messy hair. "I've been here two winters now and am still not ready for it. It's like we're not even in Australia."

"Same!" Claire exclaimed, wrapping her arms around her shoulders. "I thought living through European winters, in actual snow and ice, would prepare me, but you don't expect it to be that cold when are you back Down Under. Totally throws me."

"You spent a bit of time overseas, yeah?" George asked, turning to face her properly in his seat. Claire suddenly felt very close to him; she could smell his cologne making her already dizzied senses even more on edge.

"Mmm," she replied, closing her eyes briefly, just breathing in his musky, man smell. It had been many weeks since she had last stayed over at Zac's and it was beginning to show.

"Where was your favourite place?"

"Well, that's a hard question," she said, tilting her head while she thought, before reopening her eyes. "I love everywhere I went for different reasons; they were all at different stages in my life as well, I suppose."

"What jumps out at you the most then, in terms of a good memory?"

"Well, I've always been a bit of a romantic," Claire admitted. "And it's a cliché and I really should tell you something like Northern India, Pakistan border, or something equally travel bloggy, but I remember this one time I was sitting in a little café in Florence and I felt like I was the star in my own Fellini film."

"Can't fault that."

"Another place I loved is pretty close to home here, but...living in Timor-Leste." She let herself get drawn into the web of her memories. "I was supposed to be living and working there as a scuba diving assistant, but it turns out I am pretty terrible at both of those things, so I ran the bar at the restaurant attached to the scuba diving business instead."

"That's pretty cool," George said in his quiet voice, watching her speak.

"It was a lot of fun; I had a little house right on the beach with some other guys from the company. Beautiful people, beautiful city. Weirdly hard to find cheese products…but you win some you lose some I guess."

"That you do."

"What about you?" she asked, turning to study his impassive face. "What brought you to Canberra?"

"The usual, employment," he said, taking a long sip from his beer.

"Do you think you will stick around long?"

"Not particularly, I'm happy to move on. It is nice being close to my family, but I'm pretty happy to give anything a go. I won't be in Canberra forever."

"Why? Where are you going?" a high-pitched voice asked, interrupting them. Claire jumped, looking up to see Harriet staring intently at George, one hand on her hip, twirling a lock of her blonde hair with the other hand.

"Ahh, nowhere." George looked a bit shocked at her having approached so quietly.

"Good," she said sweetly. "You will be able to come get a drink with me then if you aren't going anywhere."

Claire took another long sip of her wine, transferring her gaze to the dancers in front of her.

"I did say I would buy you a drink, remember?" Harriet added, her flirtation levels now reaching dangerous heights. Claire began to worry she might twist a chunk of hair out.

"You did," George agreed, his eyes catching Claire's in what she suspected was a plea for help.

"Okay, let's go then!"

From the corner of her eye, Claire saw George glance at her; she felt like an awkward third wheel. Standing up quickly, she did a big stretch.

"Well, you guys have fun! I gotta get these limbs warmed up for round two."

"Great, see you," Harriet said quickly, sinking her claws into George's arm and pulling him up to follow her to the bar. He looked slightly alarmed, but Claire just stood up from her chair, wine in hand, and twirled herself back onto the dancefloor – leaving him to Daisy's younger sister's devices. *He is a big boy, he will survive*, she thought, accidentally spilling wine on the floor as Daisy pulled her into a hug. Claire laughed as she hugged her back, enjoying the music and happiness radiating from the beautiful group of people celebrating love around her.

She couldn't help but look back across to the other end of the barn, where Harriet had now dragged George and was clutching onto his shoulder tightly as she spoke into his ear. He seemed to be listening politely as they waited for their drinks. As Claire was watching, George looked up and caught her eye with his intense gaze once again. Claire held it for a few moments, before ripping her eyes away and back to Daisy in front of her. *It's not any of my business what he does or who he is with*, Claire told herself sensibly.

The party went well into the night before people started disappearing off to their respective rooms at the Cherry Tree Inn or getting taxis back to other accommodation in the main centre of town. Claire stayed right until the end, even after Daisy and Joanne had gone to bed, just buzzing around and chatting to family and friends and keeping an eye on Anna. David had gone to bed far earlier in the night, but Anna had kept on drinking quite hard; she was going to feel rotten the next day. Claire, being the good friend that she was, did not want her to drink alone so continued to help her in that department. Just before midnight, when there were only a few people left and Anna was semiconscious, Claire decided to walk her back to her accommodation. Anna did not complain as she slumped against Claire, walking the short distance to her room.

"Hey, thanks for getting me…getting me back," Anna hiccupped, as she opened the sliding door to her room on the bottom floor. "You okay?"

"Yup, see you in the morning," Claire whispered back, giving her a hug. "I love you."

"Love you too." Anna stumbled into the room she was sharing with David and closed the door behind her. Claire's room wasn't far, but she suddenly didn't feel very sleepy, she didn't want to go straight back to her room just yet. While she didn't want to admit it, Claire was very curious to see if George had indeed set up for the night in Frank…and if he was alone. *It's not that I'd be jealous or anything if Harriet was with him,* she told herself reasonably. It was just that if anyone was going to be having fun in Frank it was her, not Daisy's now slightly annoying younger sister. Claire decided there was no harm in just popping by to check he was alright.

George had parked Frank in the orchard, a hundred metres behind the barn. The fairy lights from the reception illuminated the darkness like a great beacon of light, and the silver of the moon brightened the pathway through the garden to where he had parked. Claire took her shoes off, feeling the cool tingling of cold beneath her toes. She sighed in relief as she stretched her feet out, finally free from a day trapped in high heels. Walking over to Frank, she could see his pop-top was raised, a light gently shining from inside.

"Hey," George said in surprise, when she came into his line of view; she'd caught him in the act of taking his shoes off. He was sitting on the rock and roll bed, which had been stretched out and covered in blankets and a few pillows; he must have stored them under the seat. Claire poked her head through the open side door.

"Just wanted to see what Frank looked like when he's being a campervan and not a wedding car." She smiled at him, stretching out her toes in front of her.

"Well, strangely there isn't too much difference," he noted. "Have you slept in him yet?"

"No, not yet," she said. "I figure I am going to have more than enough opportunity to live that when I can't afford a hotel in a few months."

"I've had a bit of a lie down; I think Frank is pretty comfy. You will be totally fine."

"Did you have a nice night?" she asked, swaying slightly on her feet.

"I had an awesome night." He frowned slightly. "Can you take a seat? All that movement is making me dizzy and it will probably end up a bit grassy for you."

"Hmm, this is possible," she muttered, sitting down on Frank's wooden floor.

"Did you have a good night?" he asked, climbing up on the bed and taking his shoes off and loosening his tie.

"Yeah, it was great," she slurred happily. "It's just so nice to see Daisy like that, so happy, so in love. You know, when Daisy first met Joanne, I remember she told me that she knew she was the one. That she knew she would love her."

"Love at first sight, not common these days." He nodded, giving her one of his not-so-rare – as it turned out – warm smiles.

"Yeah, rare and very special," Claire agreed. "I remember we had been facetiming when Daisy told me about her, she said she was a little scary but in a sexy way and that she was the person she wanted to marry."

"Scary but in a sexy way, now that's a description."

"Like smudgy eyeliner, the morning after."

"What?" he asked, laughing in surprise.

"Oh, I don't know, I don't really know what I'm saying..." she laughed.

"Well, either way, it was a lovely evening, so please tell Daisy thank you again for letting me be a part of it."

"Oh, I have no doubt you will be able to tell her yourself," she replied slyly. "What with her sister Harriet being so interested in everything you seem to do."

"Ah, yes..." he laughed awkwardly, taking his tie off completely. "That obvious, was it?"

"Like a brick to the face."

"She was a nice girl," he said diplomatically.

"Oh, really? Just a nice girl?" Claire giggled. "I would say that she would be more than just a nice girl where you are concerned."

"I suppose," he replied, aloof.

The world suddenly seemed to spin, and Claire felt very dizzy. She grabbed the side of the cupboard next to her to stop herself from being pulled down into a whirlpool.

"Woah," she said, clutching the cupboard to slow the swaying. "I think those couple of extra glasses of wine have just really hit."

"Did you want to lie down?" George was frowning with concern again. "Come up here, I will swap places with you."

"No, no," Claire said, in what she hoped was a sober-sounding manner. "It's fine, I'm fine."

"Get up here," he demanded, climbing down off from Frank's bed and scooping her up into his arms. Claire was momentarily shocked at how quickly it happened, especially in such a confined space.

"Woah," she murmured, as George laid her down on the bed.

"There you go," he said quietly. He took her place, sitting cross-legged on the floor next to her.

After a few moments, he stood up. "I'll go find you some water."

"No, no...It's fine...I'm fine..." she mumbled, her vision

swimming as her hands clutched at the bed beneath her in an attempt to once again find stillness.

"You say that."

George left, disappearing into the night. Claire rolled onto her side, feeling the world slip around her in long spirals of confused motion. She groaned softly and closed her eyes to try and still the movement, but that didn't do much to help. After what felt like an eternity, George reappeared from the darkness, holding two bottles of water and what looked like a packet of chips.

"This is the best I could do, sorry," he said, holding up his findings. "Everything else has been packed up. They are very efficient here."

"That's fine...I'm fine..." she muttered, glad that he had returned.

"Here, drink this," he ordered softly, holding out one of the bottles of water. Claire sipped it dutifully, closing her eyes to again soften the motion.

"Sorry you have to see me like this," she groaned. "I was like totally sober...only like...ten minutes ago!"

"Of course," he humoured her.

"It's when all the fun and dancing stops that the alcohol creeps up on you," she grumbled, sipping the water slowly. "And I ate so much bread and everything."

"There is no justice."

"Right?" she agreed, taking another sip of water.

George didn't seem to mind that she'd arrived unannounced while he was getting ready for bed. He sat back down on Frank's floor again quite happily, his head resting against the passenger-seat chair, one leg stretched out the side door onto the grass below.

"Hey, thanks for today," Claire said, drawing his attention back. "I really appreciated you coming out all this way to help with the driving. I know Daisy really appreciated it too."

"No problem," he said casually. "I had nothing on anyway, happy to help."

"I bet your normal clients aren't this much hassle."

"Well, I tend to only fix their cars, not drive them to their friend's magpie-infested park ceremonies."

"I forgot about that, I hope you aren't too scarred."

"It was fun. The physical scars will heal. Just not the emotional ones…that magpie got me good."

Claire laughed. "After such a near-death experience, does that mean I've made it past client to maybe friend?"

George studied her for a moment before responding, his face as impassive as ever.

"Yes, I think that would make sense."

"Excellent!" she cried, setting her water bottle down on the kitchenette basin. "You won't regret this; I have been told that I am a moderately okay friend to have around. I will make you feel better about your life by comparison."

"I don't know about that – I would be pretty happy with myself to have this orange beauty."

"That is true," Claire conceded. "Frank is the one exception. Did I mention I live with my parents, though?"

"Not as uncommon as you'd think."

"Damn, well, I'm plenty messed up in other ways."

George just laughed softly under his breath. "If you say so."

They sat in silence for a few more moments, and Claire opened the packet of chips he'd brought her. She ate a few, and the spinning began to subside.

"Want some?" She held out the packet.

"Sure." George relocated to the end of the bed next to her to reach the chips. They sat in comfortable silence, with Claire unashamedly hogging most of the chip packet. She studied his face, slightly bewildered to think that the person who she had bumped into at Repco a few months ago would now be at Daisy's wedding with her, eating snacks in the back of her Kombi van. Life had a funny way of surprising you. As she watched him some clouds must have shifted in the sky outside, and the moonlight seeped through the curtains of the van and played across his face.

He was beautiful, Claire found herself realising. She did not know how she had ever found him grim or unhappy. He was a lovely, proud, reserved man who was also kind and decent and generous. He also didn't hit on nice, unsuspecting baristas at yoga as far as she knew.

"Are you sure you are okay to sleep in Frank for tonight?" she asked, not really sure what she was offering.

He met her eyes and held her gaze a moment before responding slowly.

"I'll be okay for sleep."

"Alright then," she said, suddenly feeling a little awkward. "I guess I should be getting back to my room now."

George didn't say anything, he merely nodded slightly. Claire got up, spinning head notwithstanding, and climbed out of Frank. She felt relieved that she didn't have to oust Daisy's younger sister from the back of her van, although as she walked away she couldn't help but feel a little disappointed also – if for an entirely different reason.

CHAPTER 15

Rust-free Removal, Just Add Romance

Surely there was nothing strange about taking your mechanic, who had fed you chips while sloshed at your best friend's wedding only mere days before, on a weekend away with you? After the night of Daisy's wedding, Claire had driven home to Canberra in Frank with George. Despite being spectacularly hungover, they had talked most of the drive back, and that talking had now extended into a several-days-long Messenger chat. Such consistent texting was now beyond anything that could be construed as just 'casual chitchat', or so said Anna. Claire was less sure. When he invited her back around to his work, however, saying he had some spare parts for Frank that would otherwise go to no use, she began to think maybe Anna could be right.

"Do you have the weekend off?" George asked, his eyes crinkling into a smile after lifting the spare tyre into the back of Frank.

"Which weekend?" she asked, frowning, her mind losing track of their conversation at the sight of George, bare-armed in a singlet, effortlessly lifting all that weight with one hand.

"The one in approximately two days time."

"I don't have any shifts until next Wednesday, actually. Ainsley is doing some renovations."

"Kismet," he said. "That's settled then, we have to go to Old Bar."

"An old bar?" she asked, perplexed. "I'm happy to go to any bar."

"Old Bar Kombi Festival," he corrected. "It's an annual thing, just popped up on my Facebook. I haven't been before, but I have seen photos."

"Where is it?" her interest peaking. "I've never been to something like that before either."

"It's literally in Old Bar; you need to brush up on your geography before your trip. It's a mix of car show and small-town market festival," he explained, wiping the dirt from the tyre onto his overalls. "I don't know if we will be able to get any accommodation, though. Want me to call the caravan park? It is right on the water. The surf is good there too."

"Sure," Claire decided spontaneously. "Not doing much else and a bit of a road trip will be good for Frank anyway. How far away is it?"

"Six-and-a-bit hours…"

"Lordy," she whistled. "So, a good test for how Frank is running then!"

"If he can get us there and back, I think you will have a bit more confidence in your Western Australia trip."

"Oh wow, this is exciting!" she said, hopping from one leg to another. "Frank's very first festival and it's for Kombis!"

When she was travelling, going on spontaneous trips with almost-strangers was never something you questioned; it was all part of the experience and fun. However, since she had been home in Canberra – essentially reverting to her former teenage self's life – her expectations of normality had been a little different. It felt exciting to be throwing caution and routine to the winds once again and taking an impromptu small beachside adventure.

Over the next two days, Claire went shopping to try and set Frank up for his very first official camping trip. She bought some brand-new pillows, a couple of big, thick, woolly blankets and some new material for curtains. Claire also bought some simple camping equipment, consisting of two cheap fold-up chairs, some knives and forks, and what she was very excited to see was a mosquito net. She didn't know how to make it useful for her van, but she figured it was better to have one than not.

Using charm to bribe her father, Claire got his help in sewing the curtains to fit on the same system as the previous ones had. She had dragged Harvey along to Spotlight to pick out some fabric, and in the end chose a yellow, green and white swirling pattern that she thought looked suitably psychedelic. Frank was a child of the sixties, after all.

Weddings were not fair for single people, though; all that love and lifelong commitment stuff being spouted. It was no wonder people immediately jumped at the closest willing participant to dull the reminder that their own special day was nowhere in sight. This flirtation with George had been a wonderful distraction from the pain and humiliation of finding out she was Zac's Canberra mistress – but was it anything more than that? Could it be? Considering she was about to pack up her van and disappear off along the coast of Australia.

Typical. She could be single for an entire decade and then spend a few months back home and it's all 'boys' this and 'settling down' that and 'what are you meant to be doing with the rest of your life?'

Claire and George had arranged for her to pick him up on the way. He lived in a share house in Queanbeyan with some other people from his work. George said he didn't mind living there; he was barely around anyway, as he spent most of his time off work on the coast. When Claire pulled up, she couldn't help but think how different the small miner's cottage –with its two quaint chimneys, a small fence and overgrown garden filled with beautiful yellow sunflowers – looked to Zac's meticulously pristine, modern apartment. She shook her head, as if to shake off the thoughts of her former flame. That didn't take long, however, as the front door to the cottage opened and George walked out, his face alight with a broad smile at the sight of both Claire and Frank.

He had a gym bag over his shoulder, and Claire felt her stomach fill with butterflies as he strode over to the idling Frank and popped his head through the passenger door.

"Hey there Kombi lady, I'm still okay to grab a lift?"

"Oh, you can tag along I suppose," she teased back, shrugging indifferently.

Opening the side door, George threw his bag on the floor. "I'll just grab the boards, be two seconds."

"Boards?" Claire asked, perplexed, as he ran around the side of the house, emerging moments later with two rather worn-looking surfboards secured under one arm. Claire couldn't help but notice how his broad shoulders were able to make such a feat look easy. Climbing into Frank, he pulled the rock and roll bed out so it laid flat. Then George closed that door, opened the back and slid the two boards in on the bed.

"There," he said with satisfaction, after climbing into the front passenger seat and slamming the door closed. "Frank was never complete without them; he is truly a restored child of the seventies."

"Sixties," Claire corrected. "Is it too late to tell you that I am possibly the world's worst Australian and do not know how to surf?"

"Really?" George raised his eyebrows in disbelief. "How did you get away with that overseas? The tanned, surfing, kangaroo-riding Aussie is our greatest and most beloved of stereotypes."

"I lied," Claire joked. "But I grew up in Canberra! The lake doesn't naturally present itself with many swell opportunities."

George laughed. "That's okay, I can teach you."

Opening Google Maps on his phone, George put in 'Old Bar'. The navigation system came up with six hours and fifteen minutes from his house.

"Ouch." He looked over at Claire. "You ready for a long drive, boss?"

"I'm ready," she nodded. "I just hope Frank is too!"

"Oh, he's ready," George assured her, patting Frank's dashboard. "He's spritelier than both of us."

"Well, as you are nav you can be DJ as well," she said, putting Frank into first and steering out of George's street. "My music is woeful and if we play it, I will die instantly of shame, potentially also killing you in the process."

"Fair."

"Oh, I should have asked the other day," Claire said, just remembering. "Did that caravan park have a spot for us? I was looking on the event Facebook page and everyone seemed to think it would be impossible...I just assumed we'd figure it out when we got there."

"Oh, yeah..." George scrolled ahead on Google Maps, "...just keep going straight here until you get to Sutton Road."

"Gotcha."

"Ahh, yes, caravan park," he said, putting his phone down. "We got very lucky. The website said booked out, but when I called the site, the woman I spoke to said they had a couple of people pull out ahead of this weekend. She said if I had called any earlier, or last week, it would have been a no-go."

"The universe is rewarding our spontaneity!" Claire cried cheerfully, turning down the aforementioned road. It felt nice to drive Frank out of Canberra, it felt right, as if he was finally escaping back to where he wanted to be. "This is what I keep telling Anna, be less organised."

"Question on that, you don't have to answer it though."

"Mmm?"

"Hope you don't mind me saying it," he said slowly, as if choosing his words carefully. "I just noticed at the wedding...doesn't matter actually."

"No, come on then, spit it out!"

"Nothing, nothing really." He shook his head quickly. "Was there a town you wanted to stop at for lunch?"

"Nice redirect." She raised an eyebrow at him. "However, as it is concerning food, I shall allow it."

"Sydney's too busy, maybe between there and Newy?"

"Newy?"

"Newcastle...Honestly, Claire, you need to do that road trip and get your lingo up." He shook his head sadly. "Going to have to chat this out with Harvey."

"Fair enough, it is his fault."

The next few hours were uneventful but very relaxing. George played music and Claire got used to driving Frank on the highway. While she was enjoying the drive, sitting on 90 kph and chattering away to George – when they didn't just sit in silence – she was also enjoying the music and the sunshine and the wind blowing in through the open windows. She did conclude that Frank would never be able to stray anywhere off the far lefthand side of the highway. Behind her, several cars would get close, wait several moments and then overtake almost immediately. Even large trucks, which she would normally overtake without a second thought, were flying past Claire, Frank and George as they slowly made their way up further north from Canberra. Some cars would wave as they went past or even beep, smiling as they looked at Frank – which made Claire laugh and smile in return.

"Can you believe this?" she said excitedly, as a young family all cheered and waved madly at her as they flew past. "I feel like a celebrity!"

"People love old cars, especially Kombis," George replied,

winding his window down and waving back to the kids as well.

"I'm just glad they are beeping because they like him and not just because they are angry at how slow we are!"

"I guess people expect a Kombi to be slow," George reasoned. "If you were in an old Mustang, they would probably still love him, but maybe that particular expectation wouldn't be there."

"Do you think we will see any other Kombis on the road?" she asked with excitement, beginning to think about the festival ahead of them. *Maybe they would have some Australia-lap tips for her?*

"Definitely, I reckon." George nodded his head. "Probably after Sydney."

"Everything good happens after Sydney," Claire muttered darkly, thinking about running into Zac on Daisy's hens' night those few months ago.

"Hey, the beaches aren't bad."

As it would happen, Claire's negative energy towards Sydney must have manifested, because as they were approaching the outskirts, about to pass through Pennant Hills Road, cars began to jam up bumper to bumper. George opened his Google Maps again and groaned at the sight of the strong, red line denoting traffic all along the road until the turnoff to Newcastle.

"This is insane," Claire exclaimed, slowing right down to a crawl. She nervously kept Frank idling in neutral until it was time to inch forward.

"Old cars do not like this kind of traffic," George mentioned casually, glancing over at the dashboard in front of Claire.

"Oh, God, he hates it...I can feel it just holding the gearshift," Claire fretted. It probably sounded like an odd thing to say, but it was true – she could sense when Frank was struggling. It was like a feeling, a vibration, or maybe an offbeat rhythm to the engine.

"He will be fine," George said smoothly, stretching his arms over his head and leaning back into the chair casually as if to prove how very relaxed he was with the whole situation.

"And that hill coming up! I won't even get the chance to run up some speed." Claire pointed up ahead nervously.

"You are doing great," he reassured her. "Just keep doing what you're doing."

"Poor Frank, he is only air-cooled, this idling in one spot can't be good for him…"

"I would say he has survived far worse" George yawned. "When you are this old, a little bit of traffic won't fuss you too much."

"You are doing a very good job of being calm," Claire laughed, suddenly embarrassed. "You probably think I'm being ridiculous."

"No way." He wound his window up against the loud beeping of traffic outside. "I'm just grateful I'm not the one driving."

They slowly inched closer as the sea of frustrated drivers in front of them did as well, and after what felt like eternity – but according to Claire's watch and George's song count, had only been about forty minutes – they were once again cruising up north in the far left lane.

* * *

Hours later, when they finally arrived at Old Bar, the tiny beachside town was absolutely packed with Volkswagens. Travelling down a tree-lined country road, having turned off the highway, they noticed that the houses along the way had signs out front with big peace symbols and flowers.

"Even the locals get right into it." George pointed to a giant cardboard cut-out Beetle on a signpost next to a letterbox. "That's awesome."

As they drove into the centre of town, Kombis suddenly started appearing everywhere. They were parked on the side of the road, in the carpark at Woolworths, driving ahead of them, behind them; the tiny town was just crawling with air-cooled classics. As Claire drove slowly through the centre of town, people waved excitedly and she waved back; other Kombi owners nodded at her and a few even threw up peace signs.

"This is crazy," Claire laughed. "I feel like I've joined some sort of hidden society…or maybe a cult!"

"A cult for people who like to spend lots of money on old, rare car parts."

The caravan park, they discovered, was straight through the centre of town and down on the beach ahead of them. The showgrounds were literally right next door, to the left, with large signs indicating 'Old Bar Kombi Festival this way'.

"What do you want to do?" George asked, "We can go check into the caravan park or go straight to the showgrounds. We won't be able to do much in terms of setting up camp, as we have to sleep in Frank anyway."

"Let's go straight there!" Claire decided, bouncing around in her seat. "I can't wait to see everyone else's cars!"

"You're the boss lady, let's do it," he said, laughing at her unconcealed excitement.

They turned off to the showgrounds, and as they drove into the front road a very skinny older gentleman with a long beard and a vest that read 'Event Coordinator' held up his hand.

"You a registered competitor?" he asked, looking down at Frank's side.

"Ahh…." Claire stammered; she hadn't thought about online registration!

"That's my fault mate," George leant over to speak to him. "Can we sign up here?"

"Go over to Judy over there," the man said, unfazed, "She'll take your rego details and give you a competition sticker. It's just $20 entry for the whole weekend."

"Thanks, mate." George gave him the thumbs-up as Claire drove away. Up ahead about another fifty metres, Judy slapped a No. 234 sticker onto Frank's bottom right windscreen and took down his details.

"Just follow this road along, loves," she said cheerfully, her visor and perm looking straight out of the eighties. Claire dug it.

"When you turn left into the showgrounds, just keep going until you see the next free spot. The Kombis have just been lining up next to each other in neat rows. Try to stay fairly close, we are expecting a fair few more today as well."

"Thanks a million!" Claire chimed, again bouncing in her seat from excitement. She drove Frank in through the gates and came out into the open field of the showgrounds. Row upon row of parked Volkswagen Kombi buses greeted them.

George whistled low and long at the sight. "Now, that is a lot of maintenance all in one spot," he noted.

"This is freaking awesome!" Claire cried, swinging Frank's wheel to the right to take them down a row of lined-up Kombis. They had to drive another 150 or so metres before they came to the end. Claire reverse-parked Frank next to what looked like a restored lime-green split-window barn-door.

Claire turned Frank off and they both sat in the car as another Kombi came and pulled up beside them. It was a beautiful maroon split-window bus; Claire made the appropriate 'ooh' noises as it parked beside them, gleaming in the afternoon sun.

"I was not expecting this many people, or this many cars!" Claire reached around to the back to grab her hat. "What do we do now, you reckon?"

"I think we should clean out these candy wrappers for a start,"

George said, picking up the bits of paper and empty water bottles lying at his feet. "Then maybe tidy up the back a bit and put her on show?"

"Then we can go for a walk and check out everyone's vans, yeah?" she asked, excited at the prospect of investigating the colourful lines of classic vehicles that were puttering up and down the showgrounds.

"Absolutely."

They made quick work of tidying Frank. Claire opened his side doors and George pulled his surfboards out, leaning them up against the outside of the van. Claire then put Frank's seat back up and arranged the pillows in what she hoped was a semi-fashionable kind of way. Looking around, everyone else had thought to bring along cool displays to use in setting up their Kombis. The best Claire and George could hope for was to look like a functional campervan; but even so, Claire couldn't help but be insanely proud of Frank.

"Do you think it's okay to leave him all open while we check out everyone else's set-ups?" She bit her lip, fretting a little at the prospect of something happening to Frank.

"He'll be fine," George answered reassuringly. Next to them, the owners of the lime-green split-window had returned and were setting up camping chairs next to their van. They were an older couple, in their mid-fifties Claire would guess. They smiled welcomingly at both Claire and George.

"That's a beautiful van you got there!" the older gentleman said, sitting down in his camping chair and dropping an esky by his side. "You don't see too many early-model bay-windows; most we've seen today have been seventies models, hey love?"

The plump, cheery woman all but beamed at her husband. "You don't! It is a real beauty. What year model is it?"

"He's a '68," Claire said proudly. "He was my pop's, he bought him new."

"A family member!" the man exclaimed, opening his esky and pulling out two beer cans, passing one to his wife. "Now, that is special. My name is Brian, this is my wife Shirley."

"Lovely to meet you both, I love your van as well, that is so beautifully restored." Claire stared at it adoringly. "I'm Claire and this is George."

George waved politely, happy to sit back and let Claire do all the talking.

"So, when did you take him – him? – over from your grandfather?"

"Only this year, actually," Claire said, patting Frank's side. "And yes, he's a him, his name is Frank. He was sitting in a farmhouse in Yass not moving for the past fifteen years."

"Well, you've done a great job restoring him if that's the case. Wow." Brian addressed this to George.

George put his hands in the air. "Frank here is all Claire's; she did all the work, not me."

Claire looked at George sharply. "That's not…"

"She's very modest." George looked down at Claire with his crinkly-eyed smile. "Within just a few months she's done everything to have him back on the road and roadworthy."

Brian and Shirley looked admiringly at Claire. She felt her cheeks colour pink in pleased embarrassment.

"Well, well done young lady." He nodded approvingly. "I know how hard it can be with these old cars; it's never just one thing is it!"

Having reassured Claire that they would keep an eye on Frank, even though she was sure he would be fine anyway, Claire and George went for a walk. It was a beautiful day; the sun was full in the sky and a slight breeze was coming off the coast, keeping the temperature to a lovely, almost-summer warmth. Acoustic music could be heard floating down from a stage at the other side of the showgrounds, where long lines of market tents were set up with people wandering aimlessly through them. The nearby seaside brought with it the smell of salt mixed with the freshly mowed grass from the showgrounds. Claire felt completely at peace as she walked along with George, stopping at almost every Kombi along the way and seeing what the owners had done with them. There were no two vans the same, every single one was different and set up to meet the individual quirks and requirements of their specific owners.

One Kombi they came across looked like it was completely rusted out, but George said this was just the effect they were going for – it was structurally sound upon inspection. Another was painted in rainbows and the inside was lined with purple fur. Yet another was painted bright blue, with the word 'Tardis' written along both sides. Row upon row of beautiful, immaculate bay-windows stood proudly, some with their insides done as campers and others just as buses. Claire took photos of interiors she liked as she went, along with general photos of the Kombis that were particularly cool and different. She didn't think she would change Frank's interior now, but it was exciting seeing what other people's imaginations had conjured for their own.

At one spot, they came across a woman painting a flower on the side of a matte-yellow bay-window. It looked rusty. She smiled at Claire and George as they stopped to watch what she was doing.

"Wanna paint something?" she asked, indicating a bunch of other haphazard drawings along its side.

"Are you sure?" Claire's eyes lit up.

"Of course!" the woman said. "The plan is to paint her as much as I can this weekend, just by lovely strangers such as yourselves. She is going to be resprayed within the next year or so anyway, so it's just a bit of fun."

"That is so cool," Claire breathed with excitement. She could not imagine letting anyone near Frank with a paintbrush, it would feel like sacrilege. She liked the idea of painting someone else's van, though.

Claire spent the next twenty minutes attempting to paint a horse, which she would tell George was a donkey in hopes he wouldn't judge her too much for it. George painted a rotund dog, which he said was his family's labrador, Larson. After going through all the markets and sharing a pizza from a food truck, they sat down in the grass in front of the stage and listened to a band play Foo Fighters covers. By the time they left the showgrounds, the afternoon sun was just beginning to slowly dip lower in the sky. As they were driving out, Claire could not help but smile happily to herself at what an amazing idea their spontaneous Old Bar weekend had turned out to be.

CHAPTER 16

Oh No, Not This Boy Stuff Again

George drove Frank to their camp site, negotiating his way through the busy caravan park, which was also filled with campervans. He parked Frank between a tent and another Kombi, and Claire jumped out excitedly; she had had such a fantastic afternoon and was now about to really camp out in Frank for the first time ever. The spot they had reserved was truly beautiful. It faced directly onto the beach below, with a man-made granite cliff face separating the beach from the pine trees and green grass of the camp site. A soft breeze came off the ocean, and crickets chirped happily in concert with one another in a beautiful background symphony. *It's perfect*, Claire sighed, as she opened her passenger door and did the window up. On one side of them was a large, five-person tent, and on the other, another Kombi, which must have been participating in the festival as well. Kombis made up the majority of the visitors at the caravan park.

George hopped inside Frank and pushed his pop-top up; Claire opened the back while he did that and once again took the two surfboards out, leaning them up against Frank. They could probably have fitted next to them along the internal sides of the van, but Claire was secretly a little nervous about the sleeping arrangements for the night. She had slept in vans before, even with people she knew less well than George – but there was something less casual between the two of them. Whatever it was, it remained unspoken, which meant it could all very possibly be part of her imagination. Inside Frank, George pulled out the blankets from underneath the seat and pillows and arranged them on the bed, managing to not meet Claire's eyes as he did so.

"I'm going to go have a shower," she said, with forced cheer.

"Do you need a torch or anything?" he asked, looking up at the remnants of the sun as it dipped below the horizon.

"It's called a mobile...Come on George, how old are you?" she teased, grabbing her towel, toothbrush and pyjamas before wandering off to find the women's bathrooms. The shower had a coin-operated hot-water system, which she loved – it took some of the guilt out of how long her shower was when she was actively paying for it. Taking her time to carefully brush her teeth and stare woefully at the state of her skin after so many hours in the sun, Claire walked back to where Frank was parked, using her mobile for light as it had gotten very dark, very quickly. Up ahead, she could see the light illuminating Frank's curtains; his side door still open.

She peered inside, to see George – just returned from a shower too, his hair wet and messy from what must have been an attempt at towel drying – wearing a white T-shirt and comfy-looking football shorts, lying on one side looking at his phone. He looked up at her when she climbed in and pulled Frank's door shut behind her, fussing with the lock so he wouldn't catch her eye – or her thoughts, which were very much trained on the giant man body currently taking up space in her bed. It had been several weeks since she had last stayed at Zac's, and the prospect of breaking her long stint of sex deprivation only seemed to make things harder now. No pun intended.

God give me strength, she prayed silently, *I am but woman.*

"Let me know if you want that open." She hung her towel up over the passenger-seat chair. "I just figured it will probably be cold tonight and there is something about me, possibly this pasty, translucent skin, which tends to attract mosquitos in the thousands."

"No, that's okay," he said, shuffling even further over to give her room to climb onto the bed beside him. "How did you go in that shower? Mine was freezing."

"Ahh, you weren't prepared!" she admonished. "I'm used to this paying-for-amenities business, from my many years of near homelessness."

Claire turned the interior light off and laid down next to George, intensely aware of how close his body was to hers. She pulled the blanket over her and moved close to the other side of the Kombi, facing away from him, willing her breathing to quieten down, as it sounded thunderous in her head.

"Night, George." She forced a yawn.

"Night, Claire," he whispered back beside her.

They lay there in silence and Claire attempted to focus on her breathing. Outside she could hear the crash of the waves at the beach just below; the predictable roll and crash was very relaxing. She lay there listening to it for a time, trying to calm her thoughts and force herself to sleep. This was proving futile, though, and after what felt like hours but was probably only minutes, she shifted around a little, pulling her blanket close. George did not stir beside her.

She was so close she was sure he could hear the loud pounding of her heart. He moved next to her, stretching slightly, shifting onto his side so that he faced her while she continued to lie on her back. He smelt fantastic…an earthy, musky man smell that seemed to settle in the pit of Claire's stomach and send butterflies fluttering. Outside, crickets chirped and waves crashed rhythmically. Claire closed her eyes, willing them to sleep. She wanted nothing more than to reach out and touch him; her arms raised in goosebumps at the mere thought of him only inches away.

"Claire," George murmured next to her. Claire's eyes snapped open, and she turned her head to face him.

"Yes?" she whispered back immediately.

"Do you mind?" he asked gently, holding out his arm as if to put it around her. Claire felt her heart skip as she stared into his beautiful, earnest eyes. She didn't know how she ever thought them arrogant or unkind – how could such honest eyes hold anything such.

"No," she said. "It's sweet you asked, though."

George gently reached out and drew Claire to him, turning her onto her side. Her body moulded against his and his arm locked her close against his broad chest. Claire sighed in contentment, her previous nervous energy completely draining from her body as she relaxed into the shape of his long body. It was almost a sense of relief, as if she had been waiting for him to touch her in some small way, to make some sort of advance. They had been dancing around this all week, this intimacy, which Claire for once had no idea how to instigate, as he could be so impenetrable. She had known there was something there, that she had felt more than friendship, but she had buried it, waiting for this exact moment – a touch, a caress, something to show that it wasn't just Claire who felt this way.

"Goodnight, Claire," he breathed, kissing her cheek gently. Claire's heart soared at the gesture, while her cheek burned from the soft brush of his lips.

"Goodnight, George," she replied, feeling inexplicably happy. Slowly, wrapped within each other, Claire and George drifted off to sleep.

The next morning, Claire awoke to sun peeking through Frank's curtains, a soft breeze coming through the opened windows making them flutter. George had already woken up at some point in the morning when she had still been sleeping; the bed was empty next to her. Sitting up, slightly disorientated, Claire looked around outside to see where he was, suddenly very conscious her normally curly hair was probably looking exceptionally wild.

"Good morning," a cheery voice called out from outside.

Climbing out of bed, Claire stepped out of Frank's now-open side door, stretching as she hit the soft grass outside. It was still very early. George was in front of Frank, in nothing but a pair of board shorts, his broad chest exposed. She cleared her throat and determinedly stared at his face as he smiled at her, waxing his surfboard far too happily for someone at this time of day, in her opinion.

"Good morning," she mumbled, stifling a yawn. "What time is it?"

"Ten past five." George's long arms were making quick work of his board. "Check out the surf, though."

George pointed to the ocean down below them; the waves were steadily rolling onto the beach under the beautiful, soft, golden light of the sunrise as it began to creep into the sky. The camp sites around them were still very quiet; all the other campers still in bed. *Smart folk*, Claire mused, her gaze being drawn back to the topless George. Watching him move methodically up and down the board.

George stood up straight, revealing an impressively tanned and muscular torso. Claire suddenly felt far more awake. It was evident he was a surfer – that tan wasn't coming from anywhere in Canberra.

"I did promise to teach you," he reminded her, indicating the other surfboard leaning against Frank.

"You did." She stretched her hands above her head. "Do you think it will be cold?"

"Paddling will warm you up pretty quickly; I don't have a wetsuit for you, though."

"That's okay," Claire shrugged, inspecting the surfboard in front of her. "It's about time I learnt how to be Australian, I can't keep disappointing random strangers overseas."

"Best way to start your day," George promised.

Claire climbed back into Frank and quickly got changed into her bathing suit. Picking up her phone, she checked the screen to see three unread messages. Opening it up, they were all from Anna.

Did you make it to that old car thing or are you dead on the side of the road somewhere?

Then a second message. *Hello? It's me, your best friend, the light of your life, answer me immediately.*

Anna had saved the best for last. *Right, clearly you have far better things to do, such as your mechanic. Message me so I know he isn't wearing a mask made from your skin. Love you, bye.*

Claire quickly typed a reply. *Anna! It is I! Zero car incidents and skin relatively still attached to face, sunburn aside. Just about to go surfing so will call you later.*

Surfing? Anna must have woken up early. *You can't surf.*

Duh. Love you, talk later. Claire pressed send.

Putting her phone on charge to a portable power bank, Claire grabbed a couple of towels and closed Frank's side door as quietly as she could, very aware that people were still asleep in their vans and tents beside them.

"Ready to go?" George asked, handing her a bottle of sunscreen.

"Two seconds, sorry." She squirted a huge amount of sunscreen into her hand. The sun might not be fully up yet, but her skin was so pale she was in danger of being sunburnt by the home screen on her mobile. Once she was finishing slathering her whole body in about an inch of sunscreen, George put a surfboard under each arm and they walked down to the beach together. While they were finding a spot on the sand to leave their towels, Claire eyed the board nervously.

"Okay, teacher, what's the dummies' guide to not drowning?"

"It's okay." He put both boards down in the sand next to one another. "We will do some stuff here first."

Claire tried not to show her relief. The waves did not look very large, but to her the surf might as well have been the Banzai pipeline, given how confident she was feeling. George sat her down and talked a few things through first, how rips work, currents, etc. After that, he had her practise hopping up on the board. She felt mildly ridiculous doing this, but was determined to get it right; her competitive side overriding any sense of shame at the sight of her jiggly bits – and not the good kind – bouncing around in a bikini. *He's an excellent teacher, though*, Claire thought admiringly, as he patiently took her through the steps over and over again.

Once George had decided that Claire's surfboard stand-up was looking less like the first awkward steps of a baby calf, he got her to velcro the cord to one of her ankles and carry her board down to the water. Claire gasped when she first got in, the water was freezing.

"You will warm up, don't worry," George promised, following her in without fanfare, diving under quickly and re-emerging from the chilly water, running his hands through his hair. It was incredibly attractive; Claire was in no rush to emulate him, though.

"Well, now I kind of am." Her teeth chattered slightly.

The sun was well and truly creeping higher into the sky, and the previously empty beach now had some fellow surfers on it, rubbing sunscreen onto their somehow cold-immune skin.

The water was up to their waist, their boards floating next to them, when the first wave hit, knocking it out of Claire's hand. "You can either push it under the wave or push it over," George explained, as Claire scrambled to grab it. Thank God for that ankle cord.

Claire nodded and continued to follow him out into the deeper water, holding onto the side of the board until the water came up to her shoulders. For the first wave, George had Claire lie on her board and then pushed it out for her when the wave came.

"Paddle Claire, paddle!" he called out, as she flailed her arms through the water.

"Okay, now UP, stand up!" George called out again. Claire tried to climb up onto her knees, but she lost her balance and rolled off the side and tumbled into the surf. She emerged choking slightly, but even more determined to stand up for the next one.

"I'm okay!" she yelled out, waving her hands and pushing her board back into the surf. The next hour went pretty much the same way, and when Claire finally did stand up, she was so excited that she turned back to wave at George and lost her balance. She somersaulted into the surf, only to have the surfboard come back and hit her hard across the forehead. Claire let out a yelp of pain. A moment later, George was there, steadying her with both hands as the waves continued to roll in harder. Claire, disorientated from the unexpected blow to the head, swayed slightly as George's grip tightened.

"You okay?" he asked gently, pulling her close to his chest to ride over a wave, one arm on his surfboard and the other around her shoulders with his hand holding onto hers. His skin was warm and hard, and Claire felt the breath escape her chest at the shock of his body against her. After they were over the wave, Claire did not pull away but stayed against him, her mind racing, unsure of what to do. In the spur of the moment, she reached up and kissed him quickly on the lips. It was brief and salty and warm.

George hesitated, leaning back to study her face. She reached in once again and this time he didn't hold back but responded ardently in kind, his arm crushing her even harder against his chest. It was an incredible kiss. Claire sighed, leaning her whole body against him. George pulled away once again.

"We should probably get you back onto the beach now." He breathed heavily, trying to catch his breath.

"Why would you want to do that?" Her head was now spinning from intoxication of a different kind.

"My self-control is only so great, Claire."

"Good," was all her sluggish mind would conjure.

"And you're possibly concussed."

Claire rolled her eyes, touching her head where the board had hit. "It's just a bump – we can move past this unwarranted chivalry."

George looked somewhat doubtful, so Claire simply leant in once again, wrapping her arms around his neck. She felt the tension in his broad shoulders dissipate as she kissed him more slowly this time, her body shivering as she felt his arm pull her closer against his chest. While she was distracting him, her board slipped from his fingers as another smaller wave rolled in.

"You are a hard woman to argue with," he breathed, pulling back from her kiss and gently tracing a thumb under her chin, before reaching for Claire's rogue board. She grabbed it from him, slightly shocked at the turn their surfing adventure had taken.

"Easy, don't argue with me." *It was a simple solution, really.*

"Deal," George laughed. "But come on, let's go back up to Frank and get you some breakfast."

The rest of the morning was spent back at the showgrounds, looking through other people's Kombis. They didn't stay long, only an hour or so, before hitting the road and heading home. They talked the whole time. Claire, about all the places she wanted to take Frank in Australia when retracing her grandparents' steps. George, about his love for rebuilding cars and the unexpected problems they liked to throw at you, and about his family on the South Coast. His sister, Gail, was nearly always in Sydney now, but his parents were still firmly ensconced in the same house he had grown up in. When they finally arrived back at Claire's, it was about eleven at night and her parents were well and truly asleep. George asked if he could use her bathroom before he got an Uber back to his house in Queanbeyan.

"I can drive you home, it's okay," Claire repeated for the one-hundredth time, stifling a yawn.

"Don't be silly, it's almost midnight."

As Claire turned on the lights, putting her overnight bag down next to the kitchenette, his eyes quickly took in her little granny flat.

"So, do you mind if I use your bathroom?" he asked.

"Go nuts." Claire sat down on the end of her bed, completely exhausted from the long drive home.

George reappeared a few moments later, rubbing his forehead and yawning, looking equally tired. Claire had taken her shoes off and was now lying fully in bed, too tired to get properly undressed or have a shower. George came and sat on the edge of her mattress, looking down at her with a smile.

"Thank you for the weekend," he said.

"I was about to say the same thing to you." She reached out and put a hand on his leg. George yawned once again.

"Did you…did you just want to stay here?" she asked timidly. They had only just 'slept' together last night, but that had been in a van – this was a bed. A real bed. It felt far more serious.

"You wouldn't mind?" he asked, surprise crossing his face.

She shook her head, pulling him down onto the bed. George opened his arms and gathered her into a hug, her head resting on his broad chest.

"Claire," George said.

"Yes?"

"How on earth is a girl like you single?"

Claire snorted. "I think you just answered your own question."

"No, honestly." He laughed. "Not married in any of those countries you left behind?"

"Unfortunately not," Claire replied, her mind going to Zac. She hadn't expanded on what had happened between them to George, only that she had been seeing someone but it had ended. It just all felt a little too fresh. She didn't want George to think she was hung up on him, and a small part of her was still embarrassed and a little hurt.

"Well, that makes this a little less complicated then," he said, stroking the hair off her face and leaning down to kiss her softly, then more urgently. Claire responded in kind, no longer feeling tired. It did not take long to settle things; George did not go home that night.

CHAPTER 17

Mr Long Black, Extra Froth

The countdown until Claire left for her trip was on. At first it had been a vague date, 'around November', but then her parents and even Ainsley started tactfully ignoring her original plan. They started doing things like organising Christmas lunch, and Ainsley even began rostering her on for shifts in December. Claire decided she needed to be firm, decisive, and so she picked November 15, giving her three weeks to finalise everything and hit the road. She was excited about this at first, having finally made a drive-out decision. The days seemed to have sped up extra quickly now though, and Claire felt the pressure of November 15 beginning to loom closer and closer.

Ainsley – who was now openly flaunting her blossoming relationship with the baker across the road, as Claire had originally suspected – had very specific thoughts on Claire's road trip.

"Two weeks, I give it two weeks," she predicted, lounging in an empty chair and sipping a coffee. The café was empty that afternoon and Claire was humming to herself happily while wiping down the bench.

"Your faith in me is inspiring," Claire replied dryly.

"Oh, I have nothing but faith in you. In Frank, however…That old van of yours is going to break down or catch fire or both and you will be stuck in some godawful Wolf Creek situation in the middle of nowhere. Far safer to just stay here."

"I would think you'd be well shot of me by now."

"Nonsense," Ainsley said. "You are my favourite curly-haired barista."

Out front of the store, a tall blond man was peering through one of the glass windows, looking straight at Claire behind the coffee machine.

"Is that...?" Ainsley asked, perplexed.

"Yup," Claire confirmed, her stomach dropping at the very sight. *What the absolute hell?*

Zac had opened the front door to the café, striding in determinedly after locking eyes with Claire. She was frozen; her hand paused midway through wiping down the bench.

"Claire," he breathed. "Can I talk to you?"

Behind him, Ainsley widened her eyes, and mouthed, 'Do you want my help?' Claire shook her head slightly; she was curious to hear what he was doing there.

"Do you mind if we go outside?" Zac asked, indicating the empty footpath out front, glancing back at a blatantly glaring Ainsley.

Claire nodded, not trusting herself to speak just yet while the shock of his presence wore off. It hadn't been long, but she had already started forgetting what his face looked like up close; she had almost forgotten how handsome he was. It was funny how the mind chose to retain only what it wanted to. George's face suddenly loomed to the forefront of her mind. *Focus, Claire,* she hissed at herself inwardly. *Do not be sucked in by his handsome juju!*

Besides, George was handsome as well *and* he wasn't a cheating narcissist.

Going outside, Zac loomed over Claire, staring down at her intently.

"Claire..." Zac seemed to have lost his words, now that he had lured her out of the store. He must have been worried he would not even get that far.

"Zac." She crossed her arms defensively. "What are you doing here?"

"I miss you," he said straight away – not beating around the bush on this one apparently.

"Cool," she replied impassively. "Have you told Abbie that?"

"That is over," he said quickly. "I ended it."

"Sorry to hear that." Claire was not ready to believe him. As if someone would ever end anything with a beautiful creature like that.

"It's true, we are finished, done."

"Again, sorry to hear."

"What I'm trying to say...I want to give things a try again."

"Zac..." She tapped her foot, becoming exasperated. "We never really began in the first place, no point returning to something that never had the chance to happen."

"You don't understand," he whined. "Abbie and I...Abbie and I have been together a while and then I had to move to Canberra; long distance was really hard."

Claire raised her eyebrows sceptically.

"Or at least it wasn't, until I met you..." He took a step towards her, changing tactics.

"Zac, I'm going to stop you right there." She raised her hand as a barrier between them. "Whatever was happening between us – which, from memory, was just a lot of sex and takeaway – could not be more totally *over*."

Zac's face fell. She had forgotten how handsome he was; she had been focusing so much on how hurt she was by finding out he had a partner that, in her head, she had painted him to be some kind of horrible, hideous beast. Only he wasn't, he was gorgeous and had warm eyes and a natural charm. It was confusing and unfair; Claire wished he had just looked like the ugly bad boy she had painted him to be.

"Claire..." he breathed, reaching out to grab her hand. "I missed you, I really did. I was surprised by how much actually."

"You're only human," she muttered, moving her hand out of the way.

"I know you are leaving soon..."

"Huh?" she asked, confused. "How?"

"Saw it on your Instagram..."

"Bloody Instagram," she cursed. "Well, I'd just ignore that if I was you, that website's caused you enough problems."

"I don't want you to go," he pleaded, his tone containing a whine she couldn't remember hearing before.

"What?" she snapped, throwing her hands in the air. "I am so confused. What does it matter if you want me to go or not?"

"We were good together, Claire."

"We were never really even together, Zac," she growled back, becoming more and more irate by the second. *What an arrogant sod.*

"Then why are you even upset with me? You just said we were never really together..."

"Okay, woah there cowboy, don't even *try* to gaslight me. You need to take this all back a notch."

Zac suddenly stepped in and grabbed her arms, his face reaching down towards hers. Claire had not been expecting this and she was momentarily paralysed; Zac's face was only inches from hers as her body immediately stiffened against this unwanted advance. Behind them, somebody coughed loudly.

Zac froze. Looking up, his face registered shock. He dropped his arms from around her.

"George...?" he muttered, bewildered.

"Huh?" Claire asked, spinning around to see George standing a mere five metres away, his gaze moving between Claire and Zac; his face was impassive, except for a furrowed frown.

"How do you...do you know each other?" Claire asked, looking from one man's face to the other.

With one last look of disdain at Zac and not even a glance at Claire, George spun on his heels and strode away to his car, parked on the other side of the road.

"What is happening?" Claire asked, dazed and uncertain about everything that had just taken place. She looked up at a bewildered Zac. "How do you know George?"

"Him?" Zac scoffed, his face contorting with dislike. "I...I knew his family."

"This is crazy," Claire breathed, swaying slightly. "I need to go after him."

"Him?" Zac all but snarled, his handsome face twisted in anger. "Why? Who is he to you?"

"Zac," she said sharply, her hands on her hips. "I don't know what you thought you would achieve by coming here today, but just in case I was not clear enough – leave me alone, I am not bloody interested in you."

"Fine," he spat, all traces of his cool, calm demeanour gone. "Good luck finding anyone better that would want a nobody barista anyway."

"Nice," she replied, fuming. "Now kindly fuck off, I've got coffees to make."

When Claire marched back into the Bookshop Café, her whole body shaking with a mixture of fury and adrenaline, Ainsley away from the window, where her nose had been pressed only seconds before.

"Did my eyes deceive me...wasn't that the mechanic bloke you're dating?" Her voice was breathless with excitement.

Long

"It sure was," Claire said through clenched teeth, walking straight out to the back kitchen to retrieve her phone. No missed calls or messages, nothing from George. What was he doing there and how in the hell did he know Zac? There were too many unanswered questions; her hands trembled as she typed him a message.

Hey there. Why did you leave just before? I was just getting rid of a pest when you arrived. Can I give you a call after work? I finish at four.

Claire waited with her phone in hand for a minute or two to see if he would respond. When her phone stayed silent, she messaged Anna in frustration.

Call me tonight, I have goss. Not good goss, the annoying man-child kind. Talk later.

Claire put her phone back in her bag and walked back out into the café, where a small line for coffee was starting to build up. Ainsley was at the counter, taking orders, her eyes lighting up when she saw her.

"You okay, Claire?" She completely ignored a customer holding cash out in front of her. "You have approximately twenty minutes of self-reflecting time before I demand a story from you."

"I'm okay, Ains." Claire re-tied her apron around her waist and went straight over to the coffee machine where a stack of orders had built up along the counter. She threw herself into making them, trying to calm her mind and stop it going at a million miles an hour with the all the thoughts running through her head.

Zac had broken up with his girlfriend, the Instagram goddess, who Claire had now taken to stalking only now and then as opposed to daily. Zac wanted to get back together with her, even though they were never really together. Claire couldn't help but feel that was more to do with his depression about losing the blonde bombshell and less to do with her and her short mop of curls and probably too big of a butt. Not the good, gym kind of butt either, but more the *I'm addicted to peppermint chocolate and have an aversion to exercise* kind.

Claire was proud that she had kept her calm with Zac, even when he tried to kiss her. Horrible men should not be allowed to be handsome; it is both confusing and makes hating them difficult. Not that disliking Zac was in any way difficult, then or now.

Claire frothed some milk and poured it into the awaiting two takeaway cups, handing them over with a smile to a hopeful older gentleman. She continued to quickly work away, replaying the confrontation over and over in her head. It was making her so worked up she wanted nothing more than to go home, curl up in bed and have an angry cry. With George. George...how had he known Zac, and how had Zac known George? A friend of the family...his family or George's? Claire wished she had pressed the issue more; she wished she had chased George down the street so she didn't have to stand here and fret about it now.

Finishing up several more coffees, she quickly ducked into the kitchen to check her phone in her bag. No messages or calls from George, just one from Anna.

I demand more information immediately.

Zac showed up at work...I'll tell you more later.

Hey! Anna quickly replied. *You have to give me more than that!*

Claire put her phone back in her bag, her anger at Zac suddenly turning cold at the prospect of no message from George. He had left very quickly; he hadn't even looked at her. She had been facing away from him, so maybe he had only seen her being unwillingly pulled into a kiss from Zac – not her look of shock or disgust. Panic began to set in, as Ainsley called out to her from the front room. Claire ran back out, to see a small crowd filling the small café, all seemingly lining up for coffee orders. Ainsley was at the counter once again; she saw Claire's face as she came out.

"You okay, love?" her curiosity from before turning to concern. "Do you need to go home?"

Claire looked at the busy room around her. There was nothing more she wanted to do than get on her bike and race over to see George to tell him exactly what had happened, in case he was thinking the worst. She couldn't do that to Ainsley, though.

"No, it's okay." She hurried back over to the coffee machine. Her hands were slightly numb with shock at the events of the day.

"They're not worth it, love," commented an old woman at the front of the line, ordering a coffee from Ainsley. "If it's a boy, you will live longer without him."

"I think it's actually two boys, so you are probably twice as right." Ainsley handed the old lady her change. She raised her eyebrows in appreciation and gave Claire a wink. Claire glowered at Ainsley and went back to making her coffees.

Later that afternoon, after she had finished work, Claire called Anna and explained the events of the day. Anna told her not to worry, just to text George and then give him some space. Claire did as she recommended, but did not receive a response. She resisted the urge to get into Frank and just drive to his house; like Zac, they hadn't really established what they were, so it wasn't as if they were breaking up, was it?

Stop trying to downplay the situation. You two HAD laid down a few things – just not a relationship status, she reminded herself, as she sat on her bed, staring forlornly at her silent phone.

CHAPTER 18

Ice Cream Is Better Stolen

Claire sat in the living room with Harvey, watching *The Bachelorette* and eating her weight in peppermint chocolate that she had found on sale; no longer caring about the ever-growing size of her thighs in her current state of man-induced misery. Harvey sat in the chair next to her, sipping his tea and commemorating each scene with strong fervour.

"Ooh, just you wait, Claire. You watch – he is definitely going home. Cannot stand him. Look at the way he is walking, like he's trying to be even bigger than he really is. She can do so much better," Harvey said, pointing at the television.

Claire grunted in agreement and continued to demolish her feelings via sugar.

"And every time he does a piece to camera, it's almost like he's trying to see his own reflection in the lens…"

"Mmhmm."

"Now, James on the other hand, I can definitely see Faye with James. Such a nice man, he is far better than that vile Kyle."

Claire muffled a series of noises in response.

"…honestly, I don't know how anybody watches this show, it's just ridiculous."

Claire raised her eyebrows at her father, but chose not to respond this time.

"So," he asked, dragging his eyes away from the screen as an advertisement for pools – while Canberra was still freezing, mind you – appeared. "You still set on the 15th?"

"Like you wouldn't believe," she said dryly.

"Hmm," he replied, concerned. "Still going alone…George not going with you?"

Claire almost laughed at his probing question; Harvey could definitely tell something was wrong. Her inhalation of snack food was probably a good indication. That man knew how to read an emotional binge from his daughter when he saw it.

"Definitely still alone. It was never going to be any other way."

"Well, that is a shame," he said, sipping his tea. "Your mother and I really liked George."

"Who did I really like?" Dianna called out from the kitchen.

"George!" Harvey yelled back. "You really liked George, remember!"

"Oh yes, George!" Dianna called back. "Yes, I really do like George!"

"George is a great man, very respectful, very useful too."

Claire groaned at the repeated reference to he who should not be named right now. It had been several days with no word from George, and Claire was progressing through the many stages of grief via sugar and trans fat.

"Dad, George and I are not on speaking terms right now," she replied miserably, unceremoniously stuffing another three squares into her mouth.

"What? Why ever not?" Dianna asked, walking into the living room and sitting down next to Harvey with a cup of tea as well.

"Because men, no offence Dad, are idiots," Claire grumbled in response, almost choking on a chunk of Cadbury.

"Well, she's got you there, Harvey," Dianna said, raising her eyebrows in amusement.

"You two seemed to be getting along very well..." Harvey said, probing further.

"Oh, yes, very well," Dianna murmured. "I was getting used to giving him a wave every morning when he tried to sneak down the side of the house."

"Mum!" Claire cried out, blushing.

"Yes, a very nice boy," Dianna said with a sly smile.

"Like your mother said," Harvey threw her a sideways look, "you two were getting along very well, did something happen?"

"Well," she said. "If you must know, Zac came by my work the other day."

"He didn't!" Harvey said in shock.

"He did."

"What? What's this? Who's Zac?" Dianna asked sharply, looking from Harvey to Claire.

"The gall!" he said.

"I know!" Claire replied angrily.

"What is happening?" Dianna interrupted, annoyed at being left out.

"He was Claire's clean-cut former flame."

"Oh well, yes, or something like that..."

"How have I never heard of this?" Dianna asked, looking across to her husband. "More importantly, how have you heard of him?"

"Claire and I have gotten very close," he replied smugly. "When we were fixing up Frank, she told me about him."

"Well, there you go." Dianna laughed. "Here I was thinking you were off staying at Anna's all those nights. The pieces are suddenly all coming together."

"He was a total schmuck though," Harvey explained. "He had a girlfriend in Sydney, Claire says she is famous."

"Only on Instagram," Claire corrected him quickly. "Not really

214

famous, not like a celebrity or anything."

"And you were the mistress, were you?" Dianna asked pointedly.

"Mum! You're not a mistress if you don't know about the other woman!"

Harvey nodded to his wife. "She was definitely the mistress."

"Dad! You are supposed to be on my side!" *You raised this mistress, bloody traitors.*

"Anyway," Harvey said, filling Dianna in on all the gossip. "Claire found out this Zac character had a girlfriend and then proceeded to eat every carbohydrate in the house for a few weeks."

"Was that when she decided to try and swindle some free mechanical work out of poor George?"

"Yes, would have been about then, I think," Harvey replied. "Was it about then, Claire?"

"You two are unbelievable," Claire grumbled, a smile breaking across her face. "And if you must know, it may have been about the time of Daisy's wedding…"

"…and we've seen you two skulking around ever since," Dianna continued. "So, what happened, this Zac character turned up to your work and then what?"

"Well, he said he had broken up with Abbie…"

"Wait – who's Abbie?"

"The woman whose boyfriend Claire was seeing."

"Ahh, right, carry on."

"…and I told him that basically he and his breakup could go take a flying leap…"

"That's my girl," Harvey chuckled.

"…and then Zac decided that I must have been playing some very confusing game of hard-to-get and that it would be the perfect opportunity to lean in for a kiss…"

"Oooh, I can see where this is going."

"…which, would you believe, was the moment that George must have decided to visit me at work…"

"Oh no, poor George," Harvey sighed.

"…and caught me in what must have looked like a massive pash but was just me being generally frozen in shock."

"What did he do?" Dianna asked, leaning closer with interest. "Did he make a scene, break you two up? Did he punch this Zac character?!"

"No, that's not George's style." Harvey shook his head sadly. "He is a gentleman."

"Unfortunately, yes," Claire said, her voice almost breaking. "He just stood there quietly; by the time I noticed he was there, he just looked at me briefly and then turned around and left. I tried to call out to him, but I was still awkwardly entangled in Zac's bloody arms and didn't know what to do."

"Did you call him?" Dianna asked.

"Only a billion times," Claire said. "And texted him about a billion more."

"I'm sorry, Claire-Bear," Harvey said. "I know you liked him a lot."

"I bloody did," Claire said, annoyed. "I'm frustrated at myself for even getting into this situation in the first place. I was never staying in Canberra – what was I doing getting attached to him anyway?"

"You can't help who you fall for," Dianna mused wisely. "And besides, you are at that age."

"Age? What age?" Claire squeaked. "I am still in my twenties!"

"I know, love," Dianna sighed, sipping her tea. "You are very young, you are still my baby, don't get me wrong. But you are almost thirty. You travelled for so long…"

"What are you saying?" Claire demanded, defiant. *If she mentions my ovaries, I swear…*

"Just that you don't have that same aversion to anything *fixed*, like you used to..."

"What is she on about?" Claire growled at Harvey, not wanting to hear what her mother was saying to her right now.

Harvey cleared his throat, looking from his wife to his daughter, probably afraid of getting caught in the crosshairs.

"I think, dear, what your mother is saying..." he chose his words carefully, "is that you are just maturing."

"Maturing," she said, woefully. "I am getting old."

"No, no, it's nothing to do with ageing..." Dianna said, frowning with disapproval at Claire's theatrics. "I've noticed it a lot, you are far happier to just spend time with us, to just relax. When you were younger, you were so worried about seeing the world. It was almost like you were in such a hurry to get everywhere at once you couldn't sit still, you couldn't be present at home with us like you are now...it was always work, work, work, save, save, save and then go, go, go."

Claire slumped deeper into the couch; she understood what her mother was saying to her, but she didn't want to acknowledge the truth in her words. She knew she had been that way – that the urge to disappear, to pack up and see something she had never seen before, had been all-consuming for her. Maybe this change in attitude *was* something to do with getting old, or more 'mature', as her father so eloquently put it.

"It's not a bad thing, dear," Harvey said kindly. "I have had an absolute blast hanging out with my favourite middle child these past few months. I'm super proud of everything you have achieved with Frank as well, and I feel very privileged to have been a part of it."

"Thanks, Dad," she mumbled ungraciously, breaking off a few more pieces of peppermint chocolate and shoving them in her mouth.

"You are welcome," he said, clearing his throat. "Anyway, after all that *Bachelorette* excitement I think I might go and read for a bit."

"Yeah, and the TV reality show sounds pretty entertaining as well," Dianna said slyly.

"Mum!"

"Okay, okay…I'm going to bed, see you in the morning."

Harvey hugged Claire and then he and Dianna both left the room, leaving her to stare at the advertisements alone. It wasn't until Barry's face and his Tyrepower advert popped up that she felt it was time to make a move. She sighed, picked up the remainder of her chocolate and decided to raid the cupboard for more comfort food to take back to her room in the backyard, where she could wallow in peace, without her well-meaning albeit judgy parents.

As she laid in bed, having created a food moat around her, there was a knock at the door. Claire's heart jumped in her chest. *Could it be George?* she thought frantically. *Had he finally read her messages and wanted to talk?*

Claire all but ran to the door, pulling it open quickly to reveal a very red-eyed Anna.

"Mind if I wallow for a bit?" her friend asked quietly, her voice husky.

"Of course," Claire replied, looking concerned. "I'm eating my way through half a tub of Dad's hidden ice cream if you want to join."

"Ahh, I love a bit of forbidden cookies and cream," Anna said, dumping her bag on the floor and climbing onto Claire's bed. Claire went and got another spoon from the kitchenette and climbed in next to her.

"What are you watching?" Anna asked, stuffing a spare pillow behind her head and digging into the ice cream with Claire.

"*Love Actually*," Claire said, hitting play.

"My favourite Christmas movie."

"It's just the right amount of humour-meets-romance to help spur on the self-loathing."

"Perfect, I knew I'd come to the right place."

They sat in comfortable silence, eating ice cream and watching Hugh Grant fumble adorably over his words, both of them booing at Alan Rickman when he gives that expensive necklace to the short-haired floozy from his work. Claire appreciated Anna's company; it was so familiar having her there, watching TV and eating Harvey's stolen cookies and cream that he kept at the back of the freezer as if to trick Dianna into not seeing it. It was just like in high school, although Claire had actually had a room in the house back then, not a shack in the backyard.

"I finally told David," Anna said quietly, just as the credits rolled, signalling the end of the film.

Claire almost choked on her spoon.

"You did?" she spluttered.

"Oh, yup," Anna replied, digging even deeper with her spoon this time, filling her mouth. "It was probably the most horrible thing ever."

"What happened?" Claire asked, hoping her surprise did not register too much on her face and upset Anna. She knew the affair couldn't go on forever without something changing; she just didn't think Anna would actually leave David.

"Well," Anna said, watching the screen. "I came home from work and David was there, sitting on the couch. I just kind of stood in the doorway for a bit staring at him…"

Claire listened intently, watching Anna as she spoke every word.

"…probably a bit creepy, but it was just a weird moment. I stood there staring at him, in his socks, on the couch, and I realised I didn't feel anything. Nothing. No love, just indifference."

"I'm sorry, Anna…"

"Honestly, don't be, I don't deserve it," she said. "So, anyway, I just kind of walked over to him and sat down. He asked me what was wrong and I… I said I wanted to break up."

"How did he take it?"

"To my surprise...he wasn't surprised at all," Anna said. "He just kind of nodded and said he knew that things had been bad for a while. I asked why he never said anything, and he said he didn't really know what to do or say."

"That's horrible."

"Yeah. It gets worse," Anna said, hugging herself with her arms. "It was like a flood gate had been opened after that...I told him I had been seeing someone, had been seeing someone for a while..."

Claire gasped, "You did?"

"Yeah," Anna said, her face crumpling. "I may not love him anymore like that, but seeing his face when I said those words...it will haunt me, Claire...David never deserved that."

"I'm sorry, Anna."

"I think I managed to compartmentalise so well, to just mentally separate what was happening so well, that when the two worlds crashed together, I wasn't prepared for what seeing his pain would do to me."

"Did he...did he get angry?"

"No," Anna said sadly. "He just looked really wounded and sort of...nodded. We sat in silence after that. I just kind of cried for a few hours and he went into our room. I left him there. I assume he is still there."

"Do you regret telling him? Now that it's all out in the open?"

"For him, I wish I hadn't of. He didn't deserve that, Claire," Anna said. "But for me, I'm glad I did. The secret was eating away at me, you saw how I was becoming. It's selfish, but I almost feel... relieved?"

"I get that," Claire nodded. "You've been holding all of this inside of you for so long....you could never have done it forever; you would have imploded."

"Yeah, it was getting to be a pretty close thing."

Claire gave Anna a hug, holding her friend close. Anna hugged her back tightly. Claire could feel her tear-wet cheek against hers as she continued to gently cry. They broke apart and Anna wiped her eyes.

"Even though that must have been completely horrible, I'm glad you made a decision Anna," Claire said. "Does Paul know? Is he still keen on marriage and all that do you think?"

"Oh, Paul? I broke up with him too."

"What!" *She really had been behind on the goss lately.*

"Yeah." Anna laughed bitterly. "A few days ago. Cut it away for good."

"Why didn't you tell me?"

"I feel like I burden you with all of this so much already," Anna said. "And I kind of wanted to just give it a few days, you know."

"What happened?"

"Nothing in particular, really...I just realised that what I was feeling for Paul wasn't anything real, it was just the excitement of something different. He is a lovely man, do not get me wrong, but it was no way to start a new relationship. I think I just need to be by myself, be single for a while you know."

"I totally understand," Claire said. "When was the last time you were single? Uni?"

"Pretty much," Anna said. "I just kind of jumped headfirst into the first serious relationship I had. I think I wanted to make something stable; maybe it's a hang-up from my parents' divorce, who knows... but I never had those independent, single years to 'find myself' or anything like that. Not like you did, with all your travelling."

"And look where that's gotten me," Claire replied bitterly. "Right here, eating ice cream with you and sulking over a man."

"Damn, you're right. Aren't we the pair?"

"A real messed-up duo."

"So, what's the plan for you now, anyway?" Anna asked, digging into more of the ice cream in the tub on Claire's lap.

"Finish up my last few shifts at the Bookshop, invest in a good-quality mattress softener to take the edge off Frank's leather seats, and hit the road to Western Australia on the 15th."

"That is getting close…"

"Bloody oath it is."

"I will miss you, you know, but I've been missing you for a while now."

"You should come meet up with me somewhere, for a weekend or something. I have a feeling Mum and Dad will magically appear at every second town I pull into."

"Deal. I'll drag the newlywed along, she's been MIA since she found true love and happiness and all that."

"Deal. Now pass me those chips. I wanna see what it's like if I dip them into the ice cream."

"Um, how are you single again?" Anna asked, laughing.

Claire shrugged, her hand already halfway into the ice-cream container.

"It's a damn mystery."

CHAPTER 19

Trusty Frank and the Long Road Ahead

November 15 crept up on Claire very quickly. With only two days to go, she still didn't feel prepared to leave. Sitting in the kitchen with Claire, Harvey was going through his daughter's to-do list with strict determination.

"Okay," he said, frowning at the messy, handwritten list. "You've listed gin twice here…"

"I know." She nodded seriously.

"Okay…and yup, dry food, good idea…"

"I figure if I run out of money, I can live off Maggi noodles."

"Thrifty, I like it…hmm…and you have all your blankets, etc., so that should be fine…" Harvey muttered, more to himself than Claire. "Do you have a jump-starter kit?"

"I do! Well, I do now…I stole Mum's," Claire said, proud of her ingenuity. *Such organisation!*

"Excellent," he said, reading further down the list. "Just the one spare tyre?"

"Nah, I've got that other one in the back-rear corner, as well as on the bumper bar, remember?"

"Yup, gotcha…What about…clothes? Are you bringing much?"

"Hardly any," Claire admitted. "I'm leaving most of what I have here with you guys; there just won't be all that much room once I fill the cabinets with dry food and all of your stolen toilet rolls."

"No, no, that's smart," Harvey said. "You seem to have it all in order. Have you mapped out a proper route yet?"

"Well, I don't want to make anything too solid..." Claire explained. "I feel like it will take away from the whole bohemian vibe of the thing. The only thing I know is I'm stopping in to visit Nan, show her Frank and get the details of those second cousins I might still have in Perth. Then visit Lynette in Sydney, before truly heading off after that."

"Oh, God, between your nan and your sister, your first year will be spent all within two hours of Canberra...not that I'm complaining."

"Don't you worry about that," Claire said. "I've got a foolproof plan to escape them. It involves driving off in the middle of the night, having left a cute but sentimental letter on their kitchen benches about yearning for the open road, etc."

"That will infuriate them both and my mother will hate it," Harvey said, pushing his glasses up. "I love it."

"The last thing I really need to do is get an e-tag for the tolls around New South Wales, it's hard to avoid them."

"You can just take your mother's spare one."

"But won't the charges then pop up on your account?"

Harvey waved his hand dismissively. "Do your worst. If it sends us destitute, I will just write you out of our will."

"Well, I guess I'm pretty much sorted, then," Claire said, mentally working her way down her list of things to do.

"What are you up to tonight? Your mother and I are going to watch *The Bachelorette* if you want to join us here in the main house."

"After the flack I copped last time? I don't think so." Claire laughed. "Besides, Anna is coming over and we will probably just watch it in my room with copious amounts of alcohol."

"How is Anna going?" Harvey asked, sounding a little concerned.

"She is good, she has found a new place to live; her and David are just going through the whole splitting-assets debacle."

"Well, I hope it works out for her. I always said she and David weren't right for each other, they got together far too young."

"Sure you did, Dad," Claire said, amused. Harvey had never said any such thing.

Back in her room, Claire prepared some snacks on a plate and made herself a drink while she waited for Anna to arrive. She had been deliberately keeping herself busy this week – mostly with as many last-minute shifts at the Bookshop Café as she could squeeze in, and with Frank preparations – to keep herself from thinking about George.

George had not messaged her or called her since the morning out the front of the café with Zac. She, on the other hand, had called and messaged him plenty; even resorting to what could have been an embarrassing drive-by of his share house in Queanbeyan. She had thought that if she had just happened to be driving in the area and he was getting into his car or something out front of his house, it wouldn't appear creepy or stalkerish. However, as she was creepily driving past slowly in her very non-subtle bright orange Kombi van, which he knew intimately, she realised how absolutely batshit insane she would look and just kept on driving.

Making another drink for Anna in anticipation of her friend arriving shortly, Claire sat down on her bed and turned on the television.

Moments later there was a knock at the door. Claire jumped up and picked up Anna's gin in preparation, flinging open the door to reveal a very handsome, very still, very unexpected mechanic. George stood in the doorframe, filling it with his gorgeous shoulders, his dark eyes staring hard into her own.

Claire didn't know what to say; she was completely taken aback by his presence. He glanced at the glass half-extended in her hand. He looked so handsome, so tall. She wanted to throw it down and jump into his arms...but at the same time sock him in the face for ignoring her. All of these emotions fought silently inside her while she stared dumbly at him, frozen at the door.

"Sorry to show up without calling," he said, his face expressionless. "Do you mind if I come in?"

"Of course," she croaked, willing her throat to begin working again.

George stepped into the flat, making it feel smaller as he seemed to do to every room. Claire placed the gin on the kitchenette counter and wandered over to the bed, sitting down as he did the same on the couch. She didn't know what to feel, apart from a little overwhelmed from the surprise and a little bit of relief that he was finally here, in front of her again.

"When do you leave?" George asked politely, his face an impenetrable mask.

"In a couple of days," Claire said, smiling back politely in return, as if a mere week before they hadn't been ripping each other's clothes off in a desperate frenzy.

"All set?" His back straight and hands resting politely in his lap, as if he'd just arrived at a job interview.

"Dad is getting me there," she said, trying to be cool and unemotional, as if she didn't just want to fling herself across the couch. "I'm getting more and more terrified at the idea of fuel prices, but that will just be part of it."

"The amount you will save on accommodation will make it all even out," George said, repeating previous conversations they had already had, to fill the space.

Claire nodded. "That's the plan."

They sat in an awkward silence for a moment, Claire's mind racing as it tried to catch up with the surprise of having him in her room.

"Umm," she said, fiddling with her hands. "Just so you know... that day with that guy...I didn't, I wasn't..."

"I know," he cut her off quickly, his eyes boring into hers. "I get it, I read your messages."

"Oh," she said, disappointedly. "I wasn't sure. You never texted back."

"There was a lot to respond to."

"Ugh." Claire blushed, inwardly squirming. "Sorry about that."

"No, don't be...it's...I am..." George said, clenching his jaw, looking like he was trying to say something but unable to form the words.

"Under no obligation to say anythi-"

"I care about you a lot, Claire," he said forcefully, as if he was reciting a speech that he had prepared in his head and needed to get out. "I didn't realise how much. At first, I thought that maybe you wanted to get back together with him, that I had just been an easy distraction."

"You were more than a distraction," Claire said, her heart lifting with each word he said, feeling more confident. "You still are. I care about you a lot too, George. I am so sorry that you had to walk in on that...scene."

"Don't apologise, it was what it was."

"Still, I felt really bad about the whole thing..."

"No, I probably should have gotten in touch with you earlier," he said. "I just felt I had left it a bit too long, processing, and then I felt like you probably deserved an explanation in person."

"Okay..." *So this wasn't a tear-your-clothes-off chat, it's an explanation chat?*

"There is something I have to tell you, Claire, about Zac," George said.

Now it was his turn to look uncomfortable.

"Like how on earth do you two know each other?"

"Well, I've known him through my family for years now," he explained. "He was dating my little sister."

Little sister? Claire felt the room about her grow cold.

"I told you about her, she lives in Sydney now. She's a student, studying to be a nurse."

Claire's mind was busy imploding. "You mean ... Gail?"

He nodded. "Well, her name is Abigail, actually, but everyone in my family just calls her Gail."

How could this be possible? Abbie? The perfect pizza maker?

"I remember you telling me about a guy, and then later again about another girl in Sydney. I didn't think much of it – just another immature idiot who didn't realise what he had. Then when I saw him with you, it clicked."

George looked at Claire's stunned face, as if trying to read what was going on in her mind. Claire assumed it must have been obvious, considering the open-mouthed stunned mullet she was impersonating.

"I was angry," he admitted. "Furious. Both at the idea of my little sister being hurt, as well as the sight of the same scumbag...touching you." He waved his hand awkwardly.

"Is that why you ignored me?" she asked, finally finding her voice.

"It was," he said. "I was just trying to process...the coincidence."

"I think that's what I'm doing now..." she muttered, putting a hand to her forehead.

"Abbie and Zac broke up a few weeks ago; she broke it off with him, said she had suspected something was going on. She can do way better than him."

Ain't that the truth, Claire thought, going red in the face. How had she gotten herself into this mess?

"George…" she said, not sure what to say. "I feel terrible…I'm so sorry about Abbie."

"It's not your fault." He shook his head quickly.

"Still…I just…it's just way too weird."

"It is very weird," he agreed.

They sat in silence. Claire felt very strange. She had spent the past week missing George, wishing he would call. When he had arrived, she had been ecstatic; now she had every delicious inch of him in front of her and she was just sitting by, lamely. *Did I break a mirror or something?* Claire wondered in irritation.

"Did you just come by to talk about Zac?" she asked, hoping that the disappointment hadn't crept into her voice.

George didn't answer straight away. She felt her heart sink.

"I…it…that was a big part of it. I wanted you to know why I have been so distant."

"Oh," she said quietly, nodding. "Well, thank you for letting me know."

"That's okay."

"And I'm sorry again about your sister."

"Abbie is my little sister, but she is still a big girl. Even though she has been a bit sad, she will be fine."

They were both silent again for a moment.

George suddenly sat up a little straighter and cleared his throat.

"Well," he said, speaking to Claire as if she was a distant acquaintance, "good luck with Frank and your travels. I'm sure you will have an amazing time."

Claire felt her breath catch. He was leaving, and he had visited just let her know she had been the mistress in the relationship of a close family member of his. No big, magical, happy ending, no declarations of love. Claire felt deflated; it was too much emotion to deal with while coming down from the high of her sugar binge.

"I will," she replied, swallowing. "Thank you for everything you did for Frank."

She looked up from her twisting hands to lock eyes with an intensely staring George. Claire thought she saw a flash of anger, of indecision, pass over his face before it once again became impassive.

George went to stand up, and spontaneously Claire moved across to the couch and grabbed his hand. He went completely still as Claire leant in, unsure of what she was doing. His whole body was tense, as if wound up and under strict control. She hesitated, before giving him a kiss on the cheek.

"You have been special to me," she said earnestly. "Good luck with everything."

She let go of his hand and George nodded curtly, as if unsure what to say. He stood up abruptly and left.

A moment later, her door flew open again. It was Anna.

"Was that brooding male who just stomped down your parents' driveway who I think it was?" she demanded, dropping her bag on the floor.

Claire just nodded.

"And you aren't chasing after him?" Anna asked, making a beeline to Claire's kitchenette.

"Zac's Instagram model is his sister."

That stopped Anna right in her tracks; she stood still, staring back at her.

"No way."

"Yes way."

"No way!"

"Mmhmm." Claire nodded, her eyes welling slightly.

"Damn, Claire!" Anna exclaimed, suddenly peering out her window as if to see Abbie standing there with George. "You really know how to get tangled up in a mess. I should know, I'm an expert."

"We all have our strengths," Claire said, tears beginning to roll down her face.

"Oh, no," Anna said, looking horrified. "I'm rubbish at this, please don't cry."

Claire quickly tried to wipe the tears away, feeling foolish.

"Here!" Anna cried, handing her the glass of gin sitting on the kitchen bench.

Claire laughed. "Sorry, I'm being ridiculous."

"No, you are not," Anna said, pouring herself another. "Let's get drunk and you can tell me everything that just happened, because the rollercoaster of your love life makes me feel better about mine."

Claire threw her glass back, choking slightly as the gin burnt the back of her throat.

"Okay, I'm ready."

CHAPTER 20

The Adventure in Between

Today was the day, the day Claire would set off on her Australian road-trip extravaganza. Her mother had taken the morning off work to say goodbye to her, and Harvey had been up for hours the night before, ensuring Frank was packed with everything that she might need and more. Claire had been through Frank already that morning, just to check that her father hadn't gone overboard – he only had a little engine, after all, he didn't need to carry any additional weight – but Harvey had done a great job. There were things he had managed to squeeze in that she hadn't even thought about, like mosquito repellent, small disposable gas bottles for the stove, and extra towels. He had also stacked her cupboard with toilet rolls, sunscreen and even baby wipes. Harvey had been exceptionally practical in covering all bases to ensure Claire was well looked after.

Her mother, on the other hand, had given her a bottle of Canberra Distillery French Earl Grey Gin and a promise to utilise physical restraint on Harvey if he tried to stow away in the back.

"If you run out and need more you will just have to come home," Dianna said, sounding suspiciously sentimental as Claire stashed the bottle away in one of Frank's kitchenette cupboards.

"Or if you just want to," Harvey added quickly. "You can come back any time."

Claire laughed, "You two! I swear, I will feel almost missed!"

"Of course we will miss you, you ridiculous child," Dianna said, pulling Claire into a big hug. "When this thing finally does break down and you are stuck in some small backwater town without reception, just know your father and I will come find you if need be."

Claire laughed and hugged Dianna back tightly; her mother, ever the pragmatist.

"Dee," Harvey frowned. "Don't say such things; we cannot curse her trip before it begins!"

"Curse! Goodness gracious, Harvey, you need to stop watching midday television."

"You learn lots of useful things," he said sourly. "You never complain about the things you *do* like that I buy…like that peel-"

"Trying to leave without saying goodbye?" Anna said dryly, appearing around the side of her parents' house with Daisy.

"As if we would let you!" cried Daisy, running over and giving Claire a big hug.

After many more hugs and protestations from her parents, Claire started Frank, letting him warm up for a minute before she pulled out of the driveway, waving to her parents, Anna and Daisy who had arranged themselves on the front lawn.

"Have fun!" Daisy yelled out.

"We'll miss you, Claire-Bear!" Harvey called, waving madly.

"See you in half an hour when Frank breaks down!" shouted Anna.

"Love you guys!" Claire cried out from her open window, beeping Frank's horn. "See you later!"

Claire drove down the street, watching her little family fade in Frank's rear-view mirror. She put on the radio and tried to calm the mixed feelings of excitement, fear and a little bit of loneliness at saying goodbye in Frank all by herself. When she thought about how far she and Frank had come since she first met him in her nan's back shed, it tended to make her mind wander to thoughts of George; seeing him the other night had stirred up a lot of feelings she was still trying to repress. So, Claire turned the music up on Frank's radio and tried to drown out her mixture of intense, different feelings. *Focus on your adventure*, she chided herself, *not painful bloody men*.

Finally getting out of Canberra itself, Claire took the Sutton Road turnoff, remembering the last time she had driven through there was with George, the weekend he taught her to surf. It was strange, the six months she had spent at home was never supposed to have been a journey. It was supposed to have been her respite time, her recharge before taking on a new adventure. She could never have imagined that the adventure she *didn't* expect to take was one into love. To stop her mind wandering back to George, she turned her attention to the landscape on either side of her, thinking about how much it was going to change as she visited all the beautiful, individual Australian states.

The sun was bright, reflecting light off the lush, green, sheep pastures on either side of the road. As she drove down the small windy road, going slowly, even for Frank, Claire couldn't help but again feel a little lonely. She had this beautiful van, all this beautiful countryside, and an empty road ahead of her. Previously, she had preferred to travel solo – that way you didn't have to rely on anyone – but at that moment, after having set down some roots in Canberra over the past few months, Claire couldn't help but want to share it with someone else.

As she turned a bend, Claire noticed a hitchhiker ahead of her, thumb out, all but standing in the middle of the road. She slowed right down to a crawl as she came closer. It was a tall, dark-haired male, wearing sunglasses, with a gym bag slung over his shoulder… he kind of looked like George, but that was probably just her mind playing cruel tricks on her.

Claire pulled Frank off to the side of the road, and the man walked around to the passenger door's open window. Claire blinked; her stomach turned ice cold in shock.

It was George.

"Thanks for stopping," he said coyly. "I was getting a bit worried there for a while."

"What are you doing here?" she asked, feeling numb.

"Was hoping I might be able to catch a lift," he replied casually, leaning one arm on Frank's roof and peering in at Claire.

"A lift?" she repeated, dumbfounded.

"Yup."

"To anywhere in particular?" *This was insanity.*

"Just as far as you want to take me, really," he replied earnestly.

"I am so confused…" she said, unable to take her eyes off him, wondering if he was just a figment of her imagination. Had living with her parents for so long in her late twenties driven her mad?

"Can I jump in?" he asked, opening the back door and throwing in his gym bag.

Claire tried to gather her thoughts, unable to make neither head nor tail of what his presence meant. "Are you going to Sydney?" she asked, confused, thinking he might be on his way to visit his sister. *Surely, he wouldn't be hitchhiking though?* She wasn't thinking straight.

"I can go to Sydney, if you want to take me to Sydney."

"Yes, but…" Claire said, suddenly feeling frustrated. "What are you doing here, climbing into my car?"

"Looking for you."

It was all too much for Claire; she turned Frank off and took a minute to sit in her seat and process what George was saying.

"Do you mind if I hop in?" he asked again, indicating the empty passenger seat. Claire nodded numbly, her brain trying to understand what was happening. George was here, found lost on the side of the road, asking to get a lift, sitting in her van and very much not a figment of her imagination – unless she *had* finally slipped into that chaotic world of madness.

"Looking for me?" she repeated, staring at George beside her.

He looked so gorgeous, in a simple white shirt and shorts, his dark hair slightly messy, as always, his face open and honest; his eyes penetrating hers. She couldn't believe she ever thought this man to be anything less than beautiful. She couldn't believe he was sitting with her in her van. She had missed the grumpy sod.

"I was," he said, staring intently into Claire's eyes.

"On the side of the road?" she asked.

"Well, I knew this was the one way you had to come to go through Sydney. There would have been no point in taking any other route."

"How long have you been out here?"

"Well, only about forty minutes…"

"Why didn't you just call me? Or turn up to my parents' house?" she asked. "Or just stay, the other night?"

"Look, it was a bit of a stab in the dark, to be honest. I thought it might be, well, romantic," he said sheepishly, scratching his chin.

"Romantic?"

"Yeah, grand gesture and all that."

"Oh, cool," she said awkwardly, suddenly worried she was ruining the moment. Claire didn't know how to act; she was used to being left on 'read' in Messenger by boys, not ambushed on highways.

"And then I thought, if I turn up at your parents' house or somewhere closer to the city, you might just tell me to get stuffed and grab an Uber. However, if it was somewhere slightly in the middle of nowhere, I figured you are be far too kind and good to just leave me there," he explained, looking smug. "It was all very deliberate."

"Where is your car, then?"

"I sold it – to Barry."

"Why did you do that?" she asked, her mind just completely going into overdrive.

"I figured he'd give me a good price, and quickly. He's a great guy."

"But why did you sell your car?" *Was this some sort of early midlife crisis?*

"Well, I figured I wouldn't need it anymore – and any extra money that can go towards illegal camping fines, the merrier."

Claire's heart soared a little more with every word he said. She still wasn't convinced it was real, but she wished it was.

"I also just sold all my furniture to my roommate," he continued. "I wasn't on the lease there, so it wasn't really an issue."

"Right," she said, still in shock.

"The only thing I was a bit sad about was my surfboards, but I figure I can just buy more on the way."

"On the way to where?" she asked sharply, now well and truly jolted from her initial shock.

"Wherever it is you are going."

"Oh, is that so?" Claire asked coyly, her heart pumping madly. "That sounds like quite the permanent situation."

"It could be, if that's what you wanted..." George said, finally having the decency to look nervous like she was.

Then he continued, his voice a bit softer and lower, as if to emphasise that his words were for her and her only.

"...because that is exactly what I want Claire. I'm sorry for walking out the other night and for being an idiot in general. I want to be with you, and Frank, for as long as you'll have me."

Claire felt her eyes welling and tried to will herself to be calm. All the loneliness, the stress, felt like it was rising into her chest in what would no doubt be one big, ugly cry.

"You say this now," she said, wiping her eyes, "but you haven't met my nan yet."

"Grandmothers love me ..." George shrugged, with the all unfounded confidence of a man who had clearly never met Beatrice Baxter.

"So…all the stuff from before, with Zac…you are okay with that?" Claire asked timidly.

"I was always okay with you, Claire," he said, looking embarrassed. "It was me that was being an idiot. I was angry at Zac. And angry in general; I don't like complications. The drama of it all kind of freaked me out. I'm pretty ashamed of how I acted, ignoring you like I did."

"It's okay, it's not like we were together or anything…"

"Don't make excuses for me, Claire," he said, his voice sincere and serious. "We were together – it was early days, yes, but it wasn't nothing."

"I just can't believe you did this," she said, laughing at how absurd it all was; she just wanted to move on from the whole Zac debacle altogether. "You just uprooted your entire life, grabbed a bag, all to catch a lift in a van that might have missed you."

"You know what they say, take the leap and all that." He shrugged.

"What would you have done if I had driven by you?"

"Oh, I had a very solid back-up plan…" he said jokingly. "Become a real hitchhiker and get a ride to Sydney and then just meet up with you when you visited your sister."

Claire laughed, the ridiculousness of the whole situation taking over.

"Once I snapped out of it and realised that I was about to lose you, Claire, I would have followed you anywhere," he said with sincerity. "You are a very special person; I knew this as soon as I met you that day."

"At the mechanic's?" She frowned, tilting her head.

"No, even before that, when you were hogging up the line in Repco."

"I can't say the same," she teased, shaking her head.

George laughed, leaning in slowly, looking a little nervous as he kissed her gently on the lips. Claire did not pull away, but closed her eyes, letting the events of the day just wash over her in a wave of unexpected joy and happiness. She pulled back, holding his hand and gazing at him for a time. He just stared back. They both smiled.

"I guess you can come along," she said, rolling her eyes in a pretence of annoyance.

As Claire pulled off the side of the road and shifted Frank into first gear, she looked over at George next to her, smiling happily as he wound the passenger-door window down to lean his arm out. She still had no idea what she wanted to do with the rest of her life, she was still degree-less, career-less and had just traded in a room at her parents' for no room at all.

She didn't know if Frank would make it all the way to Western Australia, if her meagre savings would keep them from starving, or if things between her and George would last – but at that moment, she did not care. Claire was happy, Claire was free, and Claire felt her heart pounding with the call of adventure that lay ahead of them. Beside her, George put a hand on her leg and smiled at her with his beautiful, warm brown eyes. She smiled back and looked to the road ahead.

It was empty, but she felt full.

"Want me to DJ?" he asked, plugging his phone into the aux cord connected to Frank's stereo system.

"Something that'll make me happy," she instructed.

"You got it, boss."

Years later, when they would look back on the photo album of their trip, Claire would say that is exactly what he did.

Author Chloe Stevenson lives in Canberra with her two fluffy mops, parading as dogs, and her 1977 Kombi van, Sadie. Chloe is a communications advisor, an Air Force officer, a terrible gardener, and a lover of all things literary, vintage and wretchedly colourful.

Cover by Lisa White
lisawhite.xyz

Internal design by David Potter
transformer.com.au

Edited by Casey Luxford
thehumblequill.net

Illustrations by Jamie Lawson
blackbirdcamperco.com

Printed and distributed by Ingram Spark
www.ingramspark.com

First edition 2021

ISBN 978-0-6450761-2-7 (pbk)
ISBN 978-0-6450761-0-3 (digital)

Printed in Australia
AUHW010637170321
342731AU00001B/1